Love

For All Time

NATIONAL BESTSELLING AUTHOR

Deborah Fletcher Mello

MaGREGOR PRESS

Published by MaGregor Press

ISBN-10: 0-9979481-1-6
ISBN-13: 978-0-9979481-1-0

A Love for All Time

Printed in the United States of America
First printing, June 2004
Second printing, September 2016

For my father,
Walter Louis Fletcher
Who set the standard
And my baby sister, Tealecia Fletcher,
For living by it

ACKNOWLEDGMENTS

First and foremost, I give thanks to God for His many blessings, for only through Him are all things possible.

I have to thank Mary Vickers for getting through those rough drafts. I truly valued your opinions, and I am exceptionally grateful for your candid insights.

I want to thank my mother-in-law, Mrs. Constance "Pinkie" Mello, whose love for her late husband, Lionel Mello, and her dedication to her family have been shining examples for us all to follow. To my Bermuda family, I love you very much and I am so proud to have been a part of your clan.

Thanks to Jacquelyn and Roy Barrett, Bridget Wilson Hall and Anthony Hoxter, Karen and Dan Eudene, and Sharon and Abraham Broomes. Each of you, and all of my other favorite couples out there, have been great sources of inspiration. May true love continue to be yours, now and forever.

Thank you, Matthew Mello, for keeping up the grades even when I wasn't looking over your shoulder. What did I do to have such a great kid like you?

And last, but certainly not least, to Jody, Allan Jr., Christopher, Paul, and Carmen Mello. Thank you for being the incredible people you are. I am proud to claim you as mine. May you each know love and companionship that will last you an eternity.

CHAPTER 1

Camille Martin ignored the telephone ringing in the background. The day had been long, and at that very moment the last thing she wanted was to be bothered by one more person wanting an ounce of her time. It had barely been thirty minutes since she'd come through the door of her town house, dropping her gray silk blazer in the entrance and kicking her high heels off in the wide hallway. She inhaled deeply, then took a long sip of the Courvoisier that darkened the interior of a Waterford goblet.

When the answering machine clicked off, Camille took another sip of her cocktail, grateful for the drone of silence that followed. Leaving an imprint of MAC lipstick against the rim of the glass, she dropped it onto the cherry-wood table beside her and rubbed her eyes, oblivious of the eye shadow and mascara that embellished her face. Drawing her manicured fingers across her wide cheekbones, over her ears, to the back of her long neck, she kneaded the tightness that lay heavy against the width of her shoulders. The pressure of her hands felt good against her tired flesh as she pinched and pressed the tense muscles.

As her amber-colored eyes swept around the room, she was suddenly dismayed at the mess she'd managed to accumulate in the short time she'd been home. Her clothes wove a path from the front door to the bathroom and back to the kitchen. Her Charles Jourdan handbag and an assortment of packages had been dropped to the floor in the entranceway. A white silk blouse lay tossed over the end of the chenille love seat and her plaid silk pants lay in the bathroom doorway. The sight mocked the pristine perfection she demanded of the Merry Maids cleaning company that serviced her twice weekly. Nita, the robust Hispanic woman with broad smile who kept her home spotless, would not be amused.

Rising from the comfort of her seat, she set out to clear up the mess, kneeling down to pick up her possessions in nothing but a royal-blue Victoria's Secret satin bra and matching thong. She relished the ability to languish so wantonly with much appreciation, having been told by many of her married friends that such was a luxury only single women who lived alone could afford.

As she hung the Chanel suit in the walk-in closet, the telephone rang, again, the harsh jingle intruding upon the quiet. She rolled her eyes in agitation. Crossing over to the other side of the room, she leaned to see whose name appeared on the caller ID, becoming even more aggravated when the neon light flashed *Out of Area*. She stood by the bedside waiting for the answering machine to pick up.

"I'm not able to answer your call, but then you already know that. Leave me a message and I'll get back to you. Bye." *Beep*.

Her sister's voice called out from the recorder, "Hey, Camille. Pick up the telephone. Hello? Camille? I know you're there. Pick up."

A man's voice rang out from the background, "Maybe she's not home?"

"Oh, she's home. I know her. She's right there listening. Camille? Pick up the telephone, heifer! I know—"

The answering machine clicked off, followed by a loud beep, cutting the woman's comments short.

Camille Martin smiled. She knew how much it upset her sister for her not to answer her calls on the first ring. Taking a seat on the side of the bed, she barely had to wait a minute before the telephone rang again. She listened as the answering machine clicked on, played its message for the caller, and then beeped.

"Why don't you have a machine that will let me speak until I'm finished? Even better, pick up the phone and talk to me, 'cause I know you're there. I know you're ignoring me. Hello? Hello? Well, forget you then. I just wanted to give you my good news."

Sighing, Camille picked up the receiver to answer the call. "All I want to hear is that you sold that jazz triptych, and at least a half dozen of the paintings you took with you," she said nonchalantly. "Otherwise, I'm really not interested."

"Well, hello to you too, little sister," the other woman responded. "How are you?"

"Why are you bothering me, is Zina? You know I had a rough day today."

Zina Martin laughed into the receiver. You need to lighten up. All work and no play is beginning to make you a dull pain in the you know what. Besides, I know you didn't do anything today but give Darrow orders." Zina mocked her. Hang that there, Darrow. Up on the left, Darrow. Down on the right, Darrow. What can be tiring about that? Oh, I know! Your hips must be sore from holding up your hands all day!" The young woman's vibrant laughter echoed from the telephone.

Camille sucked her teeth, shaking her head from side to side. "If all you called for is to give me a hard time, then I'm hanging up."

Zina was still laughing, the man in the background chuckling with her. Camille could hear the two of them giggling as they shared some secret she was not privy to. The rise of excitement in her sister's voice intensified.

"No, fool," Zina responded. "I called to tell you my news." The vibrancy rose with the enunciation of each word as the woman shouted into the receiver. "I got married last night!"

Camille could feel herself swallowing, a lump caught deep in her esophagus. She sat up straighter on the bedside, the muscles along her neck tensing up again, the pressure against her temples beating against her brow. "You did what?" she asked, the tone of her voice tainted with dread.

"I'm married! I am Mrs. Antione Foggo! We wanted you to be the first to know. Well, the second. I called Daddy first. Hold on. Antione's right here. Say hello."

The deep vibrato of a man's voice rose from the receiver. "Hello, Camille. Your sister has made me the happiest man in the world!" the man said breathlessly, his excitement as intense as that of the young woman who stood pressed at his elbow.

Camille was at a loss for words. She could feel herself smiling weakly into the telephone as she struggled to find her voice. "Hello," she said at last. "I'm sorry, but what's your name?"

"Antione. Ann-tea-on. Antione Foggo. I can't wait until we can meet each other in person."

"I'm sure," Camille responded tersely. "Would you put my sister back on the phone, please?"

She could hear the duo sharing a quick kiss as the man passed the telephone back to his new bride.

"Isn't he great!" Zina gushed.

"Have you completely lost your mind, Zina? Who is this man, and where did you meet him?"

"Here at the show. It's been wonderful, Camille. He's wonderful. I can't begin to tell you how in love I am."

"Zina, I swear you don't have the sense God gave a green apple." Camille could feel her blood pressure steadily rising, tension pressing at the orbs behind her eyelids. Catching herself, she inhaled deeply, then slowly exhaled, containing the rise of her voice as she purposely changed the subject. "How was the opening?"

"Great. We did very well, as a matter of fact. Eight of the paintings sold the first day. I actually need you to have Darrow ship two of the new ones from your inventory. One of the buyers wanted to take immediate possession of her pieces and I want to fill in the wall space. Charlene isn't concerned, but it bothers me. I know that witch will hang someone else on top of me if she thinks she can get away with it," Zina finished, speaking not so kindly about the curator of the gallery who is hosting her in Santa Fe.

Camille nodded into the receiver. "I'll do it first thing in the morning. When are you coming home?" she asked.

"Antione and I are going to spend a few more days here," Zina responded with a light giggle. There was a mumbled exchange between the couple on the other end, and Camille could almost envision the man's touch that caused your sister to breathe heavily, a low laugh easing past her lips.

Turning her attention back to their conversation, Zina continued to speak. "It is my honeymoon, you know," she said facetiously, as though her sister needed to be reminded. "We'll be back on Sunday. Make a nice dinner for us, Camille. I want you to welcome him properly. Okay?"

Camille shook her head. "You can't be serious?"

"Please, Camille. Be happy, and do this for me? Love like this only comes around once in a lifetime. I'll see you Sunday, Camille. Love you! Bye!"

Camille continued to hold the telephone to her ear, an abrupt dial tone echoing from the other end. Dropping the receiver back onto the hook, she could only shake her head in disbelief. Her sister had completely lost her mind. The telephone once again interrupted her thoughts. This time her father's name flashed on the caller ID.

"Hi, Daddy," she answered as she pulled the receiver back to her ear.

"Have you talked to Zina?"

"She just called me."

"What in the hell is that girl thinking? Do you know this man?"

"No, sir. I've never met him."

Dr. Louis Martin cussed, his deep baritone voice resounding with annoyance on the other end. "I cannot believe this. Your mother must be turning somersaults in her grave."

"Zina says she's in love, Daddy."

"Baby girl says she's in love every other week."

Camille couldn't help laughing, a low chortle she knew instantly would annoy her father.

"This isn't funny, daughter," he responded, his tone short. "It's not funny at all."

"I know, Daddy," Camille said, fighting to stifle another giggle. She coughed lightly into her cupped hand. "Excuse me, Daddy. Sorry about that."

"Are you doing okay?" he asked.

"Yes, sir. I'm just fine."

"Well, Zina said you're doing dinner Sunday. I guess we will have to figure out how to get her out of this mess then. I'll speak with Lawrence tomorrow about having this thing annulled."

"Yes, sir."

"Macaroni and cheese and some fried chicken would be nice to have on Sunday. Maybe some of your mother's peach cobbler?"

"Whatever you want, Daddy."

After a moment of brief reflection, the man continued. "Haven't had any collard greens in a while either. Collards sound good to you?"

"If you say so, Daddy."

"I'll invite Lawrence and Kitty to join us. It'll be easier if he's there when we discuss this problem with Zina. And please, use your good china."

Camille rolled her eyes, sneering ever so slightly as a hint of sarcasm rose in her voice. "Yes, sir, Daddy."

Not missing a beat, her father reprimanded her as if she were still four years old. "Watch your tone, young lady. I'm still the head of this family no matter what you or that sister of yours wants to think. You will not disrespect me. Is it that understood?"

"Yes, sir," she said, her tone apologetic. Without seeing him, Camille could sense her father nodding, a stern expression gracing his face. "I didn't mean to be rude, sir," she finished.

"How was your day?" he asked.

"It was fine, sir. Everything go well for you today?"

"I had a good day. Not as bad as some, and definitely better than others."

Camille smiled. "I'm glad to hear it. I will call you tomorrow. Okay, Daddy?"

"That's fine. I'll be at the hospital most of the morning, then back in my office in the afternoon. Love you, daughter."

"I love you too, Daddy."

This time, Camille left the telephone off the hook. Heading toward the kitchen to refill her glass, she could only continue to shake her head. The whole family had completely lost their minds.

CHAPTER 2

Standing in the front foyer of her home, Camille took in the view as she hoped her guests would. Panning from the doorway, down the hall into the open living space, she wanted to insure that everything was in place when her sister arrived with her new husband. The interior walls were lined with her growing collection of artwork. Paintings were hung precisely at eye level with the room's lighting aimed at just the right angles. Originals by Kadir Nelson, David Wilson, and Olivia Gatewood hung to the right of the entrance. Two original roof Russell Williamses, one Synthia Saint James, and the Joseph Holsten's were hung on the left. As you entered the living room, the walls were lined with exquisite abstract renditions by Zina Martin. Ornate sculptures sat on top of marble pedestals, further defining Camille's love of the arts, and enhancing a magnificent collection of antique mahogany furniture. The woman had impeccable taste, and her showmanship was both expensive and upscale.

A mixture of soft jazz and blues, all her father's favorites, played in the background, the Bose CD player controlling the mood of the moment. Camille inhaled deeply, wanting to ensure that the aroma of fried chicken didn't over power the subtle scent of lavender oil that flowed from room to room. The dining was set for ten and four bottles of vintage Dom Perignon, courtesy of her father, were chilling in the wine bucket. She was pleased. Glancing at the clock, she checked that nothing was left to burn in the kitchen, then rushed into the bedroom to shower and dress.

Since Zina's call on Wednesday, Camille had tried to envision the man who had so enraptured her sister that the woman acted impulsively. But Zina had always been impetuous, her erratic behavior and actions sometimes as abstract as her artwork.

Zina was known to follow her heart first, never allowing her head to lead the way. Men had always flocked to her and she'd been able to pick and choose a man as her heart desired. Her father had been right when he'd said Zina was in love every other week, but never before had she fallen hard enough to even consider marriage. Their father had always bet a dollar to a dime that Camille would've been married well before Zina.

Camille sighed. Instead, here she was, thirty-one years old, without any prospective husband material in sight. Even if their father hadn't, she herself had figured out long ago that it would be her sister, Zina, who'd be first. She knew that not only would Zina be the first to marry, but also she would be the first to have children, and if necessary, the first to divorce. She knew this because Zina was always the first to do everything. Camille had grown accustomed to walking in her sister's shadow, following the lead that Zina inevitably took.

Zina Martin never thought twice about doing anything. There was never any second guessing or reconsidering with the woman. She never hesitated when something moved her. No matter how foolish. Camille, on the other hand, never acted without thinking through every possible scenario, and always with her father's approval at the forefront of her mind.

It had been that way since she was six years old and Zina was eight. Zina had picked all the prize-winning roses off Mrs. McDonald's rose bushes. Mrs. McDonald had lived in the house next door to their parent's home in Raleigh. Her father had been livid, having told them countless times to stay out of the McDonald's yard. At that very moment, Camille had decided she never wanted her father to ever be that angry with her. Zina, of course, couldn't have cared less. She had wanted those roses, and those roses were going to be hers, no matter what the good doctor had said. Their father's anger was only a momentary disruption for Zina, and one she didn't mind having to deal with. Father and daughter had waged daily battles ever since, Louis Martin saying don't, and Zina doing it anyway. Camille, on the other hand, had been more than obedient, never wavering from her father's choices for her.

Camille stepped under a wet spray of water, relishing the warmth of a quick shower. Filling a bath mitt with lavender soap, she drew the scented suds up the length of her body, intoxicated by the fragrant scent. Camille loved the aroma of lavender, and had made such her signature fragrance. The smell of lavender was the only memory of her mother that still lingered with Camille, not having faded to a dull black and white like most of the others. The aroma of lavender brought clarity to the few remembrances of her mother that she still had. The scent had clung to the older woman's clothes, her hair, the cleavage between her breasts, the curve of her wrists. The fragrance warmed Camille, just as her mother had.

Stepping out of the shower, she wrapped a large white towel around her body, brushing at the damp moisture against her skin. Her hair was wrapped neatly beneath a silk scarf, and she loosened the tie at the back of her neck to let the jet-black strands fall down past her shoulders. Shaking her head from side to side, she was satisfied with the light curl that remained, grateful that there would be no need for hot rollers and the curling iron. The doorbell rang just as she sat down at the dressing table in her bedroom to apply her makeup. Looking at the gold and diamond watch on her wrist, she shook her head. There was only one person on tonight's guest list who would arrive an hour early without giving it a thought. Camille was ready to kill her sister, and as she made her way through the living room and down the hallway, she was glad for the opportunity to do so before everyone else arrived.

She began ranting as she threw open the front door. "I cannot believe you. You call four days ago to see you marriage some man you don't know; then you disappear, don't call, don't answer your cell phone, and now you show up here early."

As Zina pushed her way inside, she leaned to kiss her sister's cheek, hugging her warmly. "Hello to you too."

Camille peered out toward the street, glancing past the large topiary bushes at the front door. "Where is he?"

A Love For All Time

"Picking up his brother, Dante. They shouldn't be too far behind me. I told him to get here about fifteen minutes early."

Camille shook her head. "I cannot believe you did this. You know Daddy is absolutely furious."

Zina shrugged. "What else is new?"

Camille studied her sister closely. Her older sibling was dressed in casual denim jeans, a bright white peasant blouse that fell off her shoulders, and tan Timberlands. Her thick, jet-black hair was pulled back in a neat ponytail that fell to the middle of her back, and the only makeup she wore was a light coat of lip gloss. She and Camille shared the same dark complexion, their coloring a rich, robust coffee with no cream. They both had the same full lips, mountain high cheekbones, blue-black hair that fell past their shoulders, and the same broad noses. The only difference in their features was their eyes. Zina's were large and round, a deep, dark ebony inherited from their father. Camille's were narrower, slanted ever so slightly, and a pale shade of hazel like their mothers had been. Zina looked relaxed, and not like a woman who was about to introduce a new husband to a host of family and friends for the first time. Camille could only shake her head. "So, give me the details," she said finally, heading back through the house.

Tossing her oversized tote bag onto the sofa, Zina followed her sister into the bedroom. "He's wonderful, Camille."

"What's his name again?"

"Antione. And please, don't embarrass me by mispronouncing it."

Camille rolled her eyes as she sat down to apply eyeshadow and liner to her lids. A light coat of mascara to her lashes followed. "Antione. Antione. Antione. Okay, I've got it. So where is this Antione from?" she asked, emphasizing the proper pronunciation of the man's name.

"He has a home right here in Raleigh, but his family is originally from Bermuda."

"Family?"

"Father, brother, grandmother, and a ton of uncles, aunts, and cousins. But he has no baby-mama drama and no ex-wife woes."

After patting at her lipstick, Camille swung around toward her sister, who'd stretched the length of her body along Camille's freshly made bed.

"How old is he, where did you meet him, and why in the world did you marry the man so quickly?"

Zina giggled as Camille rose to peer into her closet, searching for the perfect outfit to wear. "He's thirty-two years old, we met in the airport gift shop, and we sat together on the flight. Girl, he had my ticket upgraded to first class so I could sit with them!" Zina exclaimed with a wide grin as she continued. "And I married him because I knew before we landed in Santa Fe that he was a man I wanted to spend the rest of my life with.

Camille turned to stare at her sister. "Thirty-two? He's younger than you? she asked, mildly surprised.

Zina nodded, her head bobbing up and down on her shoulders. "Is there a problem with that?"

Camille shrugged. "No, not if you don't have one." She returned to getting dressed, pulling two dresses out of her closet and laying them across of the bed. Glancing toward Zina, she asked, "You are going to change, aren't you? Daddy will have a fit if you come to Sunday dinner in jeans."

Shrugging her shoulders, Zina rolled onto her stomach, pulling a pillow beneath her head. "Daddy will be too busy trying to find fault with this marriage to worry about what I'm wearing. Besides, I'm comfortable. We're having a family dinner in your home, not entertaining the ambassador of Never Never Land at your father's estate. So please, leave me alone."

Camille shook her head, finally deciding on the Diane von Furstenberg wrap dress. It was tailored enough to be tasteful for an elegant dinner, yet casual enough for entertaining family and close friends on a Sunday afternoon, she thought to herself. Her father would also approve. Since Zina seemed determined to keep the man ranting and raving, Camille figured she'd at least give him one less thing to complain about. Standing five feet eight inches tall, Camille opted for flats instead of a higher heel. She couldn't have her feet hurting, if she was going to get through the rest of this day, she thought after careful consideration.

Zina lifted her head off the pillow and rolled her eyes, unimpressed, as Camille belted the rose-printed dress around her waist and spun about in front of the full-length mirror. Shifting her body for the third time, she pulled her knees to her chest.

"Are you tired?" Camille asked.

"Whipped. Antione and I haven't gotten a whole lot of sleep the past few days."

Camille laughed. "It's like that, is it?"

Zina laughed with her. "Morning, noon, and night."

Camille dropped down to the bedside, rolling to lie beside her sister, clasping her hand like they used to do when they'd been little girls. "Are you sure about this, Zina?"

Her sister nodded. "It feels right, Camille. I love them and I'm sure he loves me."

"But you don't know anything about him. You've known him for what now, one week?"

Zina shrugged. "I feel like I've known him forever. I can't explain it, Camille. We just bonded and it was the most natural thing for us to do. When he asked me to marry him, I didn't hesitate to say yes. I haven't felt this good since I don't know when. I know it's right. I can just feel it." She smiled broadly, squeezing her younger sister's hand.

Squeezing back, Camille grinned. "Well, if nothing else, big sister, you do keep us entertained. I just hope you're Mr. Antione knows what he's in for."

Camille adjusted the pillows against the sofa for the umpteenth time as Zina stood guard in the window. They were both praying that Antione and his brother will arrive before their father. Dr. Louis Martin would be more inclined to hold his tongue while there was company to entertain.

Zina suddenly jumped in place, clapping her hands together. Racing to the door, she threw it open before the doorbell could bring. Camille followed the excited voices that came through her entrance into the foyer. As she approached, she saw the Zina had thrown herself into the arms of a tall black prince who stood majestically in the entranceway. Camille caught her breath, inhaling sharply, instantly understanding what had captured Zina's attention. Zina's grin stretched from ear to ear as she grabbed the man's hand and pulled him inside.

"Hey, baby," she said, wrapping her lips around his, her body folding into him as he pulled her close. They held the kiss for what seemed like an eternity, until Camille cleared her throat, drawing attention to the fact that she was standing there. Coming up for air, Zina continued to grin broadly. "Darling,, meet my sister. Antione, this is Camille. Camille, this is Antione."

Camille smiled warmly, extending her hand politely. "Hello, Antione. It's a pleasure to meet you."

The man laughed, a deep, robust laugh, as he pulled Camille into a heavy bear hug. "We're family now, little sister. Only hugs and kisses for us."

Camille continued to smile as she patted him lightly against the back, her eyes falling on the other dark stranger bringing up the rear. This man smiled broadly, perfect white teeth gleaming against his indigo complexion.

"And this is Dante. He's the oldest," Zina continued, pushing her new brother-in-law forward.

"Hello. And only by one year," he said, also leaning to give Camille a hearty embrace. "We're a very warm and fuzzy family, Camille. We do a lot of hugging and kissing. You get used to it after a while."

Camille nodded her head, eyeing him suspiciously. "Okay," she said slowly.

Zina laughed, reaching out to lightly pinch her sister's arm.

"Well, welcome, both of you. Please come inside and have a seat," Camille responded, rising at the bruise Zina had inflicted.

"Thank you," they responded in unison.

Antione stopped to admire the artwork before taking a seat. "Are these yours, darling?" he asked leaning toward Zina.

Zina smiled. "Yes, they are."

"May I?" Antione asked, turning his attention to Camille as he pointed at the artwork.

"Oh, please. Look around. Make yourselves comfortable. Can I get either of you a drink?"

Antione shook his head. "No, thank you."

"Not just yet," Dante answered. Camille smiled politely as a Zina pulled her husband and his brother along to show them the collection of artwork. Quietly, she studied the two men, inhaling the beauty of them like much-needed oxygen. They both stood well over six feet tall. Their complexions were akin to dark wood, Antione's a polished cherry and his brother's a deep, rich ebony. Dante was thinner than Antione, who clearly spent a fair amount of time in the gym perfecting the mass of muscles that adorned his body. Where Dante supported a clean-shaven head, Antione was crowned in dreadlocks that stopped just above his waistline. The snakelike mass was braided down his back, the ends that wrapped neatly with twine and cowie beads. He was also wearing casual jeans, a white T-shirt, and Timberlands that matched her sister' s. Dante was dressed more conservatively in tan Dockers, a navy blue polo shirt, and leather penny loafers, without the penny.

Camille was suddenly taken aback by the energy the newlyweds exuded. They were a beautiful couple, and Camille marveled at how Zina glowed beside this new man of hers. They fit comfortably as they laughed and chatted quietly together, almost forgetting that she and Dante were in the room with them. Dante came to stand by her side.

"So, Camille. Are you an artist also?" he asked, attempting conversation.

"No, Zina got all the talent in the family. I have a degree in art history from UNC – Chapel Hill and I own an art gallery in their Durham. My forte is artist management and career guidance."

Dante nodded. "Well, you have a magnificent art collection."

She smiled, welcoming the compliment. "Thank you. So, what do you do?" she asked.

"I'm an attorney. Antione and I have a small law firm right outside Cary, near Fuquay Farina."

Interjecting from across the room, Zina laughed. "Small? That's a joke? These two brothers head the largest black-owned law firm in the area. They specialize in medical malpractice. They employ some sixteen attorneys, and there are only three partners."

Antione grinned, joining them on the living room sofa. "Foggo, Foggo, and Mayes is small and still growing."

As he wrapped his arms around Zina's shoulders, kissing her on the cheek, the doorbell rang. The two sisters caught each other's eyes, silently acknowledging their father's punctuality.

"And that would be Daddy." Camille smiled, glancing quickly at her watch. "Are you two ready for this?"

Antione grinned. "Don't you worry, Camille. Your father and I will get along just fine."

In the entranceway, Camille paused briefly, adjusting her dress and running her hands through her hair before opening the door. Swinging the door open, she greeted her family warmly. "Hi, Daddy. Hello, Aunt Kitty, Uncle Lawrence."

Louis Martin filled in the doorway, his oldest friends in the godparents to her and Zina standing directly behind him. A large man, Louis Martin stood imposingly. With his ultraconservative grooming from the tip of his precision haircut to the toes of his black leather shoes, the two women instinctively knew what to expect from their father. The man's expression was predictable, the stern lines of his face almost too somber for comfort, until he smiled, revealing deep set dimples in his full face. The beginning of a potbelly was tucked neatly behind a tailored gray suit. A crisp white shirt and bland, gray-striped necktie completed his attire. A wide gold wedding band wrapped around his thick ring finger was his only other adornment.

Kitrina and Lawrence Chambers were an elegant couple, the epitome of the elite black bourgeois circles they ran in. Uncle Lawrence stood as tall as Louis, but lacked the body mass his friend possessed. Pencil-thin, he seemed almost fragile in comparison to the other man beside him. His wife was a true petite, her four-foot-eight-inch frame barely weighing in at one hundred pounds. It was obvious that they had all three just come from church, Lawrence in a similarly tailored suit to Louis's, and Kitty dressed in an expensive silk dress the color of maize, which complimented the yellow tones in her honey complexion. Camille gestured for them to come inside.

"Hello, daughter. Don't you look nice?" Louis said, reaching to give her a kiss as he hugged her tightly. "We missed you at service this morning."

Camille smiled. "Yes, sir. Took me some time to get everything ready today. I'll be there next week, though," she said, her tone apologetic.

He nodded his head. "Is your sister here?" He asked.

"I'm right here, Daddy," Zina said, rushing to create father.

Camille reached out to hug both of her godparents. Zina followed suit.

Before Camille could close the door, Darrow Holiday, a longtime friend and the director of her gallery, came walking up drive, meeting the Reverend and Mrs. James Baker at the entranceway.

Warm greetings rang throughout the room as old friends and family exchanged hugs and hellos. As the noise slowly died down, Zina pulled Antione to the center of the room, clasping his hand tightly beneath her own.

"Everyone, I'd like you to meet the love of my life, my husband, Antione Foggo, and his older brother, Dante Foggo. Antione, Dante, this is my father, Dr. Louis Martin, my godparents, Kitrina and Lawrence Chambers, our family minister and his wife, the Reverend James Baker and first lady Mrs. Gail Baker, and last but not least, a family friend and fellow artist, Darrow Holiday."

Dr. Martin extended his hand to Antione. "It's a pleasure to meet you, young man, and may I say a definite surprise? I'm sure you can appreciate that we're a little stunned by this sudden development."

"Thank you, sir, and yes, I can. It was a surprising to Zina and myself as well," Antione responded, meeting the man's intense gaze with one of his own.

An awkward silence filled the room. Camille rushed to ease the tension. "I think a toast would be very appropriate right now. Let me get everyone a glass of champagne so that we can welcome the newlyweds properly." Rushing into the kitchen, she kept her ears prepped for one of her father's outbursts.

Lawrence's baritone voice filled the room instead. "I've actually had the pleasure of meeting both these young men."

Dr. Martin turned toward his friend, crossing his arms in front of his chest.

Dante nodded. "That's correct. We faced each other in a civil case a year or so ago, if I remember."

"That's right. You two were representing a patient who was suing Triangle Hospital. You won quite a sizable settlement for your client, if I recall."

The two brothers smiled, both nodding.

Lawrence continued. "Your firm has quite an impressive track record. We tried to lure you both to my firm at one point, when you are starting out. Since then you've outgrown us, and then some."

"We've done quite well," Antione said. "We're both very proud of all we've accomplished."

Gail Baker interjected, "It is so nice to see young black men doing so well, and in such a noble profession."

"Well, I don't know how noble it is," Lawrence said with a wide grin.

They all chuckled.

Antione smiled. "Thank you," he said. "Our father instilled a strong work ethic in us. We have great respect for what we do, and we believe in doing it well."

Dr. Martin nodded his head approvingly. "Two lawyers in the family. Your parents must be very proud."

Antione responded, "Our mother and our younger sibling died during childbirth when we were both babies ourselves. Our father and our paternal grandmother raised us. It was one of the first things Zina and I shared, having lost one parent early and having the other raise us alone." He looked directly at Dr. Martin as he spoke.

Mrs. Baker clocked her teeth. "Oh, my. We're so sorry to hear that. I know your mother would be very proud of you two. Your father has done a fine job."

"A fine job," her husband echoed.

Dr. Martin cleared his throat. "My daughter tells us your family is from Bermuda?"

Antione nodded. "Our father is. Our mother was originally from South Carolina. She was born and raised in a small town right outside of Charleston. Dante was born on the island, but mom had me here in the States, in South Carolina."

Dante interjected. "Our family home is on the island, though. We grew up there until Dad sent us both off to boarding school. Then after graduation and law school we opted to open our practice here, but we go back to the island frequently."

"Where did you two go to boarding school?" Lawrence asked

"New Hampshire, sir. Phillips Exeter Academy."

"Very impressive," Lawrence said, throwing Louis a quick glance. "Very impressive indeed."

"And college? Kitty asked.

"I graduated from Duke University," Dante responded.

"I'm a Harvard graduate, ma'am," Antione answered.

Zina squeezed his hand, boasting proudly. "Antione actually holds two degrees. He graduated with a degree in medicine from Harvard medical school, and then went on to get his law degree at the law school."

"Praise be!" Reverend Baker exclaimed. "God is good!"

"All the time, husband! All the time!" His wife said, clapping her hands excitedly.

Camille smiled approvingly, leaning to peer into the living room as she eavesdropped on the conversation. She watched her father closely as he took in this new information about his daughter's husband and family. She knew he couldn't help being impressed, but as usual there was no display of emotion registered on his stern face. The group continued to make small talk as Dr. Martin stood off to the side observing.

Joining her in the kitchen, Darrow reached out to help Camille with the glasses.

"Well, ain't been no fireworks yet," he said in jest, grinning at her broadly.

"Keep your fingers crossed that it stays that way," Camille responded.

Darrell lowered his voice, leaning in to whisper to Camille, "those two brothers are sure 'nuff easy on the eyes, girlfriend. But I hate to say it. I think big brother Dante is more my type than he is yours. I hope you didn't get any ideas about that one before I got here." Darrell snapped his fingers, arching his eyebrows in her direction.

Camille chuckled. "Down, boy. Do not get started. There is plenty enough drama happening already."

Darrow laughed.

"Here," Camille said passing him a tray of crystal glasses. "Take these out and I'll get my father to pop the cork on this bottle."

Darrow gestured for Dr. Martin as he walked from the kitchen to the living room. "Dr. Martin, Camille would like your help in the kitchen, sir."

The man nodded, smiled politely, then excused himself from the room.

Camille smiled as her father came to her side. "So, what do you think?" she asked curiously.

Dr. Martin shrugged. "No opinion yet. He's employed at least."

His daughter narrowed her eyes. "I like him, Daddy. He seems to really be in love with Zina, and she with him."

Dr. Martin scoffed. "He's only known her for a week. What he loves he can get down on Angier Avenue for twenty dollars."

Camille shook her head. Passing the champagne bottle to her father, she bit her tongue, mindful not to say anything that might provoke his ire. Instead, she asked, "Will you make the toast or do you want me to?"

"I haven't lost my manners, Camille."

"No, sir."

Back in the living room, Camille filled each glass, then joined her father, who stood beside Antione and Zina.

Everyone in the room lifted their flutes toward the couple.

Dr. Martin started, "Since the day she was born Zina has been an unexpected tidal wave on a warm summer's night. She is stubborn to a fault and that hard head of hers has been the bane of her soft behind. She has challenged me most with her impulsiveness, and admittedly she has scared me to death more times than not. Zina has always bobbed and weaved when you wanted her to walk the straight and narrow. Nevertheless, she's been my baby girl since the day I laid eyes on her in her other's arms, all shiny and new, like a copper penny. So handing her to another man is not an easy thing for me to do, and most particularly since these circumstances are so untraditional. But I've had to learn from her experiences and…" He paused, emphasizing his last words. "Her mistakes."

Dr. Martin paused again, then cleared his throat before turning to his new son-in-law. "Antione, I hope to come to know you as my daughter feels she knows you. I give her to you, admittedly with much reservation, but I'm going to trust that you will do right by my baby girl, and that you will make her happy. Because if you don't, I will hurt you. Understand, that if you do anything to harm my child, you will have me to deal with."

Camille grimaced, squeezing her eyes closed as her father continued. Antione smiled, nodding his head in deliberation as Zina shook her own at her father, giving him a look that said she was not all amused.

"May you two find happiness and joy in each other. May you bring happiness and joy to each other. May you be to each other all that you can possibly be, now and forever. God bless you both and welcome to our family, Antione. I personally look forward to the opportunity to know you as my son."

Camille wiped a tear from her eyes as they all drew their glasses to their lips. Dr. Louis Martin never ceased to amaze her. As Antione pulled Zina into a warm embrace, Camille wrapped her own arms around her father.

"Why don't we enjoy dinner? she said, leading them all toward the dining room. "Reverend Baker, would you do us the honor of blessing the meal?"

Dinner had gone better than expected, and after a dessert of warm peach cobbler and Breyer's vanilla ice cream, Camille's guests had gathered in small groups around her home. Her father, Antione, Lawrence, and Reverend Baker had taken up residence in her office. Dante and Darrow were huddled in conversation in the kitchen, and she and Zina were chatting with Mrs. Baker and their aunt Kitty. Camille sat prepared, just in case, keeping one ear open to the conversation the women were having, and the other listening for any raised voices coming from her father or Antione.

Suddenly Zina shrieked, shouting Camille's name with excitement. "Camille! I cannot believe I forgot to tell you!"

"Tell me what?"

"Who Antione's father is!"

"His father?"

"Yes. That's why Antione was headed to Santa Fe in the first place. He was meeting his father there. His father had an exhibition opening at the Plummerhill Gallery."

Camille's eyes widened, her curiosity piqued. "Who's his father?"

"Vincent DeCosta!" Zina clapped her hands like a small child. "The renowned Vincent DeCosta is Antione and Dante's father."

Dante laughed out loud as he and Darrow entered the room, rejoining them. "He really isn't all that," he said, joining in the conversation.

Mrs. Baker shook her head, confused. "I'm sorry, girls, but who is this Mr. DeCosta?" she asked.

Camille set the coffee cup she'd been holding on the sofa table behind her. Her mind's eye began gathering data like a well-tuned computer, every minute detail she could remember flashing through her thoughts. "Vincent DeCosta is own of the most talented black sculptors of this millennium," she answered. "He creates these massive pieces of sculpture that are just out of this world."

"Didn't he do that metal piece that sits in front of the Heritage Cultural Center?" Kitty asked.

"Yes, ma'am," Camille answered.

"If I remember correctly, he was under consideration for featured artist for Central University's auction and fundraiser last year," Kitty said. "Unfortunately, he couldn't accommodate our schedule. We're hoping to get him next year though."

Camille's head bobbed up and down. "Are you heading the committee next year, Aunt Kitty?" she asked, momentarily digressing from the conversation.

"I'm not sure, darling. I'm so overextended as it is that I don't know if I'm going to be able to take on any more. Would you be interested?"

"No, thank you," Camille said with a definite shake of her head.

"Well," Zina interjected, giddy with excitement, "you have to see the works Vincent had in Santa Fe.

He had these incredible fused glass and metal figures that stand some four and five feet high and wide. They were just out of this world! He invited me to do a show with him in Bermuda," she said smugly.

"Wow!" Darrow interjected. "But if anything I read has been true, they say Mr. DeCosta is somewhat of a recluse?"

Dante shook his head. "Not really. Dad kept a very low profile when he first started showing his work, but that's because he wanted to be valued first and foremost on his talent. Black artists have never gotten the recognition of their white counterparts, and Dad knew that for him to be successful, he had to cross over into a market that might not have been accepting of him simply because of his ethnicity. He wasn't actually reclusive; he just didn't take many pictures and made himself conveniently unavailable for certain shows and openings. It seemed a little crazy at first, but it worked. Now folks are lined up trying to get one of his works."

Lost in her thoughts, Camille reflected back on the one and only time she'd been in the presence of Vincent DeCosta. The attractive black man had been lecturing at the Durham Hayti Center when she'd been a student at the University of North Carolina. From the student union flyers that had been distributed, she and her friends figured he'd be entertaining eye-candy for a boring Tuesday evening. In addition, the three-hour event would garner them not only some free food, but an extra grade in their women's studies course. But the experience had initiated her changing her major from mathematics to art history, the man's magnanimous presence having a profound impact.

Her recall of the moment was vivid. DeCosta had given a powerful dissertation on the history of black women artists that had stimulated her intellect and incited her curiosity. Afterward there had been a dinner reception in his honor. They had bumped into each other at the buffet table. Camille had been sufficiently embarrassed when the plate of tossed salad she'd been holding, its contents slathered in blue-cheese dressing, landed against the front of his cashmere sweater and wool pants. The embarrassment had been further compounded with sheer humiliation when they'd both reached to wipe at the offending stain at the same time and her gold charm bracelet had gotten hooked against the zipper of his slacks. The moment had been surreal, her hand groping his crotch haphazardly as they struggled to free him from her grasp. Finally, after unclasping the hook, Camille had escaped out the side door, leaving her bracelet and Vincent DeCosta behind.

The memory of the moment made her laugh out loud. Catching herself, Camille shook her head from side to side, focusing her attention back on the conversation. "I know," she said, hoping her voice didn't betray the momentary distraction. "I've been at the back of that line waiting until I could afford one of those works."

Dante laughed with her. "Well, I think you just might qualify for a family discount now. In fact, I can just give you one. Antione and I have tons of his stuff!"

Camille spun around in her seat. "I don't understand. If he's DeCosta, where did Foggo come from?"

Taking a seat beside her, Dante explained. "DeCosta is my grandmother's maiden name. Dad chose to use DeCosta when he started showing professionally. Foggo is actually our mother's maiden name and for whatever reason it's what they put on our birth certificates."

"A family secret, perhaps?" Camille asked, her eyebrows raised suggestively.

Dante chuckled. "You never know. Every family has them," he said with a smile.

Camille grinned back, shaking her head in his direction.

"So, what do you think about a show in Bermuda?" Zina asked.

"Well, Zina, I'm sure Mr. DeCosta was just being polite, you being the new daughter-in-law and all," her sister responded.

Zina shrugged, rolling her eyes. "Maybe, but he bought tickets for you and me to meet him in Bermuda next week to make all the arrangements. And he bought them before his son and I got married, thank you very much. So it sounds like it may be a bit more than polite to me."

The two women locked eyes for a brief moment. With nothing else to say, Camille could only shake her head, her thoughts lost on the prospect of seeing Vincent DeCosta again in person.

CHAPTER 3

The commotion coming from her kitchen pulled her up and out of her bed earlier than she wanted to be up. Searching for her slippers, she tripped on the hem of her bathrobe, banging her knee into the nightstand. It was only half past nine, the cleaning service didn't work on Mondays and she had the day off herself. Camille was not pleased as she limped down the hallway, rubbing at the injury to her kneecap. In the kitchen, Zina was banging pots and pans under the cabinet.

"What are you doing here and how did you get in?"

"You didn't answer the door so I used my spare key. Where's the blender?"

"Top left cabinet. Why?

"Breakfast smoothies, of course. I bought bananas, strawberries, and protein powder."

"I hate you," Camille pouted, turning an about face and heading back to the bedroom.

"Hey, don't go back to sleep," Zina called after her. "I figured we could go running and then to the gallery. I need to get some work done and we have to plan our trip."

"What trip?"

"Bermuda, fool," Zina responded, giving her a full commentary about the tropical paradise that sat just mere miles off the coast of North Carolina.

Camille turned again to stare as her sister tossed fruit and yogurt into the blender and proceeded to mix the ingredients into a smooth concoction. "I really hate you," she said finally, resuming her trek back to her bed.

"Don't say hate. Daddy doesn't like that word," Zina grinned at her back, her eyebrows raised ever so slightly. "Wouldn't want you to make Daddy mad, now, would we?"

Camille flipped her sister her middle finger. "Why are you up so early?"

"Antione had to go to the office today. He had to file some court motions or something. He was up and out at the crack of dawn, and I don't like sleeping by myself."

"You've been sleeping by yourself since forever. What's so different about it now?"

"Antione."

Camille rolled her eyes, her pout deepening. She poked her lips out like she'd done when they were small and she couldn't get her way. This made Zina laugh out loud. Ignoring her, Camille finally made it back to the confines of her bedroom, dragging her feet against the hardwood floors. Back in bed, she pulled the covers over her head, shutting out the bright light peeking through the windows.

She wanted to scream. Her older sister was now married. The woman had a man. But not just any man. She had an intelligent, self-employed, financially secure man with a sense of humor, faith in God, and a body that could make a standing bowl of concrete quiver with anticipation. To top it off, the woman was in love, the man was in love with her, and it had only taken her two days.

Camille's last date had barely lasted two minutes. Her recall of it made her wince with bitterness. His name had been Peter Something-or-other, a blind date arranged by her friend Jackie. The man had met her at Martino's, one of her favorite restaurants, dressed in knockoff Sean-John jeans, a too-small Lycra muscle shirt, and a forty-ounce bottle of brew clutched in the palm of his hand. Within minutes of being escorted to the table by the hostess, the man had squeezed himself into the booth beside her, putting a kung fu grip on her lips as he pulled her hand down into his lap. Her escape had involved the prongs of a fork, an exceptionally loud exchange that had silenced the restaurant, and management asking them both never to return again.

Since that miserable date there hadn't been a prospective man around for another, let alone one who would not only last longer than two minutes, but was interested in committing the rest of his life to her. What was fair about that? Camille hated to admit that she was a bit more than jealous. In fact, envy was weighing heavy on her spirit, and all she wanted to do was go back to sleep and dream up her own personal Prince Charming.

"Get up," Zina said, pulling the covers from around her and dropping them to the floor. "What's wrong with you?"

"Leave me alone," Camille answered, rolling into a fetal position, a pillow pulled close to her chest. "I'm mad."

"Why?"

"'Cause I don't have a man, and I have to sleep alone."

Zina crawled into bed beside her. "And this is different how?"

Camille glared up at her. "You make me sick," she said, bursting into giggles with Zina.

Zina pulled back her shoulders, coming to a sitting position on the bed. Imitating her father, she dropped her voice down low, shaking her index finger in midair. "I'm not happy about this, Zina Michele. You never stop to think. At least this man seems to have his head on his shoulders. Maybe a man like him is what you need. At least this man seems to have his head on his shoulders. Maybe a man like him is what you need. At least he doesn't have any body piercings like that last freak you dated. I'll wait and see before I pass final judgement, but I'm not happy about this."

Camille laughed loudly as Zina brushed her finger under her nose like their father did. Brushing at the fine line of hair he called a mustache. "Oh, goodness," she said, gasping air to catch her breath. "You are so wrong!"

Zina shrugged, dropping back down against the pillows. "When all was said and done, I actually think Daddy approved. I think he was surprised that Antione was as conservative, and professional, and as upstanding as he is. So what do you think about my new husband."

"I like him, Zina. I think he's a great guy, and I was surprised as hell that you actually married a really great guy."

Zina laughed. "You know what, Camille?" she asked, not bothering to wait for a response. "Antione is so much like Daddy. They have the same high moral principles. The same drive. The same high expectations. It's almost scary.

Camille inclined her head, both women falling quiet as they reflected on Antione and their father. It was no surprise to Camille that Zina had married a man like Louis Martin. The first man the two of them had fallen in love with had been their father. Since then, they'd measured all the men that came into their lives by the standards he set. The type of man he was, and how he had been in their lives, dictated what they demanded and expected a man to bring to the table. And Louis Martin had demanded and expected a great deal.

Camille fought back to when their mother had been alive. Whenever she and Zina had complained about their daddy, the woman had laughed, easily extolling the virtues of her husband, telling them both how lucky they all were to have a man like Louis Martin, who loved them.

Louis Martin was a man who relished fatherhood. From the moment Zina had been conceived, he'd accepted the position wholeheartedly, wearing the role of like a second skin. He had carried the weight of fatherhood and walked the walk of parental responsibilities with the grace, and charity, and an extremely firm hand. He had been steadfast in his support and love, and both women knew Louis Martin would be there, without fail, no matter what.

Looking at Camille, Zina shook the hair from her eyes. "Well, emulating our father won't be easy for any man. But I think Antione will come darn close. I love them so much. He's everything I could ever have wanted in a man, and then some."

Smiling, Camille squeezed Zina's hand. "You and Antione seem perfect together. I'm so happy for you."

"I told you, and I can't explain it. It's just right. But tell me what you thought about Dante."

Camille cut her eyes at her sister. "No."

Zina laughed. "I think he liked Darrow anyway."

'So did Darrow."

Sixty minutes and eight ounces of protein drink later, Camille and Zina were racing through the streets of downtown Durham. Zina led the way as they jogged past Brightleaf Square toward Main Street, and around to the Durham arts Center. Camille finally collapsed on the steps of the government building. Zina paced the sidewalk in front of her, two fingers pressed to her neck, the other hand resting on her left hip.

"You should check your pulse," she said as Camille gasped for air.

Camille rolled her eyes in response. "How are we getting back home?" she asked, panting heavily.

"Running. How else?"

"I don't think so, unless you plan to carry me on your back."

Zina shrugged, resting her hands on her narrow hips. "Can you walk at least?"

"A slow stroll."

"Fine."

"Okay."

Zina reached out her hand to pull Camille up and onto her feet. Within minutes, the slow stroll had increased to a moderate jog as a Zina led the way through town and back toward Bridle Wind Drive.

The doorbell ringing pulled Kitty Chambers over a from her Rose beds as she hurried through the house toward the front door. Peering through the door's glass sidelights to the front porch, she smiled as she reached for the knob to pull the entrance open.

"Hello, darling," she greeted, reaching out to give Camille a deep hug. "What a surprise!"

"Hi, Aunt Kitty. I'm not interrupting, am I?"

"Never. Come right in," the woman said, gesturing for Camille to come inside. "So, to what do I owe this honor?"

"I was headed to the gallery to get some paperwork done and thought I would stop to say hello."

Kitty nodded as she guided Camille to the backyard and resumed her gardening. "Lawrence abandoned me for the office this morning, so I figured it would be a good time to cut my roses back and weed out my flowerbeds."

"The gardens look wonderful," Camille said, appraising the perfectly sculpted hedges, lush green grass, and abundance of color that filled the rear yard.

"Thank you, baby. My gardening gives me great pleasure. It's wonderful relaxation."

"It amazes me that you're able to find time with everything you have to do."

Kitty laughed, nodding her head in agreement. "It amazes me also," she said with a low chuckle. "Can I get you something to drink? Have you eaten

A Love For All Time

breakfast?" she asked as she pointed Camille to a seat around the patio table

"I'm fine, thank you."

Kitty studied Camille closely, noting the eyes that seemed to flicker back and forth in search of something. The expression across her face was heavy, and Kitty knew that some issue was weighing heavily on the young woman's spirit. "Do you want to talk about it?" Kitty asked, her gaze searching Camille's face for answers.

Camille sighed, her eyes meeting Kitty's briefly. "Just feeling a little low today. It'll pass."

The older woman slowly shook her head from side to side. "Are you and Zina at odds again?"

"No, ma'am. Actually, quite the opposite. Things are good between us, and she seems to be really happy since she got married."

"Her young man is quite impressive. Your uncle Lawrence and I really liked Antione."

Camille smiled a weak smile, the edges of her mouth barely bending upward. "Yes. He's quite the catch," she said with a heavy sigh.

Kitty smiled. "Is that a touch of jealousy I hear your voice?"

Camille looked up into her aunt's face. "I don't want to be jealous, Aunt Kitty. I'm really happy for Zina, but..." She paused, not quite sure how to finish her statement.

"But you wonder why it wasn't you," Kitty said, finishing the comment for her.

"Am I being selfish?"

"No, baby. You're just wondering why this blessing fell into Zina's lap and not yours. Wondering, perhaps, when it will be your turn."

Page 39

"So, when will it, Aunt Kitty? It seems like everything just drops right into Zina's lap, and I sit around waiting for things to maybe pass by my way. I swear, she's had a date every weekend since she was sixteen. I've lost count of the men who've fallen head over heels in love with her. Now she's married to this great guy and I can't find a brother to buy me a hotdog on Saturday night."

Kitty laughed. "When it's your turn, Camille, it will happen. You can't force it. God does things in His own time. You know that. The right man will come along soon enough and he will drop right into your lap the way Antione dropped into Zina's."

Camille rolled her eyes. "I guess." She inhaled a deep intake of air. "Do you remember when I was in school and I told you about losing my charm bracelet at that arts seminar?" she asked, feeling better as she changed the subject.

Kitty thought for a brief moment, squinting her face in deliberation as she reflected back. As the memory came back to her she nodded her head and smiled. "I remember. Something about tossing food onto the speaker and then getting your bracelet caught on his clothes, correct?"

Camille nodded. "That man was Antione's father."

Katie laughed loudly. "You're kidding me, right?"

"No, ma'am," Camille said, shaking her head. "It was Vincent DeCosta."

Wiping at the wave of tears that had risen in her eyes, Kitty continued to giggle softly. "Well, let's hope when you two meet he doesn't remember you."

Camille laughed with the woman. "Let's say a prayer, too," she exclaimed.

CHAPTER 4

Dr. Louis Martin paced the floor of his office, his arms folded tightly in front of his chest. His thoughts were on his daughters, Zina especially, and this man she'd met and married after barely knowing him an hour. He sighed deeply, blowing his Zina sigh, the one that rose from the pit of his abdomen, spreading up and filling his chest with sour air before blustering loudly past his full lips. If either of his daughters were to cause him to have a heart attack, it would surely be Zina.

His thoughts were interrupted by the buzz of his intercom. Crossing over to sit behind the large mahogany desk, he pushed the response button.

"Yes, Mrs. Jenkins?"

"Attorney Chambers is here to see you, Dr. Martin."

"Thank you. To send them in."

A moment later, Lawrence opened the large door and entered, closing it behind him. "How are you this morning, Doc?"

Louis shrugged. "How do you think? That child is going to drive me crazy."

Lawrence laughed. "It could have been worse. She could have married an unemployed serial killer."

"How do we know he isn't? We don't know anything about him!" Lawrence exclaimed, throwing his hands up in the air in exasperation.

Lawrence laughed again. "Actually," he said, dropping a manila file onto the desk in front of his friend, "we know quite a bit about the young Mr. Foggo. And I can assure you, after reviewing his file you'll see that you have nothing to be worried about. At least no more than any other father who has finally married off his firstborn child worries about."

Louis flipped through the pages before him, studying the documents slowly. Every other moment or so he'd lift his eyes toward Lawrence and nod his graying head.

"Okay. So what now?"

"Lawrence dropped down into the leather chair in front of his friend. "Now nothing. Louis, Zina is thirty-three years old. She's grown. At this point you just pray that your daughter has made a wise choice and will be as happy as you and Sarah were."

Louis closed the file of paperwork, flipping it onto the corner of the desk. He rose from his seat, pacing the floor again.

"I should have expected this. I should've been prepared."

Lawrence shrugged, amused by his friend's anxiety. They'd been best friends since they were roommates at North Carolina Central University, and Lawrence was used to Louis's anxiety over Zina, having shared each moment with him since the day the child was born. He shook his head. "It will be okay, Louis. how is Camille?" he asked. "is she seeing anyone?"

"Camille is good. She doesn't give me an ounce of trouble. Everything is always well with Camille."

"Everything?"

Louis eyed his friend cautiously. "Everything. Or do you know something I don't?"

Lawrence shook his head no. "Not a thing. It's just…" He paused.

"Just what, Lawrence? Spit it out."

"Well, Kitty expressed some concerns when we got home last night. You know how Kitty is. She is always worrying about those girls. She thought Camille seemed a little distant, like maybe there was something bothering her."

"No. Camille is fine. Probably just worried about Zina like I am."

Lawrence nodded his head. "If you say so."

Louis sat back down. "Well, the boy's got an impressive portfolio. He's been well educated, and he's never been in any trouble. What about the rest of the family? Anything on them?

"Nothing really. Dante's history is as impressive, and I didn't look for anything on the rest of the family. Didn't figure there with anything there to find that would make any difference to Miss Zina. Like I said, stop worrying. I personally don't think you could have gotten a finer son-in-law if you had picked him out yourself. I really like the young man myself. Kind of reminded me of you at his age."

Louis grunted, leaning back in his chair as he clasped his hands in front of him. "Well," he started, turning to stare wistfully out the window behind him, "at least I'll be able to give Camille the wedding her mother wanted them to have. I know she won't sneak off and marriage some man without my being there." The room filled with silence as the two men fell into their own thoughts. A moment later, Louis turned back to face his friend. "I can count on walking at least one of my daughters down the aisle. Camille won't disappoint me.

Lawrence smiled, silently hoping his friend would never have to eat the words he'd just spoken.

CHAPTER 5

Camille stared out the airplane window as Zina and Antione wrapped themselves around each other in the seats beside her. The lovebirds had actually made her nauseated with all the handholding and face sucking they'd done since the flight had taken off. All this public display of affection was beginning to wear on her nerves and when she'd said so, the two had only laughed before ignoring her completely.

Drawing her attention back to the yellow-lined paper in her lap, she studied her notes, jotting down additional thoughts in the margins. Zina turned to stare down at what she'd scribbled, reaching out to point your finger at one passage in particular.

"Why those pieces? I was thinking I did do a whole new series for the show."

"Do you think you'll have time, Zina? Mr. DeCosta said he'd need at least fifteen paintings from you."

Zina nodded. "Darrow is going to stretch the canvases for me, and he's promised to have them done within the next three weeks. I don't see any reason why I can't get them done."

Camille leaned forward in her seat, looking toward Antione over the top of her tortoiseshell reading glasses. She raised her eyebrows and Zina's direction before speaking. "You never had a distraction like a *husband* before. It may be different this time."

Antione laughed. "Don't put me in this."

Sitting back in her seat, Camille shook her head from side to side. "Do you even have a theme? Any clue about what you're going to paint?"

As Zina shook her head. "No. But it will come. I'm not worried. I'll get them done. I've already started some preliminary sketches and I'm ready to get going. I just want to have all new work for this show, Camille."

Camille nodded, scratching out the list she'd written minutes before. "That's fine, but you know the caliber of work that's expected, and they will all have to be finished by mid-June so that I can get them framed and shipped in time. Have you thought about show title? Mr. DeCosta said he was going to leave it up to you."

Zina shrugged. "That's what I have you for."

A liquid-filled voice floated over the intercom, interrupting the conversation. "Ladies and gentlemen, will be starting our descent into Bermuda. If you will please restore your trays and return your seats to an upright position. The captain has turned on the seat belt sign, and everyone should please buckle their seatbelts." The voice paused. "Weather conditions are optimum for landing, and if you look out the window on your left you will be able to see the island below as we make our approach."

The airplane bounced ever so slightly. The engines seem to rev louder as the landing gear beneath them dropped into place. Camille turned to stare out of the window.

The liquid voice continued. "The time in Bermuda is twelve-thirty eastern standard time, and the temperature is eighty-three degrees Fahrenheit. We appreciate you traveling with us today, and hope you will join us again on your next flight. Thank you for flying American Airlines."

Zina grabbed her sister's hand excitedly as Antione leaned to point down to the rush of color that suddenly raced to meet them. The vision below was breathtaking, the rich green land rising like magic from the depths of the deep blue sea. The contours of the cerulean waters punctuated the soft pink sand beaches, the mass of islands shimmering like precious gems dropped atop a background of blue satin and green silk. Camille could feel a warmth of tears pressing at her eyelids, and she had to smile, her own excitement starting to mount as she thought about this impromptu getaway. A four-day weekend in Bermuda, and the unexpected opportunity to meet Vincent DeCosta. *It couldn't get any better*, she thought to herself.

She and Antione's father had spoken twice on the telephone since Zina had announced the prospect of this show. Their conversations had been easy-going, the laughter abundant. She was duly impressed by his professionalism, and his expertise fascinated her. She welcomed the opportunity to benefit from his knowledge, and looked forward to personally connecting with an artist of his stature. Whether her sister knew it or not, Camille was fully aware that opportunities like this didn't come along often.

This exhibition was DeCosta's annual showcase for the Somerset Gallery. This was where his career had begun, where he'd first shown his work publicly.

It was the one and only venue where he always introduced his new creations. The gallery owner, a woman named Lydia Quinn, had represented him exclusively ever since. Camille and to Lydia had spoken only once, the woman's proper British accent edged in formality. Lydia was not familiar with Zina's work, and Camille could tell instantly that the woman had doubts about Zina's showing with. DeCosta. It was clear that Lydia Quinn was very possessive about her artist, and she didn't welcomed his sudden interest in the works of his son's new wife.

But Camille was ready for her. If nothing else, she was as passionate about her sister's talent as Lydia was about DeCosta. Camille knew that Zina ran rings around other artists. Her work was exceptional, her list of collectors duly impressive, and her career was growing steadily. DeCosta had recognized her potential immediately, and had said so, being ever so blunt about why he'd asked Zina to show with him.

His tone had been low and seductive, the subtle accent lyrical, and Camille was reminded of a popular California radio announcer she'd heard once on a well-known radio program. The man's a voice had possessed the ability to make her weak in the knees. She was surprised years later to learn that he was not to the tall, dark, native brother she'd imagined him to be, but was instead a pale Asian of average height who had beautiful eyes and a sweet smile. DeCosta's voice possessed the same potent intonation, and Camille was intrigued to finally be able to meet the man behind it under better circumstances. Camille replayed the conversation in her head, the clarity of his rich voice laced with thick honey as he spoke on the telephone.

"I don't usually show with anyone else when I do this exhibition, but I'm looking forward to showing with Zina Martin."

"Why is that, Mr. DeCosta?"

"Please, call me Vincent."

Camille nodded into the receiver. "Why is that, sir?"

She could feel the man smiling. "Because she's good. She's going to go far, and it never hurts to share the stage with someone who's better than you are. It looks good to have shown with a rising master. The competition keeps you on your toes."

Camille smiled. "But you and she work in such different mediums. I see you complementing each other rather than competing with each other."

"Don't doubt that it isn't competitive, Ms. Martin. Every artist is striving for the same thing, wall and/or floorspace. Collectors have limited amounts of both, so my work has to be better than the next artist's if I want my work to fill that space. Bottom line, if a buyer puts a Zina Martin original on a wall, and it fills a four-by-five-foot area, then the chances of one of my sculptures taking up the space in front of that area are slim or nil."

"I'm delighted that you are so impressed with my sister's artwork, sir."

The man laughed. "It's a Vincent, and I'm not impressed, yet. Every critic and collector of any importance will be at this event. This is the one time of the year that I always introduce something new, and this year I'm going to blow them away. I hope Zina is up to the challenge."

Camille laughed with him. "I just hope you are, Vincent."

Camille smiled as the plane landed. Beside her, Zina looked like she was about to be sick.

"What's wrong with you?" Camille asked, concerned washing over her.

"Did you see how close we came to the top of that car? Zina replied. "I just knew we were going to turn that Hyundai into a convertible."

Antione laughed. "The planes fly over the main road, and then onto the airports runway. It's not as close as it appears, but it can be a little unnerving the first time."

The two women nodded as Zina reached for Antione, and Camille reached for her small carry-on bag stowed away in the overhead compartment.

Stepping out of the airplane and into the open air took Camille's breath away. A breeze of warm salt air blew gently, caressing her body and causing the sun dress she wore to billow softly against her flesh. The length of her hair waved freely with the wind, and she felt intoxicated by the warmth of sunshine that rained down on them. Her heart skipped with anticipation.

Zina leaned in close to whisper in her ear. "These island men are looking at you, girl," she said, winking at the skycap, who was watching them closely. The man grinned widely, boasting an open smile of bright white teeth, and a hunger in his dark brown eyes that had them both buck-naked in his bed. "You might get lucky on this trip," Zina murmured quietly.

Camille grinned, feeling a rush of color rise to her cheeks as the man winked back. Her eyes danced with excitement as she laughed with the Zina. "You really need to stop," she said softly.

Within minutes, Antione had collected their luggage, gotten them through customs, and was talking nonstop as a small taxi, driven by a woman with a deep island accent, maneuvered them, and her car, out of the airport parking lot and onto the main road toward the DeCosta homestead.

As Antione rambled Bermudian trivia, Camille inhaled the beauty of the views. The islands vibrant green foliage swayed lazily in the breeze, the lush native landscape resonating with florae that danced in tones of tangerine, crimson, scarlet, and azure. The sweet, succulent aroma of hibiscus made Camille giddy with joy, and the fact that she could barely contain her excitement surprised her.

The women marveled at the homes that sat nestled in the rise and fall of the hills. The limestone structures sat reverent, in shades of lilac, salmon, plum, and pumpkin, holding court like intricate mosaic squares. With glimpses of sapphire ocean in the background, the impressive views blended harmoniously, offering onlookers a wonderful balance of nature and architecture. It was truly a veritable feast for an artist's eye, and Camille could almost see her sister's mind absorbing the possibilities.

"It's absolutely beautiful," she gushed before catching herself. Feeling foolish over her excitement, she turned to see if her sister and the new husband had notice, but found them locked lip to lip, oblivious of her sentiments.

Turning east toward the heart of Tucker's Town, the driver soon pulled into the gates of Art-House, which sat against the cerulean waters of Castle Harbour. Each home had a name, Camille noticed, having passed Angel's Hall, Rose Cottage, Heaven's

Hill, and many others along the way. Most had been elegant or witty, sentimental titles befitting the home or the history of its residents. She smiled, the gesture giving way to low laughter as she took in the view.

Art-House was a two-level Mediterranean wonder sprawled gracefully over the top of a high hill. Painted a soft peach with a dark green trim, the home was framed by a large piazza that swept from one side of the front to the other. Charming louvered shutters framed in the multitude of windows, and matching trellises sat positioned for the morning glories to climb. Banana trees beckoned the ocean's breeze from large stone podiums and the entire state seemed to be in a perpetual state of bloom.

"Welcome to Art-House," Antione said, tipping his hand at the taxi driver as she drove back down the drive and out of the gates.

"This is absolutely breathtaking," Camille said, spinning herself in place to take it all in.

"Is Vincent here?" Zina asked.

Antione looked at his watch. "Probably at the pool. Swimming is a daily indulgence for him when he's home. Let's go inside."

The trio stepped through the stained glass, mullioned entranceway and were greeted in the immense foyer by a very small silver-haired woman with skin the color of shiny copper, and a very large black-and-rust-colored rottweiler.

"Antione! Welcome home," she cried, reaching to pull the man into her arms.

"Hello, Nana," Antione replied, planting kisses down the woman's face. "You look wonderful." he said, stepping back to look at her. "Hey, Savage," he said, reaching out to stroke the top of the animal's massive head.

The woman rolled her eyes, flipping her hand at him. "You stop. Now who might this be?" she asked.

"Nana, this is my new bride, Zina. Zina, this is my grandmother, Mrs. Florence Gibbons, but everyone calls her Nana."

The woman reached out her arms and pulled the Zina close to her. "Hello, my darling. My boys have told me so much about you," she said, kissing the side of Zina's face. "How beautiful you are, child!"

"Thank you, Nana. I'm so happy to finally meet you. Antione has told me so much about you as well."

"Good things, I hope."

"Nothing but."

Antione sucked his teeth. "Tch. Would I do anything else?"

The old woman stepped to the side, eyeing Camille with a large grin. "And you must be this sister. Equally as beautiful, you are."

Camille smiled, nodding her head. "Yes, I'm Zina's sister, and thank you."

Antione reached out to pull her closer. "This is Camille."

Nana hugged her warmly. "Welcome, child. Our home is now your home also."

"Thank you. That is very sweet of you."

"So did you young people have a nice flight?"

"It was very good, Nana," Antione replied. "The weather was perfect and the landing was even better."

"He doesn't like to fly, you know," Nana said, guiding them toward the center of the house, into a tastefully decorated family room. "Antione is afraid of heights. Not like my Dante. That other grandson of mine has been behaving, I hope?"

"He's doing well, Nana. He would've come with us except he's speaking at a law conference in San Diego this weekend."

"Yes, he called me last night to say hello."

"Where's the old man?"

"Your father is taking his swim. I just took him something to drink. Why don't you and the girls go say hello, and I'll bring down some ginger beer for us all? You girls like ginger beer, don't you?"

"I've never had it," Camille answered.

"Neither have I," said Zina.

"Well, you will both love it," she said, heading toward the kitchen, the dog following closely on her heels. "I'll make us a light snack. I'm sure you all must be hungry for something to eat." Antione gestured for them to follow him outside.

Stepping through the large glass doors onto the stone patio, Camille was again awed by the beauty of the landscape. The outside loggia separated them from the pool area and they walked through open Moroccan arches onto the plush green grass. Camille could hardly resist the temptation to pull off her shoes to fill the lush carpet beneath her bare feet.

The deep bass of his voice pulled her attention as Vincent DeCosta called out to them. "Hello! Welcome!"

Zina grinned, waving excitedly as she and Antione rushed over to greet him. Camille stood awestruck, her legs frozen in place. She watched as the man hugged his son warmly, the laughter between them bringing through the air. He then turned, reaching out to pull Zina into an affectionate embrace. As his eyes met hers, Camille could feel a sudden rush of perspiration rise to the surface of her palms.

His smile was exhilarating, and Camille stood like a deer in headlights as he made his way to her side. He walked with an arrogant swagger, his hips moving with a stark confidence. Had she met this man on the street she would never have imagined him to be the father of Antione and Dante. Vincent DeCosta was a beautiful specimen of manhood. He carried his age with an amazing grace, easily able to pass for Antione and Dante's much older brother, instead of their father. As tall as his sons, he stood six feet five inches, a large man with a muscular build similar to Antione's. Rigorous training kept him infirm shape, the dark flesh of his arms and chest pulled tight over the granite of his muscles. His complexion was a rich, dark sable, his skin nourished by the rich sun and to the saltwater. His hair was black pepper with strands of salt tossed sparingly about, the conservative cut a complement to his chiseled features.

She stared into his blue-black eyes, transfixed by the warmth of motion that exuded from them. As he stopped in front of her, reaching out to say hello, Camille struggled not to stare down at the broad, bare chest that glistened from a faint coat of sunscreen and wet drops of water from the pool. His abdomen showcased the last remnants of a near-perfect six-pack, the taut flesh rippling in picture-perfect waves. Dropping her gaze, she fell to the nervousness only intensifying when she focused on the line of his long legs and the package of manhood that pressed boldly against the front of a pair of red Speedo's.

The man laughed in her ear as he wrapped his arms around her.

"Why are you shaking?" he asked. "I won't bite."

Camille looked up into his eyes, returning his smile. "It wasn't you I was worried about," she replied, returning his hug gingerly.

His chest pressed against hers sent shockwaves up from the pit of her stomach out into her limbs. Behind him, Zina and Antione stood amused by her reaction, her sister breaking out into laughter and shaking her head.

"Welcome, Camille. It's a pleasure to finally meet you."

"It's an honor, Mr. DeCosta. I can't begin to tell you how excited I am."

Vincent laughed. "Well, if you call me Mr. DeCosta again you might not be so excited, because I will put you out. Please, call me Vincent. We don't stand on too much formality here."

Camille nodded, inhaling deeply. "Not a problem, Vincent. It won't happen again."

"At least not for another hour." Zina laughed. "Look at you, little sister," she said teasingly. "The man's got you all giddy. Would think you never met any famous people before."

Camille blushed, the round of her face turning hot. "Shut up, Zina."

They all laughed. "Well, let me show you to your rooms so you can get comfortable," Vincent said. "You two ladies did bring swimsuits, I hope?"

Zina nodded. "Wouldn't leave home without them."

"I've got it, Pop. Nana said she was bringing out some refreshments so we'll be right back out," Antione said.

Vincent smiled. "I'll go see if I can give her hand."

Camille and Zina turned to follow Antione. Unable to resist, Camille looked back over her shoulder to find Vincent staring at her just as intensely, that magnetic smile sending waves of heat from the top of her head to the tips of her toes.

Antione led them through the house, to the bedrooms in the rear quarter of the estate. Stopping at the first one left, Antione dropped his and Zina's bags in the doorway. "This is our room, baby," he said as a Zina leads to peer inside.

Two rooms down, the door and gesturing for Camille to enter. "Camille, this one is he is. Dad's room is just at the end of the hall, and Nana this is on the other end of the house by the family room and kitchen. This is your harm, so make yourself comfortable. Don't be afraid to ask for anything."

Camille nodded. "Antione, your family is so sweet."

He nodded in agreement, pride shining in his eyes. "They're good people. Wait until you meet the rest of the brood."

Behind him, Zina wrapped her arms around his waist, reaching up to kiss the side of his face. "I told you he was wonderful," she said, her face growing with happiness. Camille couldn't help being happy with her.

"Well, why don't you two get changed?" Antione said. "I need to call and let my office know he arrived. I need them to fax me some paperwork. I'll meet you both down by the pool." He kissed Zina one last time before heading back down the hallway.

Inside the large guest room Camille fell back against the bed. The interior decor was cool and inviting. The work and furnishings in the room was a

Bermuda cedar, the rich aroma filling the air. Is whitewashed stone, texture resonating from wall to wall. A white fan spun in slow motion from the steep ceiling. The headboard, a settee, and an armchair were upholstered in an ultrasoft leather the color of mint. The window and bed coverings were all white lace. A magnificent fireplace, with a heavy cedar mantel, housed a large stone planter filled with lush green ivy that flowed up and over its sides. Carved-oak candlesticks flanked the sides, holding white candles in varying heights waiting to be lit. Above the mantle, lean metal sculptures were lined in a row, a rich patina coating the copper underlay. The pieces were divine, dancing angels in varying stages of flight. Original DeCostas, no doubt. Camille rose to take a closer look just as Zina bounded in, not bothering to knock, a peach-toned bikini and matching sarong wrapped around her lean frame.

"Why aren't you dressed?"

"Just taking it all in."

"Uh–huh."

"Why didn't you warn me about Vincent? I was expecting the man to be…" She hesitated. "… Different."

Zina laughed. "Different how?"

"I don't know. Older, grayer, flabbier, just different."

Her sister shook her head. "You didn't stop to think that a man with two sons as fine as Antione and Dante might not be a fine specimen himself? Sister, please!"

Camille giggled. "How old is he?"

"Daddy's age, I would imagine."

"Oh, don't say that, Zina!"

Her sister laughed again. "Sorry, little sister, but I don't doubt my dear father-in-law is pushing sixty if he isn't already there."

"Oh, cuss!"

"Nothing wrong with being sixty, especially when you don't look a day over forty-five."

"No. But it wouldn't be a problem at all if I was fifty-nine, and didn't look a day over twenty-five, either."

"Well, from the way the man was staring at you I don't think you being thirty-one bothered him one bit."

Camille rolled her eyes. "Antione doesn't have any more brothers he doesn't know about, does he?"

"Girl, please. What's wrong with Vincent?"

"Vincent is old enough to be our father!"

"But he's not our father. Far from it. I think you should go for it."

"Honey, hush your mouth!"

"I'm serious, Camille."

"You would be. Daddy would have a fit."

"It's not Daddy's heart we're dealing with here. It's yours. If you're interested in the man, and he's interested in you, why not? You definitely have more to gain than you could ever lose."

"It wouldn't bother you? I mean, he is your father-in-law."

"No. It wouldn't bother me at all. You just need to stop being so uptight and just run with it. You might actually have some fun for a change."

Camille sighed deeply, pondering her sister's comments.

"Hurry and change. I'm going down to the pool. I'll meet you there."

Nodding her head, Camille close to the door firmly behind her sister, then reached into her suitcase to search for her swimsuit.

CHAPTER 6

Camille started down the hallway into the family room just as Vincent strolled into the entranceway, a large beach towel wrapped around his waist, obscuring the red of his Speedos. The man smiled broadly, appraising her La Blanca retro-print swimsuit with its halter top and plunging neckline that exposed the round of her cleavage and the bare of her back. The matching skirt skated mid-thigh, revealing her long, athletic legs. The ivory fabric with the its floral palm print in rich earth tones complemented her dark complexion, the vivid brown of her skin polished from a rich lather of scented lotion.

"I was just coming to check if you were okay. We were starting to worry about you."

Camille blushed, embarrassment seeping into her pores. "I'm sorry. I was just so captivated by the artwork in the room that I lost track of time."

The man nodded, resting his palm against the small of her back. Camille could feel herself shiver beneath his touch. "Let me show you around. I've collected some wonderful pieces over the years that you might be interested in seeing."

God, please don't let me embarrass myself, Camille thought to herself, responding only with a smile and a quick nod of her head.

As Vincent guided her from room to room detailing the numerous paintings that adorned the walls and the sculptures that sat atop pedestals, Camille was in awe. His collection was incredible. Her experience and knowledge of the arts were evident as she critiqued the artwork and debated artists with him. Her initial anxiety had subsided, and she felt comfortable when he pulled her along, his hand holding hers in the living room, an arm posed around her waist in the office, a palm relaxed against her forearm as they stood in the dining room.

The man talked with his hands, and it felt comfortable when he touched her. Camille welcomed the light caresses that blessed her skin, his fingertips filled with the energy of his words and his passion for his craft and that of his peers.

"Is there anyone you don't have hanging in your home?" Camille laughed as they headed back outside. "This is truly some collection. How did you amass such an assortment of originals? I mean you have Holyfield, Bearden, Holston, and Adams…! Did I mis anyone?

Vincent laughed with her. "Just one or two, and we haven't even gone into my studio, or my other homes. But, you know that artists trade work. Some were gifts. Others I commissioned or purchased outright."

"But you even have an original Catlett and the Henry Tanner watercolor is absolutely spectacular," Camille said, clearly impressed.

"I paid a small fortune for both of those puppies, I'll have you know. I wish I could get Cosby to sell me *The Banjo Lesson*. I would truly be a happy man then."

"Fat chance," Camille smiled. "I wouldn't even sell you that one."

"Well, I'll have you know I recently acquired two new paintings when I was in Santa Fe. I am now the proud owner of two original Zina Martin's."

Camille cut her eyes at him, smirking. "And which ones did you get?"

"The self-portrait, *Independent Woman*, and the abstract, *In Retrospect*."

"Nice choices. Did she give you a good deal?"

"She did indeed."

"Remind me to speak to her about that," Camille chuckled.

Vincent wrapped his arm around her shoulder, pulling her close as they joined the rest of the family by the pool. Nana and the dog sat in the shade of a large olive tree. The matriarch dozed lightly. Savage lifted his head to acknowledge their arrival, then lay back down at the elder woman's feet, rolling comfortably onto his side.

"Nice dog," Camille said, nodding her head toward the large animal. "Is there a reason you named him Savage?"

Vincent laughed. "Yes. He was named after a sculptor whose work I admired. Augusta Savage. She actually taught art in Harlem during the Depression, but then I'm sure you know that," he said smiling warmly in her direction.

Antione and Zina lay wrapped in each other's arms on a plastic pool raft. Every moment or so Zina would reach a hand into the blue of the pool's water and draw a cooling spray of wet down Antione's chest.

"Would you like a ginger beer, Camille?" Vincent asked, reaching for a glass and filling it with crushed ice from an ice chest.

"Thank you. That sounds like it would be quite refreshing." Camille took a seat on one of the poolside lounge chairs.

"If you want something stronger I can make you a dark and stormy," Vincent said temptingly.

"What's that?"

"Ginger beer and ninety-proof Bermuda black rum."

She laughed, the sound rising from deep in her midsection. "I think I'll pass for now."

"So where did you two get lost to?" Zina asked, arching her eyebrows in Camille's direction, interrupting their hushed whispers.

"Mr. DeCosta was showing me his art collection," she answered, in that tone that let Zina know it was none of her business.

Vincent laughed. "Was it that bad? Are we back to you call me Mr. DeCosta again?"

She smiled, then winked her eye in his direction.

In the pool, Antione laughed, rolling onto his side as he pulled his wife into the water with him.

CHAPTER 7

Camille slept well. Better than she had anticipated. Despite a full day of traveling and a very long night, she felt rested, almost euphoric. They had all lounged poolside until well after the sun had dropped down out of the sky. Then she and Zina had joined Nana in the kitchen, helping to prepare dinner as the older woman had guided and directed them. When finished, the family had feasted on Portuguese chicken piri-piri, tomato rice, and fresh-baked bread, topped off with an incredible caramel custard flan. All of them had eaten until they were stuffed, savoring every morsel of the spectacular meal.

As they'd eaten , Camille, Vincent, and Nana had shared Antione and Zina stories, everyone laughing until their sides ached and tears were rolling down their faces. After helping with the dishes, she and Vincent had retired to the family room, still talking. The newlyweds had disappeared early, dropping out of sight to go do whatever it was newlyweds did, and even Nana had disappeared, leaving her and Vincent to their own devices when she said an early good night.

Camille had been fascinated by the stories he told, drawing particular pleasure from tales of his travels, his experiences in the art world, and the relationships he had with artists whose work she'd admired for years. Camille found himself hanging on every word that fell from his mouth. The man was engaging, his charismatic presence causing her to catch her breath with rising desire. For one brief moment, his gaze had been so deep that Camille found herself lost in a well of fantasy, imagining how he might feel against her. Vincent had shaken her back to reality, his words drawing a wealth of laughter from them both.

"I was glad Nana didn't serve salad tonight. Don't know if I could have survived another plate in my lap."

Camille had felt her cheeks getting warm. "I was truly hoping you wouldn't remember that," she said, her smile widening across her face.

Vincent laughed. "How could I forget! It's not often a beautiful woman throws food all over me, grabs my crotch in public, then disappears when the thrill is over."

Camille giggled with him, tossing her head from side to side as they laughed over the memory. "I can't begin to tell you how embarrassed I was."

He reached into the pocket of his shirt. "You took off so fast I didn't get an opportunity to give this back to you."

Camille reached out her hand as Vincent dropped her charm bracelet into her palm. "I can't believe you still have this," she commented, surprise gracing her face.

"After a moment like we shared, I couldn't imagine ever letting it go."

Before Camille knew it, time had disappeared, and it was well after two o'clock in the morning. Vincent had walked her to the door of her room and had wished her sweet dreams, squeezing her hand gently as he did so. Camille had tossed and turned for what seemed like hours thinking about him, twisting the gold bracelet round and round her wrist. Eventually, though, she'd succumbed to sleep, a pillow pressed tightly between her thighs.

Although she'd been lying awake for some time, it wasn't until there was a knock on the door that she thought to rise from her resting place. There was no clock in the room, and she had lost all sense of time, having lent Zina her watch the night before.

"Come in," she said, lifting herself upright on the bed.

Vincent pushed the door open slowly, peeking his head in around the large wood frame. "Good morning. I didn't wake you, did I?"

Camille smiled, pulling at the covers around her. "No. Not at all. I was just being lazy. What time is it?"

Vincent glanced down to the timepiece on his wrist. "Ten-forty."

Camille shook her head, pulling a hand to her face. "How embarrassing. You and Nana must think I'm just awful."

The man grinned. "Not at all. I'm just getting up myself. It looks like the rest of them have abandoned us, though. Nana has some charity thing she's doing for the church today, and your sister and my son have gone into Hamilton."

"They just left us?"

He nodded. "Looks that way. I thought I would make you some breakfast, then if you're interested I'd love to show you my studio and what I'm working on for the show."

"I'd like that. I'm flattered that you'd want me see your work in progress."

He shrugged, drawing her attention to his bare chest as he pushed his shoulders up toward the ceiling. "After that we can go see Lydia at the gallery and get the business taken care of."

She nodded. "I can be dressed in a few minutes."

"Take your time. Cooking is not my specialty, so it may take me a minute to figure out the stove."

Camille laughed. "Tell you what. I'll meet you by the refrigerator and we can tackle it together."

Laughing with her, Vincent nodded his head. "That sounds like a plan to me," he said, nervously twisting the doorknob. Staring, he could not help noticing the rise and fall of her breasts beneath the thin tank top that she wore. The white cotton fabric lay like translucent mesh against her skin, the fullness of her bustline pushing at the surface. An awkward silence filled the room as Vincent paused in the doorway. Camille could feel her breath slipping away as their eyes locked. She gasped, dropping her gaze to the elegant bedding wrapped around her.

Vincent stammered. "I…I'm…I'm going to go get dressed. I'll meet you in the kitchen."

When Camille looked up, he was gone, the door closed firmly behind him. Rising, she rushed into the bathroom to toss cold water against her face. Staring at her reflection, she struggled with the rise of emotion that caused her to breathe heavily, waves of trepidation dancing in the pit of her stomach. She struggled to understand the impact this man was having on her emotions.

After a quick shower, Camille dressed, then joined him in the kitchen. Vincent looked up, seeming to blush as she entered the room. Inhaling deeply, Camille smiled.

"Do you suddenly feel as anxious as I do?" he asked, breaking the silence that threatened to consume them.

Her faint smile widened into a deep grin. "Very. I feel like I'm back in high school, and you're the popular football player I have a crush on."

He laughed, the warm vibration filling the room. "Then you must be the popular cheerleader I have a crush on."

"At my age it doesn't make an ounce of sense."

He shook his head. "How old are you exactly?"

"Thirty-one. I'll be thirty-two in November."

"Ouch!" he said, twisting his face as though in pain.

"How about you?"

"I just turned fifty-four."

Camille blew the breath she'd been holding past her lips, the warm air rushing into the room. "Well, I think that settles that," she said, shaking her head. "So what do you have in that there refrigerator, Mr. DeCosta?"

Vincent laughed again, pulling open the refrigerator door. "The choice is yours, Miss Martin."

Strolling to his side, Camille peered into the cool cavity. "Are you a bacon and eggs man, or more of a health nut?"

"Well, if the truth were to be told, I usually forgo breakfast for a Coco-Cola and two Tylenols to get the day started."

"That's not good."

"Any suggestions?"

"We'll do healthy and light since you're not used to eating a big meal," she said, pulling some fruit and yogurt from the box. "Do you have any granola?"

"Does it come in a box?"

She laughed. "Box. Jar."

Vincent pulled open one of the kitchen cabinets. "Boxes are in here. Cereal is on the left. I'm not sure where the jars are kept."

Minutes later, as the duo dined on breakfast parfaits followed by two cups of tea, their levels of comfort returned. The banter between them was once again light and cheery, and Camille relished how easily they made each other laugh. When all was done, Vincent tossed the dishes into the dishwasher and led the way to his studio, a freestanding structure that sat on the other side of the private road. It was a short walk, laced with oleanders and cedar, and Camille welcomed the warmth of sunlight that followed them across the road, the aromatic hibiscus leading the way.

"Close your eyes," Vincent said, taking her by the hand as they entered the room's interior. Camille closed her eyes as he pulled her along beside him. "Keep them closed," he commanded.

Camille could hear him as he walked around her, could feel his presence as he wrestled with something large in front of her.

"Can I open them?"

"Not yet. Once second."

Camille clasped her hands together in front of her. Now?"

"No."

She tapped her foot.

"Don't be impatient," he said, leaning to whisper in her ear, his warm breath blowing lightly against her neck.

Camille inhaled deeply, suddenly unnerved by the game he was playing. "Come on," she implored. "let me open my eyes."

His presence was undeniable as he walked a tight circle around her, coming to stand behind her. He leaned his torso against her back, his hands reaching round to cover her eyelids. A shiver ran down the length of her spine.

"Okay. Are you ready?"

"Yes," she said, her voice barely audible as she fought the rise of desire that had suddenly consumed her.

"Open your eyes," he said, pulling his hands from in front of her face. "What do you think?"

Opening her eyes, Camille stared at the work of art that stood in front of her. Strolling slowly around the image, she could feel him staring at her, could feel him waiting for her opinion. Looking in his direction, she shook her head, visibly stunned.

Vincent smiled. "Well?"

A simple podium hosted the massive piece of artwork in front of her. A freestanding picture frame, forty-eight by sixty inches, designed from elaborate moldings, rotated slowly on one corner. In the midst of the frame, a three-dimensional, fifty-four by thirty-six inch brass figure of a man and woman locked in an intimate embrace pirouetted in the opposite direction, seeing to float freely in the wind. The visual was open, intricate, and incredible sensual.

"Oh, Vincent, it's amazing! How in the world did you—"

"Now, now" he said, pressing a finger to his lips. "A good artist never gives away his secrets."

She smiled. "Well, you have truly outdone yourself. You were right. This is going to blow them away."

"I have six of them completed," he said, pointing to the worktable in the corner of the room. "I only have four more to go, and then the collection is complete."

Camille pulled herself to the table to study the other structures. The frames were all similar, elegantly detailed, and finished in subtle wood tones. But it was the metal structures that captivated your attention. There were couples. Couples dancing, couples sharing a caress, all of them floating effortlessly through space, spinning against the axis of the frame. Half were completed in brass; the others had been formed in pewter. Each of the figures was elaborately detailed and precisely sculpted. The total effect was phenomenal. Hands rested gently against a breast or caressed a shoulder. Lips kissed her fingertips, and brushed the back of the knee. Limbs curved and wrapped around other limbs. Elongated appendages stretched in seductive embraces. It was the subtlety of the movement that gave the work additional dimension.

Camille marveled at the delicate balance of wood and metal that danced so effortlessly. As she studied a pile of sketches and notes that lay askew in the corner of the large table, she was amazed at how he'd so successfully transferred his vision into the dimensional work before her. "These are beautiful, Vincent."

"I'm glad you like them."

"Like them, I *love* them. They're absolutely incredible," Camille finished, returning to stand at his side.

Camille could feel her heart racing. The tension between them seemed to resurface out of nowhere. Vincent pushed his hands deep into the pockets of his linen slacks. "Well, are you ready to go? he asked, his voice cracking ever so slightly.

Camille paused, studying the lines of his face. Her eyes drew a path along the curve of his chiseled chin, up to his full lips, and over the slight arch of his wide nose. There was a maturity to the lines of his face. A maturity that validated his years of experience. Staring into his eyes, she could feel the pretense of resolution melting into oblivion. A voice in the back of her mind shouted loudly in her ear, *Don't do this, Camille. Think about this, Camille. Your father won't like this, Camille.*

When Vincent reached out a tentative hand to stroke the side of her face, the voice faded until the only sounds she could hear were the beat of her own heart and the anticipation in the swell of her breath. Pressing both hands to his chest, Camille relished the sensation of his silk T-shirt against her palms. As she walked into him, pressing her body against his, Vincent pulled her close, tasting her lips with his. The kiss was soft, a gentle brush of flesh against her flesh. They enjoyed the beauty of it, their mouths dancing like rose petals skipping in a gentle breeze.

As he pulled her tighter against him, wanting to close any gap that may have existed, Camille swore she could feel his heart beating against her breast. As the kiss intensified, Vincent parted her lips with his tongue, easing his way inside her mouth. He tasted sweet, like the honey that had flavored the cups of tea they'd enjoyed at breakfast, and she savored the sensation, fearful that it would be gone from her too soon. It seemed like an eternity before either of them pulled away, and when they did, neither one of them wanted to.

Vincent leaned his forehead against hers, clasping the sides of her face between his large hands. He inhaled deeply, then caressed her cheek with his own as the warmth of his breath blew gently past her ear. Camille could feel her whole body quiver, and she was suddenly fearful that her legs might drop her to the floor.

"You make me weak," she whispered. "My knees are shaking."

Vincent laughed, a low chuckle that made her smile. "Don't worry, I promise not to let you fall."

The embrace was as intoxicating as the kiss when Vincent held her tightly, gentle hands dancing a slow glide up and down her spine, across her back, resting lightly at the rise of her buttocks. He painted soft strokes against her skin, moving from one side of her face to the other, using his cheeks and chin as his brush.

Stepping back, Vincent cleared his throat, embarrassed by the sudden rise of nature between them. "We should be going," he said, the depth of his voice a low whisper.

Inhaling deeply, Camille fought to still the quiver of emotion that seemed to flood over her. Reaching for his hand she entwined her fingers around the back of his, then gently kissed the center of his palm. As they made their way out of the room, Camille turned to take one last look at the dancing couple locked

A Love For All Time

intimately together, then reached to switch off the lights as Vincent locked the heavy door behind them.

CHAPTER 8

"Hey there! Glad to see you two finally made it out of bed." Zina sat in the kitchen, perched on one of the cushioned stools at the center island.

"Good morning," Vincent greeted.

"Hi," Camille replied. "Where did you and the husband take off to?"

"We just drove into Hamilton to have breakfast with some lawyer friend of his." Zina I'd them curiously. "So, what have you two been up to?"

Vincent and Camille traded quick glances, as Camille shrugged her shoulders. "Vincent was just showing me his studio."

Zina raised her eyebrows ever so slightly, a sly smirk on her face. "Is that all—" she started to say, Antione interrupting as he entered the room.

"Good morning, Camille. Hey, Pop. What's going on?"

"Good morning, son. We were just about to take off for the gallery. Would you and Zina like to join us?"

Antione looked at Zina, who looked back at him. "No, thank you. I think we'll pass," Zina said, giving her husband a look that said she had something more personal for them to do.

Vincent nodded, turning toward Camille. "Let me get my things, and we can get out of here."

Camille nodded, watching as he headed out of the room toward the back of the house.

"Hey, Pop, let me holler at you a minute," Antione called, followed behind him.

Camille inhaled deeply, cutting her eyes at Zina, who sat watching her too closely. She quickly changed the subject before Zina could get started, the words perched on the woman's inquisitive tongue ready to leap. "Zina, have you given any more thought to the abstract nudes you were thinking about doing?"

Zina dropped her glass onto the counter. "Not recently. I'd really put that on the back burner since our last discussion about how they might be received. Why?"

"I think they'll be perfect for this show. In fact, I know they will."

"You saw his sculptures, didn't you?"

Camille nodded, grinning widely. "They're incredible."

Zina puckered her lips. "I want to see."

"No. I don't want you to, and if he offers, you decline. I don't want anyone to say your work was influenced by something you saw Vincent doing. Just consider doing the nudes, and take it in whatever direction you want."

"Done. I've been dying to do them. You know that. If you think this is the show they'll do well in, then I'm all for it."

"Good. You need to call Darrell, too. Tell him you want those canvases gallery-wrapped, and you want them three inches deep."

Zina raised her eyebrows questioningly. "Why so deep?"

"I want you to wrap the image around the sides. We're not going to frame them and I really want them to jump off the walls."

"Now you know you've got me curious."

"Just trust me. This will be perfect."

"What will be perfect?" Vincent asked, reentering the room, Antione on his heels.

"The show title," Camille responded, nodding her head excitedly. "I just figured out what we're going to call this show."

They all looked at her curiously, waiting for her to share the news.

Camille smiled. "A Frame of Mind. Abstract renderings by Vincent DeCosta and Zina Martin."

Vincent nodded, understanding seeping from his eyes. "I like that. I like that a lot."

"So do I," Zina added. "You done good, girl. Knew you'd get the job done."

Camille rolled her eyes in Zina's direction.

"Ready?" Vincent asked.

She nodded, following behind him as he headed out the room.

Camille called out to them just as they reached the door. "Have fun, you two, and, Camille?"

"Yes?" she responded, spinning back around to stare at her sister.

"While you're gone, why don't you tell Vincent about you are ninety-day rule?"

Vincent looked at them curiously, his gaze racing from one to the other. Antione shrugged, not understanding, but planning to ask as soon as Camille and his father were out of earshot. With the color rushing to her cheeks, Camille spun about on her heels, grabbed Vincent's hand, and rushed him out to the car.

Time seemed to pass slowly as they drove towards Somerset and the Somerset Gallery. With the restricted twenty-five-mile-an-hour speed limit and winding roads, the journey felt as if it could last forever. Vincent and Camille chatted casually as Vincent pointed out the sites along the way. With each landmark they passed-- the Bermuda Aquarium, Flatt's Village, downtown Hamilton, the harbor, and Gibb's Hill lighthouse-- Vincent regaled her with historical tales.

Neither one of them commented on what had passed between them, unsure what needed to be said, if anything at all. Camille inhaled deeply, staring out in the distance as she reflected on the memories of his touch.

Vincent found himself falling deeper into thought, and when it seemed Camille was not at all bothered by the silence between them, he allowed his mind to reflect back on the conversation that had passed between him and his son.

Follow him down the hall and into the master bedroom, Antione had closed the door behind them, dropping down onto the edge of his father's bed.

"I didn't want to ask this in front of Zina, but is there something going on between you and Camille?"

Taken aback, Vincent turned, pretending to search for something lost in the bureau drawer. "Why would you ask that?"

Antione continued, staring at his father intently. "Once or twice I sent to some tension between you two. It was just strange."

Vincent lifted his eyes, looking over his shoulder in Antione's direction. "I'm sure it wasn't anything. She and I getting along fine."

Antione paused. "Look, Pop. I know she's an intriguing woman, but she's way too young for you. I mean, she's younger than I am. The woman could be your daughter, for heaven's sake."

Vincent pushed the were closed, slamming it with more force than was probably necessary. "I don't recall asking for your opinion, Antione. It's not like she's underage. The woman is an adult."

The man shook his head. "No, you didn't and yes, she is. But I wouldn't want anything to happen between you two that might cause some conflict later between our two families when it doesn't work out. Zina and I don't need that."

Vincent heaved a heavy sigh. "That won't happen."

"Okay, but please be careful. It might not be so easy for you to... resist..." He hesitated, searching for the right words to express what he'd been thinking, not wanting to offend the man. But after seeing how his father had been looking at the woman, and how she had looked aback, he had to admit that he was more than a bit concerned.

Vincent twisted the cap off a bottle of Givenchy cologne, splashed some into the palms of his hands, and then dabbed the moisture against his neck and face. "Leave it alone, Antione. You don't need to worry."

Antione nodded his head, studying his father closely, noting that something in the man's voice told him otherwise.

Vincent shifted the conversation. "Things with you and Zina okay?"

"Couldn't be better. Her father has some issues, but I think in time he will come to accept me and the marriage."

"I can understand his concerns. It happened so fast, and if I hadn't been there to see you two with my own eyes, I would probably not be thrilled about it either."

"Zina's a brilliant woman, Pop. She's intelligent, vibrant, talented, and beautiful. I would have been a complete fool to let her get away."

Vincent smiled. "I don't think she was planning to go anywhere, son, marriage or no marriage."

Antione laughed. "Well, since I've never believed in doing things halfway, there was no point in waiting. I knew I was in love the minute I saw her."

His father laughed with him, slapping him gently on the back of his shoulder. "So did I, boy. So did I."

Turning into the heart of Somerset Village, Vincent pulled his car into an empty parking space and shut off the engine. Shifting around in his seat, he turned to look at Camille. *What a beautiful woman,* he thought, staring as she pushed the hair out of her eyes and behind her ear. Camille smiled, blushing slightly as though she'd read his mind. Grabbing her hand, Vincent squeezed it gently, then leaned over and kissed her lightly on the mouth.

"Is everything okay?" Camille asked, sensing something was on the man's mind.

Vincent shrugged. "I don't know. I'm not sure what's going on. But I feel good. I feel like everything is the way it should be." He took a deep breath, tracing circles on her upper thigh with his forefinger. "Does that make any sense?"

She sighed softly. "More than you know."

"So, what was Zina talking about when we left? What is this ninety-day rule of yours?"

Camille blushed, the rush of color warming her face. She shook her head vigorously, then took a deep breath.

"I usually wait for the right moment to share this but…" She paused, catching her breath. "It has always been my policy not to become intimate with any man until we dated for at least ninety days. Sister dearest was trying to be funny."

Vincent laughed. "Hasn't been that obvious? Before we left, Antione was asking me what was going on with us."

Camille winced. "I'm so embarrassed."

"Don't be. There is no reason. We're two adults who are attracted to each other. There is nothing wrong with that."

"My father will find something wrong with this. You and he are about the same age."

Vincent grimaced. "Yeah. It might be a problem for him."

"No might in that. It will definitely be problematic."

Vincent had stopped drawing circles on her thigh, and was gently caressing the flesh beneath her slacks with the palm of his hand. The sensation against her skin was electric. "So, why ninety days?" he asked, staring deeply into her eyes.

Camille inhaled sharply, catching her breath so that she could respond with a semblance of lucidity. "Well, it enables me to see if a man is really interested in me, or if his motives are less than honorable. If he's willing to wait ninety days while we get to know each other, then I believe the relationship has the potential to endure."

"Has it worked?"

She shrugged. "Well, I've not dated too many men, and the slim few that were willing to wait left shortly after. But they left as friends, and I think the relationships we shared taught me a lot about myself and what I want from a man I'm thinking about sharing my body with."

Camille could see his mind working as he digested what she was saying. She continued, "Me sharing my body doesn't come without a significant price, and any man who is interested in me needs to know that. I want a man's undivided attention. I want flowers, and candy, and trinkets that let me know just how much I mean to him. I fully expect to be wined and dined, and treated like the queen know that I am," she said with a wry smile as Vincent listened intently.

She continued, "I demand honesty. I want to know everything there is to know about a man I'm involved with, and in return, he can trust that I will always be honest with him. I have no tolerance for the games some couples seem to like to play with one another. Before man becomes my lover, he has got to become my friend. We need to have a mutual respect for each other. That can't happen if the two of us aren't willing to invest time and attention to each other.

"I know that not every man can handle that kind of demand. But I firmly believe that if I'm willing to give it, then I surely deserve to receive it. I think ninety days is a good start toward discovering what two people are willing to do for each other, if it's important enough to them, without it getting all muddled up with sex."

Silence filled the empty space in the car. The duo studied each other intently. Camille inhaled deeply as Vincent appraised her, his stare a blend of curiosity and intrigue. Then nodding his head, he leaned to kiss her one last time, pressing his closed mouth to hers. Grasping her hands, he caressed her fingers with his own. "You have got my full attention, Ms. Martin," he stated, his head nodding ever so slightly. "And ninety-one days from today I will be making love to you," he said firm conviction, the sultry depths of his voice lighting a low flame beneath her. "Between now and then, I have no doubts about being able to myself worthy."

Camille fought to catch her breath, forcing air into her lungs. She stared so deeply into Vincent's eyes that she could feel herself falling into the depths of them. Butterflies danced in the pit of her stomach as she thought about the promises that spilled out of his eyes.

"And then what?"

Vincent winked. "And that I hope this old heart of mine will last so that I can do it again on day ninety-two."

Camille laughed, throwing back her head with glee. "You are so wrong."

Reaching out to caress her face, Vincent warmed her with the sweetness of his wide smile. "And then, you and I will continue to explore a world of possibilities," he said softly. "We will take advantage of whatever might be waiting for us to share together. Are you game?"

Camille nodded, leaning into his touch, and without a second thought, said, "Yes, I am."

Lydia Quinn met them at the door, rushing from behind an intricately carved oak reception desk. Grabbing hold of Vincent, she pulled him into a deep embrace, more personal than professional. Camille bristled ever so slightly. Lydia was a small woman, with a pretentious disposition. Camille knew the type, and instantly disliked her. When she extended her hand, Camille smiled politely, noting the woman's resemblance to the actress Glenn Close in the movie *Fatal Attraction.*

"Lydia, it's a pleasure to finally meet you," Camille said, switching to her professional voice, the tone in octave deeper, her enunciation extremely proper.

"The pleasure is all mine," the woman responded, appraising her from head to toe. "Welcome to Somerset Gallery."

Camille smiled. "You have a wonderful space here." She looked around the room, taking note of the collections displayed. Lydia had a penchant for watercolors, subtle images of Bermuda scenery and its waterscapes. Camille wondered about the ethnicity of the artists, and made a mental note to ask Vincent when they were alone.

"Thank you. We're so excited to have your sister showing with us. Vincent has spoken quite highly of her work."

Camille nodded, reaching for the portfolio in the leather briefcase she'd carried inside. "I thought you might like to see some images." She passed the woman a large manila envelope. "I've also included some marketing materials and bio information on Zina for you."

"Let's take a seat," Lydia said, gesturing toward the two chairs that sat in front of the desk. "Vincent, darling, have you been working?" she asked, as they all made themselves comfortable.

"No. Why should I be working?"

"You promised me wonderful pieces for the show. You wouldn't want to disappoint me, now, would you?"

Vincent chuckled. "Not me, Lydia. You make me too much money to ever disappoint you."

Lydia flipped her hand in his direction. "He's so silly."

Camille gave him a look that made him laugh even harder.

"So, dear, how long has Antione's wife been painting?"

"Zina has been painting professionally for almost fifteen years now."

"Does she exhibit often?"

"Most definitely. You'll see when you review the portfolio that not only has Zina exhibited in some very prestigious locations, but she also has a very impressive collectors list."

The woman nodded her blond head, shaking her curly hair over her shoulders. "We will need to get the show's title. Vincent says he's left that up to your sister, but if it's a problem I have a few suggestions that should work."

Vincent interjected, "Done. The title has been discussed and agreed upon."

"Oh?" Lydia queried.

"Yes," Camille said. "We will be calling the show A Frame of Mind."

Lydia looked from her to Vincent and back again. "A Frame of Mind. That's very interesting. And you like this, Vincent?"

"Most definitely. It's perfect for the new works I'm creating."

"When I get a preview of these works?" She asked coyly, twisting a curl of her hair around her index finger.

"Now, Lydia you know I never let anyone see my work before I'm finished with the whole collection. And you know I definitely never let you see my work unfinished," Vincent answered.

Camille dropped her gaze into her lap, smiling slightly. Lifting her head, she looked at Vincent, her smile widening, then turned her attention back to Lydia, who was fighting to suppress an obvious pout.

"Lydia, have you established the date of the reception yet?" Camille asked.

"I was thinking the last week in June. Of course I need to clear that with your schedule, Vincent, dear."

The man shrugged.

"If it's possible," Camille said, pulling her Palm Pilot from her bag to refer to her appointment calendar, "I'd like to schedule the opening for July tenth. That's ninety-one days from today."

Without looking at him, Camille could feel Vincent smirking.

"Well, I don't think it's a problem for me as long as Vincent agrees."

Vincent nodded, sitting up straighter in his seat. "July tenth is perfect. In fact, I wouldn't want to do it any sooner and definitely no later."

"Then we're agreed. The tenth of July it will be," Lydia confirmed, jotting the date down onto her calendar.

"Great," Camille smiled, rising from her seat. "Lydia, why don't you show me around? You have some exquisite pieces here. I'd like to know more about the artists.

The two women wandered off in deep conversation, Lydia leading the fifty-cent tour. Vincent leaned forward in his seat, his forearms resting atop his thighs, his hands clasped palm to palm. As he watched Camille, all he could think to do was grin.

CHAPTER 9

She had been introspective about Vincent since she'd boarded the plane and returned home. *What in the world was I thinking, leading that man on like that?* Camille thought to herself as she turned the corner onto North King Street and headed for work. *I don't know who's crazier, Zina or me.*

She inhaled quickly, catching her breath. Thinking of his hands, she imagined warm chocolate trickling against her flesh. The slow drizzle, hot and sweet, running slowly down the length of her torso, falling in puddles against her abdomen. The image made her gasp as she glanced around quickly to see if anyone was watching her, suddenly self-conscious about the rise of heat that flushed the cheeks of her face and burned hot against her inner thighs.

Under her breath, Camille swore with much conviction as she put her steel-gray Cadillac XLR into park. Beside her, a very large, fire-engine-red Lincoln Navigator with rental tags from Triangle Car Rental had taken her regular parking space. No doubt the possession of the couple who stood peering into the window of her gallery, their noses and hands leaving print marks against the freshly washed glass. Camille sighed. She had hoped for at least thirty minutes of downtime before she would have to deal with anyone today.

She took a deep breath, ignoring the woman who studied her inquisitively as her husband continued to breathe against the windowpane. The morning had started off badly, and up until that moment had gone steadily downhill. The alarm had not gone off, and she'd been awakened an our late when Nita called out her name from the living room. After she tore holes in two pair of stockings, her period suddenly dropped four days early, staining the skirt of brand-new Donna Karan matte jersey dress. She'd had to change her clothes twice before settling on a Ralph Lauren suit that fit well and would mask of the inevitable bloating that was sure to follow. Traffic on Interstate 40 had been horrendous, and just when she thought it couldn't get any worse the warning light that she'd ignored the night before signaled that she was out of gas. Through all of it, all she could think of was Vincent and the time they'd shared together. The rest of the day was probably going to be pure hell, she suddenly thought to herself.

Camille reached in the backseat for her briefcase, then adjusted the sunshades propped on top of her nose. Exiting the vehicle, she crossed to the front of the building, flashing the brightest smile she could muster. "Jon. Elise. Good morning. How are you two doing this beautiful day?"

The woman, a tall blonde with a Reese Witherspoon haircut and pale blue eyes, smiled back. "Wonderful, Camille. How are you?"

Camille leaned to give the woman a polite hug. "Doing as well as can be expected. I'm so sorry we're late opening today. I had some car trouble this morning."

The woman's husband turned to stare first toward Camille's new automobile, and then her. "What's wrong with your ride?" he asked.

"Nothing major, but thank you for asking." Camille cut her eyes at him, the all-telling look directing the man to leave her alone. She turned to smile at his wife and then refocused her attention on him.

"So how are you doing, Jon?" she asked, leaning to give him a hug as well, the warmth more genuine, the pinch to his backside more endearing.

Jon cleared his throat, returning a look that said she couldn't fool him but if she wanted it like that, then fine. Out loud, he said, "Pretty good, Camille. We are very excited to see the new show beginning of sentence. You know we couldn't wait to get here."

"Well, we're always delighted to have you both visit with us," she said primly. Unlocking the door, Camille held it opened widely, then gestured for the couple to go inside. Stepping into the doorway behind them, she flicked on the lights and headed for the office in the rear of the building. "I'll have a pot of hot coffee ready in just a few minutes. Make yourselves comfortable, and I'll be right back to answer any questions you may have."

"Take your time, Camille. We're in no hurry," Elise called after her. "I need something special for the dining room so we wanted to get another of your sister's paintings."

Entering the office, Camille dropped her briefcase onto the desk and reached to turn on the sound system. Darrow had left a CD of women blues singers in the CD player and the booming voice of big Mama Thornton, belting out "Hound Dog," filled the quiet of the room with her deep husky voice. The music drowned out the low echo of the couple conversing in the front gallery. It would not have been her choice of music, it was fitting for the exhibition currently on display. Darrow had a knack for matching the music to the artwork, his choices sometimes as abstract as her sister's paintings.

The telephone on the desk rang and Camille reached quickly over the desktop to beat the answering machine to the draw.

"Thank you for calling Galerie Noire. This is Camille."

"Hey, Camille, it Darrow."

"Hi, Darrow. Where are you?"

"Getting off the highway now. Just wanted to see if you'd had breakfast or if I need to bring you anything."

"I'm fine. About to make a pot of coffee for Jon and Elise Howard. They were waiting for me at the door this morning."

"Sorry about that. She left a message yesterday that they'd flown in early. I tried to call to warn you but your telephone rang busy all night long."

Camille chuckled. "Don't worry about it." In the distance, she could hear her name being called. "Let me go, my friend. See you in a few, Darrow."

"On my way, boss."

Camille returned to the front gallery to find the Howard couple in deep discussion over a new abstract piece by her sister, Zina.

"Camille, this is spectacular," Elise said excitedly.

Camille smiled. "Isn't it great? Zina just completed this series. This particular piece is called *Mad Cow*."

Jon laughed. "It's perfect. I'm putting it right in the dining room."

Elise shook her head, skewing her face as if she'd been into something sour. "Are you sure? Do we really want a piece titled *Mad Cow* in the dining room?"

"I think it's perfect."

"Actually, it will go perfectly with the other pieces you've required, Elise, and the colors will blend beautifully in any room of your home," Camille interjected.

The woman shrugged, nodding slowly as her husband also nodded approvingly.

"What others do you like?" Camille questioned.

Elise pointed toward a painting on the other wall. "I love the one called *Passion*. I also like the ones by that new artist Gwendolyn Redfern. Where is she from?"

"Gwendolyn was born right here in North Carolina. She joined us about a month ago, and we're excited to be representing not only her original paintings, but also her pottery. Her ceramic work is exceptional." Camille gestured toward the back of the gallery.

Elise rushed to look at the row of pottery the lined the rear wall. "I noticed these," she said. "They're wonderful. Where else has she shown?"

"Her work has been displayed nationwide. Of course, we have exclusive representation in this area, but she's exhibiting in a number of galleries across the states. In fact, she will be showing some of her artwork at the New York Art Expo next week.

September Gallery in Boston also handles a good deal of her work."

"Does she just do originals? Jon asked.

Camille shook her head. "No. She has some giclée prints of her work, but I don't carry any. We only carry her originals."

Alisa looked up inquisitively. "What is that?" She asked. "What is a giclée?"

Camille turned her attention to the woman, gesturing with her hands as if holding a piece of paper before her. "The did giclée is French and it's a method of reproducing original artwork. The original is scanned electronically and then digitally copied onto a high-grade paper or canvas. The process has grown substantially over the last few years and the artwork produced can be incredible."

Elise nodded her head with understanding, then turned back to the pottery, pulling one of the fragile vases into her hands.

The man frowned.

Camille smiled. "I know, Jon. You don't like reproductions."

"I just don't think there's any value in them. Reproductions lack any true investment value."

"It's not that I don't agree with you, Jon. I just think that the value of reproduced artwork has to be measured much differently from that of original artwork. But it does have value."

He shrugged. "I just know that if I'm going to drop thousands of dollars on artwork I want originals, not one of a few hundred prints that might be available. When I die, and my children inherit our collection, the works will be valued based on the artists' career, their reputation in the art community, and the fact that the collection houses only one-of-a-kind originals. If I had a limited-edition print, all it would be worth is of the value of the frame, because two hundred other people will have the same."

"If it's signed, and the artist has attained some level of achievement, that in its self will give the piece value, Jon."

He shook his head. "I don't agree. I only want originals, and I'm more inclined to only purchase artists who were just producing originals. Too many African-American artists get so caught up in trying to make a fast buck with copies that they're not producing quality original work."

"Too many African-American artists could never get their work seen, let alone purchased, if they didn't do reproductions. And too many folks who can't afford to purchase an original wouldn't learn to love and value the talent in our community without those prints," Camille responded.

Jon threw up his hands. "Oh, please."

Camille rolled her eyes, then shook her head, not wanting to get into a deep discussion with the man. The two of them had been down opposite sides of this road far too many times in the past. It had been almost ten years since Dr. Jon Howard had begun collecting Zina's paintings. When he married Elise, he had commissioned Zina to do an original work as a wedding present. The duo had been avid collectors ever since, flying in from their home in Manhattan twice yearly to see Zina's new collections. Five years ago, when Camille opened the gallery to showcase her sisters talent, the Howards had been faithful patrons, by the works of several artists Camille had recommended for their collection.

"Well, Jon, I would highly recommend you consider one of her originals for your collection. The woman is extremely talented and I'll guarantee it will be well worth your investment. Next year you're going to wish you had purchased one of the paintings at this price, because it's not going to last long."

Jon nodded his head, stopping to study one of the new works more closely. "She's got great technique. I do like her oils. The imagery challenges the thought processes."

Camille smiled. "I don't know how you feel about ceramic work, but her pottery is well worth considering also. It is superior quality and falls well within the realms of fine art. And they are all one-of-a-kind."

He glanced briefly in her direction, then strode over to stand by his wife's side. They are turned toward the door as Darrow entered with a loud hello, brushing past Zina to greet their guests.

"Dr. Howard, Mrs. Howard, how are you?" The short, squat man, just a hair short of being obese, extended his hand toward John's own outstretched one.

"Just fine, thank you. How about yourself?"

"Doing very well. Ready to add one of my paintings to your collection sometime soon." Darrow laughed.

Jon smiled broadly, nodding his head in Camille's direction. "I see it won't be long now. Camille says she's scheduled your show for the end of the year."

Darrow nodded. "I'm painting now to get ready for it."

"Well, we will definitely make a point of coming back for it. You make sure we get an invitation."

"Jon, would you and Elise like a cup of coffee?"

"Nothing for me, Camille. How about you, honey?"

"I'd love a cup," Elise responded, still studying the collection of pottery.

Darrow clasped his hands in front of him. "I'll take care of it, Camille," he said, heading for the office. "One Sweet-N-Low and a touch of cream, correct?"

"That's right. You remembered," Elise said with a sugary grin. "Thank you."

Darrow grinned back. "I'll just be a minute."

"So, Jon. What can we wrap for you today?"

Jon paused, scanning the room briefly. "I will definitely take *Mad Cow*. I think we'll get those two Redfern oils also. Elise, do you want that other one of Zina's that you liked?"

His wife nodded. "Yes. I think I'm going to take these three pots, too. I do like this woman's work."

Darrow returned, passing the cup of coffee to Elise. "I'll ring that up for you. Will we be shipping it to your Manhattan home, or do you want it going to the office, Dr. Howard?"

"Send it to the house. I'm moving my office next month, so we won't be putting anything there for a while."

Camille leaned back against the large sofa that filled the center floor space of the gallery, welcoming visitors to sit and enjoy the artwork when they entered. "That sounds exciting. Are you moving into larger space?"

Jon nodded. "I've taken on two new partners since last year and we've renovated two brownstones in Harlem."

Elise rolled her eyes. "I'll never see him now."

Camille smiled as Jon pitched his wife lightly, and a large brown hand through her blonde hair. As the two filled her in on their latest antics, Camille couldn't help remembering how her father had thoughts Dr. Jon Howard would be a great catch for Zina. Her father had been John's mentor when he was at Duke University's medical school. Jon and Zina had dated once or twice, but the good doctor had been far too tame for her sister's spirit. He'd been a great fan of Zina's artwork though, and had been a staunch advocate of her talent ever since. He and Camille had also become fast friends, despite their frequent disagreements and occasional bickering.

Neither she nor Zina had been surprised when Jon introduced them to Elise, a former Miss Maryland runner-up. The woman was a long-legged, blue-eyed beauty, and with the doctor's own tall, dark features, they stood out like and orange and a pear in a bowl of apples. Surprisingly, the duo fit beautifully together like a fresh fruit salad, blended just right. The telephone ringing and Darrow's excited voice interrupted her thoughts and their conversation.

With the portable in hand, Darrow entered the room, filling it with his excitement. Donna Hightower crooning," I Ain't in the Mood" in the background befitted Camille's disposition when Darrow told her Zina was on the telephone.

Taking the receiver from his hand, Camille smiled, more for the Howards than for Darrow. "Hello?"

Camille continued to grin into the telephone. "Yes, John and Elise are right here. No, I haven't told them your news, Zina. I didn't—"

Camille's grin was starting to irritate her facial muscles. "Hold on. You can tell them yourself.

"Jon, Zina would like to say hello to you and Elise," she said, passing him the telephone.

Elise came to stand at Camille's elbow. "Darrow says Zina got married. That's so exciting! When did this happen? Who is he?"

Camille could feel herself biting the words against her tongue. "It just happened recently. They met at the show in Santa Fe, fell in love, and got married."

Elise laughed. "I just adore your sister. I wish I was more like her. She's so spontaneous! Jon and I dated almost two years before I even thought about marrying him." Elise continued laughing, giggling into the telephone when Jon passed it to her to personally give Zina her congratulations.

Jon shook his head. Camille rolled her eyes in his direction and neither said a word out loud. Camille knew he was saving his comments for one of their telephone conversations that didn't include his spouse. As Elise passed the telephone back to Darrow, she came to wrap her arms around Jon's waist. "So, Camille, are you dating anyone special? Got a man yet?" she asked.

Jon laughed. Although they had all told the woman a hundred times how much Camille hated being asked that question, she still managed to get it in every chance she got. *Probably afraid I might try to take her man*, Camille thought to herself. Elise didn't need to have any worries in that area though. Camille had no interest in going where she knew her sister had been. Most especially when she knew the man didn't have a good two inches to brag about. She and Jon exchanged a look between them.

"No one special, Elise," she said aloud, an image of Vincent suddenly popping into her mind.

"Well, now that Zina's married, we need to find you a husband."

"No, thank you, Elise. I appreciate the offer though."

Elise smiled. "Well, one of Jon's partners isn't married. Maybe one day we can hook you two up when you're in the city. I think you and Russell would make a delightful couple," she said, completely ignoring what Camille had said.

Jon hugged his wife's shoulders. "Can't beat these matchmakers, Camille. Best thing to do is just join 'em."

Camille shrugged, rolling her eyes one more time as she quickly changed the subject. "Elise, come take a look at the pottery I haven't put out yet. I think there's a piece that would go nicely with your new painting."

Relishing the magnitude of the morning's sale, Camille sent Darrow home early. Her nerves had been on edge since the Howards had left, and she couldn't bear one more question from Darrow about her trip to Bermuda. Seated behind the comfort of her large desk, she regained her composure, feeling more at ease as she flipped through the stack of mail that had been left for her. A note detailing the sale of two paintings while she'd been gone made her smile.

Rising from her seat, Camille strolled the gallery. She liked her business, felt good about the ambience she'd created within the confines of the four walls. The mix was eclectic, and elegant, and spoke volumes about the talent she represented. An aura of pride surrounded her as she adjusted a painting that lay slanting against the ivory wall. The gallery door opening and closing, and then her father's booming voice, intruded upon her thoughts, calling her to stand at attention.

"Good afternoon, daughter." Louis leaned to give her his requisite kiss and hug.

"Hi, Daddy. This is a surprise."

He smiled. "Thought I'd stop by to see how your trip was."

"It went very well. I'm looking forward to Zina's show there."

"Did you meet his people?"

She shook her head, tossing her father a wry smile. "Yes, Daddy. We met his grandmother, who is absolutely delightful, and his father, of course. The family hosted a barbecue before we left, and we had a chance to meet his cousins, and aunt's, and uncles. They were all very nice. I think you'll like them.

Louis nodded. "Well, while you two were gone I gave it some thought, and I think we should host a reception for Zina and Antione. I think we should do that," he repeated. "Officially announce the marriage."

Camille took a seat on the sofa. "That's very sweet. Have you discussed it with Zina yet?"

"Spoke with her this morning. She said she'd leave all the arrangements to you."

Camille rolled her eyes. *Like I don't have anything else to do*, she thought.

Louis continued, "I was thinking that we should throw a sit-down dinner. I have a number of business associates who should be invited, as I would imagine

Antione has too. Then of course we should invite his people. Give me a chance to sit down and talk with his father. How does he feel about this marriage?"

Avoiding her father's eye, Camille shrugged. "I don't think he has any problems with it. I mean he was there when they met and all. He seemed supportive enough."

Louis scoffed. "Doesn't make a bit of sense. How could he let them—"

Camille interrupted. "Don't start, Daddy. You know as well as anyone, when Zina wants to do something she's going to do it, and no one can stop her, most especially not a man who didn't know her for more than a day."

"Well, I would have thought he'd have some control over his son."

Camille eyed her father. "Do you think you could have controlled Zina if you'd been there?"

He shrugged. "You're probably right, daughter. That sister of yours can be a handful when she wants to be. So, what did you think of him?"

"Who?"

"Antione's father. He's an artist, isn't he?"

Nodding her head, Camille responded, averting her eyes, "Yes, he's a sculptor. I think you'll be very pleased when you meet him. I liked him a lot." She glanced over to where her father sat, checking to see if her voice had betrayed any emotion she wasn't ready to have exposed.

Louis Martin rose to his feet. "Let's plan on dinner tomorrow. The four of us can sit down and plan this reception. You pick a nice restaurant, okay?"

Camille nodded obediently. "Yes, sir. I'll call Zina and let her know."

Heading for the door, Louis turned back around calling out her name. "By the way, Camille. There is a nice young doctor who just came on staff. Stop by my office this week so I can introduce you."

Camille laughed.

"What's funny?"

"You trying to marry off your other daughter now?"

Louis laughed with her. "Can't blame a man for trying, can you?"

"Bye, Daddy, I love you."

"I love you too, honey. And remember, you stop by this week so you can meet him."

CHAPTER 10

Vincent sat alone on the loggia, the sun just beginning to set over the pool of ocean-blue water off in the distance. The start of the evening was quiet, just the hush of water crashing against the rocks and the occasional strain of a moped engine in the distance breaking through the silence.

In his lap, he fingered the pages of a book, dropped he presumed, from a pocket in her luggage. Neither of them had noticed the bound writings falling to the floor of the guest room during her departure. Nana had retrieved it from its resting place, laying the publication in his hands on her way out the door. She had smiled ever so slightly as she instructed him to make sure he returned it.

Camille had been reading *Absolute Trust in the Goodness of the Earth,* a collection of poetry by Alice Walker. Vincent had spent the better part of his afternoon reading the melodic words, wondering which ones had moved Camille, imagining that she had marveled at the same passages that he had. He smiled, laid the book down against the glass-topped table, and reached for his glass tumbler.

Nana had brewed a picture of herbal tea with just a hint of refreshment, and although the cooling elixir felt good against his dry throat, it did nothing to squelch his thirst. Dropping his face into his hands, he rubbed his fingers against his tired eyes, realizing that what he yearned for most had boarded U. S. Airways flight 1062 at the Bermuda International Airport, leaving him, and her book, behind.

Rising to his feet, he headed toward the studio and his sculpture. Throwing himself into his work would ease of the rise of frustration that seemed to be bearing down upon him, he thought, shaking the sudden anxiety that came with the memory of her lips against his, his hand atop her skin, wanting to wrap itself around her breast. He'd not thought about any one woman with such longing for some time, despite having been deemed a good catch by a multitude of prospective females wanting to tarnish the brass of the eligible bachelor title he'd held for so long. Women had, and gone with relative frequency, lasting only as long as his attention span would allow. For the most part, though, the female sex had only been a distraction that he simply had not allowed to get in his way.

But Camille had touched a nerve. A nerve he thought had been laid to rest the day he lost his wife. Vincent inhaled a deep intake of air that filled his lungs to capacity and nourished his spirit.

As he flipped through the sketches on the table, he thought about the look in her eyes as she'd walked around the infrastructure, inspecting the artwork. She had found value in what he did for a living, had validated what he loved most. Over the years, he'd discovered that many women couldn't understand his obsession with his artwork. They couldn't comprehend creativity being a means of employment. If you could contend with the feast-or-famine tide of the art world, feeling that art was a luxury for the elite and not a necessity for the average man. But for Vincent, his artwork had always been a necessity, allowing him to maintain his sanity when the world seemed most lost to them.

He said quietly, pencil in hand, drawing charcoal lines against snow white paper. Someone's jazz dripped from the speakers in the corner, but volume barely audible. He could add one more sculpture to the collection, he thought, the details coming alive in his sketch. This one would be for Camille.

As the image took shape, Vincent could feel the dynamics of the two-dimensional illustration coming to fruition. The regal beauty of an ebony queen poised seductively over her indigo prince. He was kneeling at her feet, anxious to do her bidding. The sweetness of his lips was pressed against the curve of her knee, his hand resting patiently against the back of her thigh. The delicate details of the woman's face were all Camille. And those of the passionate man waiting to please her were his.

The telephone rang just as Camille was walking customers out the gallery door. Looking over her shoulder, she watched as Darrow gestured in her direction, indicating that he would pick up the call. The newly married couple walking beside her had discovered the gallery as they were driving through town. After setting their purchase, an original watercolor, securely on the back seat of their car, Camille smiled warmly as she bade them goodbye. Back inside the gallery, she could hear Darrow's deep voice as it echoed from the back room.

"Ms. Martin should only be a moment, sir. Yes, sir. That's correct, sir. Well, thank you, sir. Hold on please, Ms. Martin is right here, sir." Darrell cupped his hand over the receiver as he mouthed in her direction, his voice dropping to a low whisper. "Mr. DeCosta is on the telephone for you."

"Vincent?"

Darrow smirked, passing her the receiver with a wide grin. "Yes, ma'am."

Taking the telephone from his hands, Camille fanned Darrow out of the room and waited as he closed the door behind him, still grinning as he scurried out to give her a moment of privacy.

"Hello?"

"Camille, hello. It's a Vincent. How are you?"

"Very well, thank you. This is a surprise."

"I didn't catch you at a bad time, did I?"

"No, not at all. I just finished with a new client and the gallery's empty for a few minutes," she answered, peeking at the security monitor focused on the inner gallery. She laughed out loud as she spied Darrow trying to dance the Cabbage Patch in the center of the room.

"Is something funny?" Vincent asked, grinning into the receiver.

"I'm sorry," Camille responded. "My gallery director, Darrow, is dancing in the center of the gallery. I just caught him on the security camera and it's a pretty funny sight. My apology though. I didn't mean to be rude."

"Not a problem. Wish I was there to see it myself."

"So, what are you up to?" Camille asked, settling herself comfortably in her seat.

"Not much. Had you on my mind and thought I'd give you a call."

"Did you now? And were you thinking about me?"

"I was wishing you were still here. There is an amazing sunset right now and I was thinking that I would love to be holding you in my arms as we watched it together."

Camille took a deep inhale. "That sounds intriguing."

"It would be."

Silence filled the space as Camille searched for words to respond. Finally, she asked, "So, what else is new?"

Vincent laughed softly, sensing her uneasiness. "I finished my collection. It's being photographed as we speak," he answered.

"Congratulations," Camille said excitedly. "You must be thrilled."

"I am. I think this is one of my best series of works yet."

"You should be very proud, Vincent they're incredible."

"Thanks. I appreciate that." Vincent paused, stopping to listen to Camille breathe into the receiver.

"You still there?" Camille asked.

"Sorry. My mind drifted for a minute."

"Can you share?"

"I was thinking about when you were here on the island. Now that you're back home I hope that what happened between us is still okay with you. I was worried that maybe I came on too strong. Now that you aren't captivated by the romance of the island you might see me differently. I just might be an old fool."

Camille smiled. "You're not an old fool. I've been thinking about you, too. I was worried that I'd thrown myself at you and you were just being polite, not wanting to embarrass me."

"Glad to know I wasn't the only one experiencing a case of new relationship anxiety."

Camille laughed. "You weren't. My stomach's been in knots since the plane took off."

"I miss you, Camille. I really do wish you were here with me."

"So do I, Vincent. I would love to be there with you right now."

Vincent could feel himself choking up. He coughed lightly, struggling to clear his throat so as not to display any emotion. "Look," he started, "I'm traveling next week. Have to be in New York to discuss the show. My flights connecting through Atlanta, but I know I can get that switched. I can get a layover in Raleigh but it's much longer. If you're willing to meet me so we can spend some time together, I can call and make the change right now. I'd love to see you."

"I'd like that. Just let me know when and where."

"Good. I'll call you tomorrow?"

"I'll be out of the gallery in the afternoon, but you can probably reach me at home sometime after seven o'clock."

"I'll talk to you then."

"Goodbye, Vincent."

"By, Camille. Speak with you soon."

CHAPTER 11

Camille was nervous. Parked in the rear lot of the Cary shopping center, she sat watching the door of Java Café as people walked in and then back out. A few carried a hot cup of liquid in their hands as they made their exit and others did not.

When she agreed to meet him, promising not to tell Zina or Antione that he was passing through town, she had not expected their encounter to feel so illicit. And she surely had not expected the emotions sweeping over her to feel as intense as they did. She'd been ecstatic when he'd called, the excitement raging when they finally said good night, hanging up some three hours later. She'd been beside herself with anticipation as she'd prepared for their date. That is if you could call this covert meeting a date. Whatever it was, though, Camille was suddenly taken aback by the rush of anxiety that seemed to increase with intensity between her driveway and the parking space she now sat in.

Tension danced in her stomach, the nervous energy pattering like moths to a single light in a dark room. She inhaled deeply, reaching over to the passenger seat for her purse. Taking one last look in the rearview mirror, she pressed a finger to her lips, brushing lightly at her lip gloss. Pursing lips together, she tilted her head, first right, then left, ensuring that her makeup was perfect. Stepping out of the vehicle, she locked the car door, then headed inside to see Vincent.

The man sat tapping his fingers against the top of the wooden table. His eyes were hidden behind a pair of sunshades, and a wide-brimmed Panama hat sat coyly atop his head. The coffee bar's decor was sparse, but comfortable, the old brick walls embracing the ambience of roasted coffee beans, decadent pastries, and an eclectic clientele. Vincent had grabbed an empty table in the center of the room, his back to the wall so that he had full view of the front and rear doors. He was excited as he glanced down to the watch on his wrist. He'd arrived early, almost twenty minutes prior to the time they'd agreed upon. Eagerness had propelled him out of the Raleigh-Durham Airport, compelling him to catch a taxi to drive three exits down Interstate 40 into downtown Cary, North Carolina. He had a five-hour layover until his connecting flight to New York, and all he wanted to do was see Camille.

As she entered the room, coming through the rear door, Vincent sat mesmerized, intoxicated by the wealth of her beauty. Camille nodded at the younger man behind the counter, smiling ever so shyly. The boy, who Vincent thought to be no older than twenty, stopped wiping at the counter in front of him, and grinned a broad, toothy smile that seemed to take over his entire face. The woman had great presence, and as Vincent waved in her direction, calling out her name, he couldn't help noticing that his was not the only appraising eye upon her.

Camille wove her way through the room toward him, the seductive sway to her full hips leading the way. Rising from his seat, he tossed his sunshades to the table and opened his arms wide. Pulling her into a hearty embrace, Vincent staked claim to her for all the world to see. Their kiss was burning, drawing the breath from them and when he finally pulled away, still holding tightly onto her, he knew he had no intentions of ever letting her go. The abruptness of that reality so shook his foundation that he almost fell back into his seat, the weight of his quivering limbs betraying his usual confidence.

Amused by his reaction, Camille beamed as she dropped onto the bench beside him. "I'm glad to see you too, Mr. DeCosta."

Vincent shook his head from side to side, his expansive smile radiating from some deep place within his heart.

Camille tucked her purse against the seat between them, adjusted the line of her linen skort, and crossed her hands on the table in front of her. "So…"

Realizing that he'd been holding his breath, Vincent expelled the warm air slowly, then took a deep inhale, welcoming the warmth of brewing coffee up his nostrils. "Would you like a cup of coffee?" he asked, gesturing for the waiter as he spoke.

"I'd love a cup," she answered. Camille quickly scrutinized the menu. "The chocolate-orange espresso, please."

As of the waiter joined them, pencil and pad in hand, Vincent ordered two cups of coffee; one espresso and one decaffeinated. As an afterthought, he added two slices of praline cheesecake. When the young man turned away with their orders, Vincent winced, suddenly embarrassed that he may have committed a faux pas. "I'm sorry," he said, the expression across his face suddenly serious. "I should have asked first. Do you like cheesecake?"

"I do. Thank you." Camille's sweet smile eased the rise of anxiety. "So, how was your flight?" she asked.

He shook his head. "Not too bad." He glanced at his wristwatch. "And we don't take off for Kennedy Airport for another four hours."

"That's a long layover."

"I hope you don't mind spending the time with me?"

"Not at all. But I'm surprised you didn't want Antione and Dante to know."

He laughed. "Why?"

Camille shrugged her shoulders ever so slightly, raising her eyebrows in his direction. "They are your sons."

"So? I didn't need to see them. I can catch up with them later. I wanted to see you."

Camille could feel her face becoming flush. "You were so secretive. Almost feels…" She paused, searching for the right word.

"Wicked?" His eyes teased her as he chuckled softly.

The young man stopped to place their order in front of them. Camille smiled up at him as he and Vincent exchanged a brief conversation about the paperback book tucked in the waistband of the man's apron. As he turned back toward the counter, he winked his eye in Camille's direction. When his back was facing her, she rolled her eyes slowly, shaking her head it Vincent.

"What? Don't you like all the attention?" he asked when the young man was safely out of earshot.

"I have no problems with attention. We women always welcome the attention we get from post-adolescent teenagers and toothless old man."

Vincent smirked, a look of amusement upon his face. He rocked back against the legs of the wing chair he sat on. "I still have my teeth."

"Do you consider yourself old?"

"Don't you? I mean, there is a twenty-four-year age gap between us."

Camille could feel him baiting her, searching out her feelings about the difference in their ages. "No," she finally responded. "I consider you ancient."

Vincent reached a hand up to his head, pulling off his hat and setting it down against the table beside his sunshades. He rubbed his palm against the wealth of tight curls. "I still have my hair. Most of it at least," he said as he brushed his fingers along the beginnings of a receding hairline. "And my original teeth, thank you very much. I look good for my age. Don't I look good for my age?" He asked, turning to face a middle-aged white woman who sat reading a newspaper at the next table.

Looking up from her reading, the woman eyed the two of them curiously, her gaze racing from one to the other, then arched her eyebrows and shrugged her shoulders as she nodded her head, the excessive length of her gray-streaked hair waving along the back of her chair.

"Ignore him," Camille said, giggling. She reached out her hand, pressing her fingertips against his upper arm. "You look good to me. Very good in fact."

He smiled, then as his memory kicked in, reached into the briefcase beside him and pulled out her book. "I almost forgot. I think this belongs to you."

"Oh, my goodness," Camille said. "I couldn't for the life of me figure out where I'd left it."

"It was an interesting read. Very deep."

Camille took a sip of her coffee, washing down a mouthful of cheesecake, the creamy substance melting against her tongue. "Do you like poetry?"

"I do. A lot. Have you read Nikki Giovanni?"

"*Blues: for All the Changes* is one of my favorites."

"I was thinking about *Love Poems* myself."

"Were you now?"

He nodded. "Maybe we can read them together sometime?"

As she gazed into his eyes, his stare penetrating, Camille suddenly felt very warm, and the cup of coffee wasn't doing much to help. She stuck another forkful of cheesecake into her mouth, her gaze falling to what remained of the dessert on her plate.

"Did I say something wrong?"

Camille swallowed hard, inhaling deeply. Glancing up, she found him staring at her intently. "I have to be honest with you, Vincent. Whatever is happening between us scares me. It scares the hell out of me," she said bluntly.

Vincent propped his elbows on the table, resting his chin against his hands. There was a pregnant pause that filled the space between them. At the next table, the rustle of newspaper made them both turn to look as the woman rose from her seat and headed toward the front entrance, waving in their direction as she left. As the door closed behind her, Vincent turned back to stare at Camille.

"Camille, I'm fifty-four years old. Like everyone else, my days are numbered, and there is no guarantee that anyone is going to bother to let me know when my time is up. Like my esteemed father used to say, there are only two things I have left to do; stay black and die. Nothing else is promised to me. So, since I may not be here tomorrow, I'm going to do everything I can to ensure that if today is my last day, then I can say I've lived it to the fullest. I will have done everything I ever wanted to do, including being with an incredibly beautiful, talented, intelligent, *much* younger woman who makes me laugh and seems to enjoy my company as much as I enjoy hers."

Vincent took a deep breath before continuing. "I don't know what is going to happen with us, but I do know that I want to explore what it is I think we're beginning to feel for each other. I really care about you. I like being with you. There's so much I want to learn about you, to share with you. So what if you're thirty-one, and I'm ancient? I haven't met any woman who's excited me this much since my wife died. But you... You excite me, and right now I want to see just how far we can take that."

"What about our families? I don't think Antione and Dante are going to be thrilled about this, and I'm sure my father isn't going to accept it at all."

Vincent reached out for her hand, sliding the warmth of his palm against the back of her fist. "How do you feel? Do you want to pursue this? Are you feeling what I'm feeling?"

Camille closed, then opened her eyes, biting down against her bottom lip. She nodded, a slow deliberate movement of her head, then leaned to brush the length of her fingers against his face. "Yes. I've never felt this way before, and I think that's why I'm so petrified. It all seems to be happening so fast, and I really don't want to get hurt."

"And I don't want to hurt you. I don't want me to be hurt. I truly believe that if we're honest with each other, and we're willing to be open-minded, you and I can have an incredible relationship."

Camille stared back into his eyes, a slight smile crossing her face as her head bobbed up and down in agreement.

"And as for our families," Vincent finished, "we can't force them to accept anything, but if this is real and if we want to make it work, I truly think they'll come around. Your father loves you. My sons love me. There might be some tension across the table come Thanksgiving, but we'll get past it. Love can do that."

Camille grinned. "Yes, it can, Mr. DeCosta. Love surely can do that."

Vincent reached out his hand, brushing his fingers down her face. "You are such an incredible woman," he whispered, his words melting as they eased past his lips.

"Stop, before you have me blushing." Camille chuckled, renting her fingertips against the back of his arm. "So," she started, "how much time do we have?"

Vincent glanced at his watch. "Almost three and a half hours to kill. Why?"

A mischievous expression crossed Camille's face as she rose from her seat. "Let's go," she said, extending her hand. "I want to see what kind of stuff you're made of, Mr. DeCosta."

Reaching into his wallet, Vincent tossed a healthy tip onto the table. Coming to his feet, he followed behind her, his hand wrapped tightly in hers as she pulled him along toward her car.

The hardwood floors of the Triangle Skate Park were fairly empty. Only a group of teenage girls who rolled in small circles at one end of the large room, an elderly man who waltzed on skates dressed in a moth-eaten tuxedo, and a family of three--a mother, a father, and a young boy with a full Afro that sat too large on a small head--were enjoying the entertainment.

Vincent laughed boldly as Camille paid for their admittance and rented two sets of roller skates.

"Do you need safety pads?" she asked, gesturing toward the wrist, elbow, and knee protectors that hung from hooks on the wall behind the attendant.

"I think I can handle myself," he answered, wrapping in arm around her waist as he reached to kiss her cheek.

She smiled, then winked at the young woman who stood watching them. "You're my witness," she said to the girl. "This man has declined protection. If he hurts himself, I am not responsible." The young lady laughed as Vincent pastor his shoes in exchange for a pair of size-eleven boots.

Taking a seat on a wooden bench, he and Camille watched as the old man danced to an amplified anthology of seventies disco music that screamed out of the speakers. The young girls were giggling as they danced around him, joking amongst themselves about his skills on the skate park floor.

"I can do that," Vincent boasted, pointing as the old-timer did a pirouette, then kicked one leg behind him, before dropping to a sitting spin.

"Bet you can't." Camille laughed.

"Bet I can."

"How much are you willing to put on that?" Camille asked, extending her hand to shake his.

"I'll bet you ten kisses I can do that."

She smiled, rolling her eyes in amusement. "Okay, but make it twenty kisses and four hugs," she responded, tying the last boot string on her skates. "At least make it worth my while."

"Deal." Camille rose, gliding off toward the center of the room. Spinning around, she dropped her hands to her hips, waiting as Vincent struggled awkwardly to his feet.

"You ready?" he called, his hands braced at his sides as though he was ready to fall.

"And waiting," Camille responded, skating closer toward him.

"Now, don't blink, 'cause if you miss it, I'm not doing it again." Vincent laughed.

"Yeah, yeah," Camille quipped, crossing her arms in front of her chest. "I'm still waiting."

Kicking his feet behind him, Vincent took off around the room. Camille tossed her head back and laughed heartily as the man suddenly proved himself proficient on the small black wheels that supported him. Skating around her, he spun in circles, skated backward, then kicked his right leg behind him, swinging his body into motion as he imitated the movements they'd just seen the other man accomplish. Camille clapped her palms together in front of her, laughing as Vincent rose, standing before her with his hands on his own hips, a self-satisfied expression gracing his face.

"Showed you, didn't I?"

"Yes, you did, Mr. DeCosta," she said, still laughing. "Yes, you did."

"Ha. You didn't think I could do it. Never underestimate a man like me, Ms. Martin," he said teasingly, grabbing her hand to skate around the room with her. "Woman, don't you know I used to be a champion roller skating king?"

"I missed that part when I read your bio, Mr. DeCosta. It must've been on that page that was missing."

"Good thing too, 'cause now I done won me twenty kisses and four hugs!" he exclaimed, grabbing her boldly around the waist.

"No, you haven't," Camille said, shaking her head. "Unfair advantage. You were a ringer. I was thoroughly misled. Under the circumstances I think the judges would invalidate that bet."

"Tough. Where are my kisses? he asked, tightening his hold.

Camille smiled as she leaned into him, pressing her lips against his. "One," she counted. "Two," she said, kissing his cheek. "Three…"

The crowd of young women gave them a round of oohs and aahs as they skated past, pointing and giggling in their direction.

The two smiled as they laughed along with them.

"Maybe better save the rest of my kisses for later," Vincent said, reaching for her hand as he pulled her along.

"There's a time limit on this bet, Mr. DeCosta," Camille responded, turning to skate backward as she watched him.

"Now, that's not fair. We never said anything about there being a time limit for me to collect my winnings."

"Oh, it's fair. I didn't know I was making my wagers against a professional. Now, that wasn't fair."

Vincent shook his head mockingly, shaking a finger in her direction. "See, now you need to be spanked."

"You'll have to catch me first," Camille said with a deep laugh, taking off toward the other side of the room.

Shaking his head, Vincent went after her, the two skating in wide circles across the floor. Slowing down to avoid running into two teenage boys who had just entered, Camille wasn't prepared when Vincent grabbed her from behind, encircling his arms around her waist. Dropping low to the floor, he fell backward, pulling her to a seated position between his legs. He breathed heavily as she fell laughing, against his chest, wrapping her own arms around his as he cuddled her close to him. Dropping her head against him, she twisted her upper body around to stare up at him. As the rest of the crowd skated in circles around them, Vincent smiled down at her, then leaned to press his lips hard against hers.

It was late, but as soon as he was settled comfortably into the suite of the Plaza Hotel, Vincent pulled the telephone to his ear and dialed. Camille's telephone number was now burned into his memory and he dialed effortlessly, his fingers skipping across the keypad. The phone rang twice before she picked it up.

"Hello?"

"Hi. Did I wake you?"

"I was trying to stay up, but I guess I dozed off."

"I'm sorry I disturbed you."

"Not at all. I'm glad you called. How was your flight?" Camille asked, pulling herself upright against the bed pillows.

"Long. We arrived safe and sound, though."

"That's good."

"Thank you for a great time. I'm glad we got to spend the evening together."

"I'm sorry you had to leave. I had a lot of fun, Vincent. I hope we get to do it again soon."

"You can count on it."

"You need to get to bed. You have a long day tomorrow."

"I just wanted to hear your voice one more time. I slip something into your pocket before I left. Did you find it?"

"No. What did you do, Mr. DeCosta?"

""Just wanted to leave you with a little something to keep me on your mind."

"Hold on," she chimed as she tossed off the covers and pulled herself up and out of the bed. Reaching into the pocket of her jacket, she searched quickly for the trinket Vincent claimed to have left. Tucked neatly into the pocket was a small white box. "Vincent, what is this?" she asked, folding herself back against the pillows as she pulled the covers back up and around her body.

"Open it and find out."

Pulling at the lid, Camille sifted through a layer of tissue paper to find a small heart carved neatly from Bermuda cedar. The tiny wooden trinket was polished smooth, the wood's grain gleaming under the faint light emitting from the lamp on her night table. Her name is engraved on one side and when she turned it over, Vincent's name was carved on the other. Camille could feel herself grinning foolishly.

"Vincent, it's adorable. Thank you."

"Sweet dreams, Camille. I'll be thinking about you."

"Good night, Vincent."

CHAPTER 12

The message on her answering machine came as a pleasant surprise. As she stripped out of her business suit, Vincent's voice reached across the room to stroke the round of her shoulders. Camille crossed over to the nightstand to turn up the volume.

"Hello, Camille. It's me, Vincent. I plan to be in South Carolina next week, and I was hoping you'd be interested in a long weekend down on my farm. Call me when you get a chance. If I don't hear from you, I'll try you again later." There was a lengthy pause, and Camille could feel him searching for his words. She reveled in the sound of his voice, its magnetic tone causing goosebumps to rise against her arms. "I miss you, baby. I hope you can get away. Well, okay then. I'll speak with you soon. Bye."

Standing in the doorway, her arms wrapped around her body, Camille wondered what South Carolina would be like during the month of April, knowing that the decision to meet him there had already been made.

Reaching for the telephone, she dialed Vincent's number. When his answering machine picked up the call, she left a message, telling him that she looked forward to spending the weekend with him. As she hung up, she looked down at her watch, realizing that the time is getting away from her, and her Aunt Kitty would soon be knocking at the door.

Thirty minutes later, as the doorbell rang, Camille had freshened her body with a damp washcloth, applied a fresh coat of deodorant and a spray of cologne, and had slipped into the warmth of a casual cotton pants set.

"Hi, Aunt Kitty," she chimed as she pulled the front door open and then closed it behind her.

"Hello, baby," Kitty said, leaning up to kiss Camille's cheek. "Don't you look pretty?"

"Thank you."

"How are you feeling today?"

"I'm doing really well this evening," Camille answered, her expression beaming.

Kitty looked at her curiously. My, my, my. This is a change. What has got you so happy?"

Camille gestured for the woman to take a seat on the sofa, dropping her body down beside her. She grinned widely.

Kitty grinned back. "Or should I ask *who* has you so happy?"

"Promise me you won't tell?"

"You know I'd never betray your confidence."

"Well, I told you that I had a great time in Bermuda and that things went really well with Antione's father."

"Yes."

"They went better than well. He and I have been speaking every day and last week he stopped here on his way to New York. We spent the evening together and had a great time."

Kitty stared at the young woman, the wide smile gracing her face fading to a thin bending of her lips.

Camille continued, her excitement spilling out into the room. "He's invited me to join him in South Carolina next week. I just called to tell him that I'd love to join him."

Kitty nodded her head slowly. Rising from her seat, she crossed over to the other side of the room, inhaled deeply, and then turned back to face her godchild.

"Camille, how old is Mr. DeCosta?"

Sensing her godmother's seriousness, Camille stiffened, lifting her body to sit upright on the sofa's edge. "He's fifty-four."

"My goodness, baby! The man's as old as I am."

Camille shrugged, not knowing how to respond.

"Is this thing serious?" Kitty asked.

"I like him, if that's what you're asking. And I know he likes me. We have a lot of fun when we're together."

Kitty's head continued to bob up and down, her expression suddenly tense. "Does your father know?"

"Heavens, no! I'm not ready for that yet, Aunt Kitty."

"Camille, I don't approve of you and this man going off to spend the weekend together. He is far too old for you, baby. You're barely thirty-one years old. You've not lived yet and half his life has already passed him by. No good can come of this."

"I really care about him, Aunt Kitty."

Kitty strolled back to Camille's side, reaching out a hand to brush through Camille's hair. "He's not pressuring you to do anything--" she started.

"No, Aunt Kitty," Camille interjected quickly. "It's nothing like that. Besides, you know I always insist on waiting…"

Kitty fanned her hand in the air, finishing Camille's thoughts. "I know, ninety days, but let's be honest, Camille. We both know that if the moment gets intense enough that a woman can get as caught up in the emotions as a man. You may not want to stop yourself and then what's going to happen? No, this is not good."

Camille bit down on her bottom lip as Kitty continued to speak

"Baby, when your mother became ill I promised her I'd keep my eye on you and Zina. I have tried to be here for you the way I know that Sarah would have been had she lived. Sarah would never have supported you becoming involved with a man as old as this Mr. DeCosta is. I don't think you understand the ramifications that could come from this, and it wouldn't be honest of me not to say something to you. I'm sure this Mr. DeCosta has experiences far beyond yours, and the likelihood of this relationship developing into something positive is slim."

Camille shook her head as she took in the woman's words. "Aunt Kitty, I don't know if this thing is going to work out or not, but I want to see where it goes. There's something about him that really moves me and I like how that feels. Maybe he is too old, and maybe it won't work out, but I will never know if I don't put myself out there to find out."

Kitty took a deep breath, wrapping her arms around Camille's shoulders. "I can't stop you, Camille. I wish I could, but at least you know where I stand."

Camille hugged her thin waist as Kitty leaned to press her lips to Camille's forehead. "Dear Lord,

Louis will have a righteous fit when he finds out!" Kitty exclaimed.

Camille inhaled sharply. "You won't tell him, will you?"

Kitty thumped her lightly on the back. "You know better than that. This conversation is between us and stays between us. When you're ready to tell your father, if there's anything to tell him, then I'll be there for you. You know that."

Camille nodded. "Thank you, Aunt Kitty."

The woman closed her eyes as she held Camille close. "I love you like my own child, Camille, and I worry about you. Just promise me you'll be smart. Don't let your emotions take control of your good sense."

"I promise."

"Now," Kitty said, pulling Camille to her feet, "let's get out of here. We still have time to grab something to eat before that movie starts."

His directions had been precise and as she pulled her car off the exit ramp, turning left at the Exxon gas station, she marveled at the beauty of the countryside that lay before her. The expanse of black road was lined with row upon row of deep green trees that draped gracefully above the roadside like a protective canopy. As the tarry pavement extended for miles into the distance, Camille felt as if she were headed toward nowhere, no visible end in sight.

Some thirty minutes and twenty-five miles later, an abrupt stop sign welcomed her to Robertville, South Carolina. Camille picked the handwritten directions up off the passenger seat, studied them briefly, and then made the quick right and left turns as instructed. Pulling onto the dirt road of Route 11, she passed the old white brick church that sat opposite a dilapidated nightclub, its faded welcome sign leaning against the front door.

Just as Vincent had said, the bright red mailbox stood out like a sore thumb in the midst of the other mailboxes that sat in a straight line across from the driveway. An-old-single-wide trailer sat to the left of the entrance way, an elderly black man in bibbed overalls waving at her from its makeshift porch. Camille lifted her hand and waved back. Following the long driveway toward the deep woods down in the distance, the wheels of her vehicle spun clouds of dust up into the air, announcing her arrival. The fresh growth of newly planted cornfields lay to the right and left of her, and as she turned her car into a deep bend, a low-country farmhouse greeted her, its clapboard exterior in need of a serious coat of paint.

Parking beside a rusted vibrant blue pickup truck, Camille beamed as Vincent made his way out of the back of the house, through a screened door, racing to greet her. "Hey, you," he sang, reaching out for her. "I am so glad you decided to join me."

"Me too," she said, throwing herself into his arms.

He drew her close, nestling his face into the thick of her hair, which blew in waves in the warm wind. He inhaled her sweet aroma, the lavender scent of her dancing in the light breeze. He had missed her, and he confirmed such with his lips, dropping his face against hers, lightly pulling at the brim of her mouth. The kiss was intense, shaking her slight frame, and when he pulled back she could feel herself gasping for air. Camille grinned, and the man returned her deep smile with one of his own.

Taking in her surroundings, Camille was overwhelmed with emotion as he pulled her along beside him, giving her a quick tour. A small, screened porch overlooked the rear yard, the landscape laden with ancient oak trees that reached high into the clear blue sky. The massive wonders were covered with thick gray moss that hung like grizzled hair on an aged body. Flowerbeds encircled the base of the massive trunks, bright pansies in assorted colors smiling above the rich, dark earth, and vibrant, green grass. Camille inhaled deeply, relishing the sweet aroma of the clean country air. She could smell the dampness of an impending rain.

She shook her head from side to side as Vincent laughed, reaching for her luggage. "So how was the drive?"

"Beautiful. Your directions were perfect. I never got lost once."

Vincent nodded as he led the way into the house. Camille followed, her eyes taking in the pair of Levi's blue jeans that fit him snugly through the buttocks and hips, and the white T-shirt spattered in paint. He had an impressive rearview, and Camille could feel her smile widening.

Inside the screened porch, Vincent dropped her bags against a paisley easy chair that sat in the center of the room. Off in a corner, a large blank canvas sat perched on a wooden easel. Paintbrushes and tubes of acrylic color sat on top of a low table to the side of the easel.

"Well, this is it. It's not much, but it's comfortable."

"It's perfect. How did you find this place?"

Vincent gestured for her to take a seat and make herself comfortable.

Camille sat down on the leather recliner, kicking off her shoes and pulling her long legs beneath her. Vincent took a seat in an old chair across from her.

"My late wife's family owned all this land. She was raised here, and Antione was actually born in the old house down the road. After she passed away, I thought about selling at all, but never got around to it. Now I'm glad I didn't. Irene's grandfather worked his whole life to buy this land. He passed it down to his son, Irene's father, and when he died he left it all to Irene. It rightfully belongs to Dante and Antione, and when they both turned twenty-one I had it signed over to them. I figured it was up to my boys to decide when and if they wanted to sell it. Then five years ago, they built this house here for me. It's become a great refuge when I just want to get away from everyone."

"So, how long were you married?"

"Six years. Dante was born in year two, and Antione in year three. She was pregnant with our daughter when she died. She suffered a massive stroke during the delivery. That was in 1974."

"I'm sorry. That must've been very difficult for you."

Vincent shrugged twisting his hands nervously in front of him. He continued talking, propelled more by his own nervousness than anything else. "I struggled for a while. Raising two boys alone wasn't easy, but I had a great support system. I eventually took the kids back to the island, and Nana was right there to lend a hand when I needed it."

Sloping forward in her seat, Camille took Vincent's hands in her own. Entwining her fingers between his, she caressed him with her eyes, the warmth of her gaze easing the rise of stress brought on by the glum memories. Vincent welcomed the comfort she offered, leaning to press his forehead against the brown of her long fingers. He inhaled deeply, then changed the subject, wanting to shift the mood that had enveloped the room.

"There are three bedrooms, two upstairs and one down the big hallway there. I've made that one up for you so you'll be comfortable. It's got its own bathroom."

Camille laughed lightly. "Thank you."

"I thought we could drive into Savannah for dinner. You know my skills in the kitchen are nonexistent."

"Are we that close to Georgia?"

"Right on the border. It's about a thirty-five minute drive into town."

"What time do you want me to be ready?"

Vincent looked over his shoulder to the antique clock on the wall. It was well past four o'clock. "Are you hungry?"

"I could probably eat?"

"Why don't we get you settled? Then we can change and head on out. We can beat the dinner rush."

"What should I wear?" she asked.

"Very casual. Like I told you on the phone, a pair of jeans and a T-shirt will get you through the weekend here."

"I told you I don't own a T-shirt," Camille responded, shaking his finger at him.

Vincent laughed. "You high-maintenance women are something else. I think I've got one or two you can borrow."

Camille winked. "Maybe later." She rose from where she sat, reaching for her bags.

Vincent called out as she made her way toward the bedroom. "Camille?"

"Yes, Vincent?"

"I'm really happy you came."

The ride to Savannah and back was comfortable. She'd not worn jeans, or a T-shirt, opting instead for a casual peach pantsuit that flattered her figure and dyed-to-match ballet flats. She and Vincent had laughed and joked easily and she had to admit that she was becoming very comfortable with him in her life. In fact, thoughts of their not being together did not sit well with her at all.

She was enthralled by the grand old gentry of historic Savannah, making a mental note to return for a longer stay the first opportunity she had. The quaint town had in inviting charm, reeking of a romantic history worthy of further exploration. They'd dined at an old boarding house that boasted of a sixty-plus-year reputation. The dining room sat in the basement of an old 1870 Brickhouse regaled with its graceful curving steps and intricate cast-iron trim. Sitting at long wooden tables that ran down the center of the room, they'd dined on lavish Southern cuisine that had been served from large porcelain containers adorned with a petite rose pattern. Camille and Vincent had filled their bellies with fried chicken, red rice, black-eyed peas, collard greens, yams, and cornbread.

Now Camille sat on the screened porch, the length of her body stretched comfortably along the window seat that curved around the front and side walls. A mountain of pillows supported her weight as she peered out into the night sky. It's dark composition was illuminated by a fading line of bright stars and an occasional crack of lightning that had announced the onset of precipitation, which had drizzled down upon them as they stepped from the car into the house.

She could hear Vincent in the other room, the weight of his footsteps creaking against the hardwood floors. Her hand rose to her breast, brushing obliviously at the rise of wanting stirred by the nearness of him. The loud crack of something falling to the floor pulled her from the distraction. Inhaling sharply, Camille reached down for a red chenille blanket that lay at her feet, pulling it up to cover the protrusion of nipple that pressed against the nightshirt she wore.

Music suddenly floated down from the ceiling, spilling out of speakers built into the walls. In the other room, the rise of Vincent's voice sang out, joining Marvin Gaye in a rendition of *How Sweet It Is*. Camille couldn't help laughing aloud. "Hey, Old School!"

"Woman, I know you didn't just call me Old School," he said, pretending to be insulted.

"I sure did. You had better leave the singing to Marvin. You sound like you're in pain in there."

Vincent stuck his head into the room. "I'll have you know I used to sing in the church choir when I was a boy."

"Operative words there, Mr. DeCosta, *used to* , and that was how long ago?"

Vincent chuckled. "You're cold, woman. Too cold." Coming into the room, Vincent set two glasses and a bottle of wine on the table, moving the paint out of his way with a swipe of his hand. "I didn't know if you wanted a glass of wine or not. I can make coffee if you prefer."

"No. The wine is perfect," she said, pumping her head in time to the music.

"So what you know about old school? I know you don't listen to good music like this."

Camille laughed again, joining in as Marvin sang *What's Going On?* Her alto voice was strong and clear, and Vincent was impressed with how well she sang. As the song finished, she snapped her finger in Vincent's direction. "Who doesn't know good music! Now, if you had some Al Green I could surely show you a thing or two."

He laughed with her. "Oh, no, she didn't. I think she just challenged me," he said, heading back into the room from where he'd just come. Seconds later, Al crooned *Take Me to the River.*" Vincent returned, standing in the center of the room as he swayed to the beat of the music, lip-synching to the song. "Can you keep up?" He asked to finally, extending an imaginary microphone in her direction. "Wouldn't want you to hurt yourself, now."

Camille rose from her seat, joining in the game of pretend. Before long they were doing an erotic duet, bouncing around the room in unison. Camille's hips swayed in time with the music, and Vincent's hips swayed in time with Camille's. When Vincent stopped to do a Temptations shuffle, spinning his body down to the floor and back up, Camille couldn't help bursting into laughter, tears rising to her eyes from giggling so hard.

"Where'd you get them moves from?"

Vincent dipped his shoulders up and down, snapping his fingers to the beat. "I was born with these moves, baby."

The tempo shifted as Al's band made him move to a slower tune, the melodic rendering of *For the Good Times* spilling out into the room. Without skipping a beat, Vincent reached out for Camille, pulling her against him, his left arm wrapped around her waist, his right-hand clasping her hand to his chest as they slow-danced to the song. As Al sang the second chorus, Vincent nestled his face into the curve of her neck, inhaling the warmth of her perfume deep into his nostrils.

Even with the rain that fell thunderously outside, its damp moisture seeping through the screened windows of the porch, Camille could feel the rise of heat invading the space. It burned hot against her skin, scorching her nerve endings, and causing the little hairs against her arms and at the back of her neck to rise in anticipation. As Vincent brushed his lips along the length of her neck, up to her cheeks, coming to rest against her own mouth, she could fully understand what Zina had meant every time she'd said rules were made to be broken. As Vincent's hands skipped up the length of her back, she knew it wouldn't take much more for her to throw that ninety-day dictum right out the window. Breaking the kiss, Camille wrapped her arms around her torso, trying to shake the spreading desire that had begun to surge throughout her body.

"I'm sorry," Vincent said, noting her sudden discomfort.

Camille shook her head, racing to ease his sudden anxiety. "No, don't be. You've got nothing to be sorry for."

"I didn't mean to push…" He paused, his arms hanging limply at his sides, his palms gesturing in her direction.

Camille reached out to brush her hand against his chest. "You didn't. I just don't want us to take this too fast, and the moment was starting to get a little intense."

He nodded, fully understanding as he shifted his weight from one foot to the other. He desperately wanted to adjust the bulge of flesh that pressed at the front of his pants, but didn't want to draw attention to his predicament by using his hands.

Camille dropped down against the cushioned seat, lifting the glass of wine to her lips. Vincent reached to refill his own glass, pulling up the wooden chair to sit in front of her.

"So, tell me, where did you get all that musical knowledge from?"

Brushing her hair back behind her ears, Camille smiled warmly, memories flooding her face with pleasure. "When we were growing up, every Saturday morning was cleaning day in our house. My mother would make me and Zina get up bright and early to help her clean the house from top to bottom. We'd start in one corner of each room and wouldn't stop until we reached the other. Mommy would play the stereo full blast while we scrubbed windows and walls and waxed floors.

"Depending on her mood, we'd listen to Al, Marvin, Smokey Robinson, The Temptations. Or if she was mad at Daddy, we'd listen to Shirley Brown and Betty Wright preach about all you no-good men. But you name it and Mommy played it. She absolutely adored Motown and it was infectious. I was only nine when she died, but Zina kept up the tradition. On Saturday mornings she'd play all of Mommy's old records over and over and over, and we'd lip-synch to the songs and pretend to be The Supremes, except our Diana was gone." Camille paused, inhaling deeply as a memory of her mother, faded gray over the years, flashed before her. The reflection brought tears to her eyes, sadness suddenly replacing the essence of desire that had surged throughout her spirit only minutes before.

A pause of quiet filled the room as the CD player switched from one disc to another. As Harold Melvin and the Bluenotes crooned *Me and Mrs. Jones*, the rain outside seemed to drip with melancholy. Vincent contemplated her expression, feeling her loss as if it was one of his own. When he met her gaze, his dark eyes stroked the lines of her delicate face, brushing at the rise of moisture that had trickled down her cheek and rested against her chin, ready to drop against the cotton of her tank top. Neither one of them said a word as Camille leaned back into the pillows, wanting to release the sudden weight that seemed to zap her energy.

Rising from his seat, Vincent reached for her wineglass, setting both goblets down on the table before heading through the door. Camille could hear him in the other room, flipping through his collection of tapes and discs. As he walked back through the door, Noel Poynter played *Night Song*, the violin strings befitting the mood. Vincent reached to extinguish the bright light that flooded the small space. Faint moonlight seeped through the thick of clouds that filled the sky, casting a translucent glow into the room.

Dropping down onto the window seat to sit beside her, Vincent curled his body around hers as she rose up to lean back against him, her head resting on his bare chest. His heart raced, beating into her ear, the palpitations marching in time to the pulsation of her own heartbeat. Outside, the rain came and went in large swells, pouring out of the sky onto the ground, darkness replacing the rise of heat with its cool infection. Acknowledging the chill, Vincent tucked the edges of the blanket beneath her, wrapping his arms around her shoulders. His hands played with the fabric of the coverlet, stroking the flat of her stomach muscles beneath her nightshirt, occasionally brushing against her breasts. He touched his lips to her ear, leaning to kiss her neck. The moment was surreal, comfort wafting between them, unspoken understanding caressing them with relief.

As Miles Davis blew his trumpet over his *Kind of Blue* CD and Donald Harrison skirted his saxophone around *Again, Never,* they talked about her mother and his wife, sharing grief that had been held for too long.

"I was so young when she died," Camille said. "I didn't fully understand the impact of her suddenly not being there. But my whole world changed. One day everything and everybody was taken care of, and the next we were all having to take care of ourselves and each other. I was a little girl with her mother, and suddenly I had to be a young woman without one."

Vincent hugged her tighter. "I can understand that. I remember the day I buried Irene and our daughter, thinking that moment would probably be the hardest thing I would ever have to do in my life. That about a month later as I was fully comprehending just how lonely was, I realized that the hardest thing I was ever going to have to do is continue living."

"I know having Dante and Antione helped a lot."

He sighed. "It did. Just like having Zina and your father helped you."

They sat in silence, listening to the quiet of each other's breathing and the whisper of music in the background. They held hands, palm to palm, caressing the length of each other's fingers. Every so often Vincent would pull her hand to his lips and plant a gentle kiss against her skin or she would brush his palm against the soft of her cheek.

When the rain finally slowed to a light trickle they were still sharing history, whispering the memories that had molded their personalities, reveling in a past that had nurtured and fed their spirits. Camille marveled at how easily she found herself opening up to him. Her usual reservations had been dashed and all pretenses had been laid to rest. She felt vulnerable, and exposed, and comfortable that he would do nothing to abuse her trust of him. Vincent was awed by that part of him that wanted her to know everything, even those things he'd chosen to forget himself.

He took a deep breath, shifting his body ever so slightly against hers. "I almost didn't have this life. I got lucky, marrying the woman I did, having my boys, being able to pursue my art. It almost didn't happen for me."

Detecting a change in the tone of his voice, Camille twisted her body around to look into his face. Though dark shadows shielded his eyes, she could feel him staring directly at her, could feel their gazes meeting under the dim moonlight. "Tell me why," she whispered.

Vincent hesitated, feeling himself being transported back to a memory and a time that he had always hoped he'd never have to revisit. Then braving the moment, he started, "I had an older brother, Maurice. The last time we were together, we were visiting in North Carolina with our father. My parents had been divorced for a good while, and my father had moved here to the States to be with his new wife. It was my thirteenth birthday, and the last night before I was supposed to return to Bermuda for the start of the school year, I was hanging out with Maurice, who was nineteen, and his best friend, Joe Louis. We were acting up, being boys, and we were pulled over by the police for speeding. This was in 1962, and of course the racial climate in the South was horrendous. The civil rights movement was in full swing and people were suffering left and right. In fact, Medgar Evers had just been killed. I remember them talking about it down at the barbershop.

"Anyway, we were stopped and harassed by two white officers, and Maurice back-talked one of them. Some words were exchanged, then blows, and before I knew what happened Joe Louis had pulled out a gun." Camille could feel the anxiety that plagued him as his body shivered against hers, trembling as he struggled to finish speaking.

"When it was over, my brother and one of the cops was dead, and Joe was gone." Vincent took a deep breath, inhaling oxygen like a drowning man, then continued with his story.

"They found more guns and some money in the trunk of Maurice's car. I was charged and convicted of weapons possession, assault, and being an accessory to the murder of the police officer. And I was given a life sentence." Vincent paused, as Camille inhaled sharply, her mind trying to absorb the information he'd just shared.

"A life sentence?" She questioned softly as though she'd not heard him correctly. "But you were only thirteen!"

His head bobbed up and down slowly. "Yes," he said, continuing, "but I only spent five years in prison. There was an attorney, a man named John Albright, who'd read about the case, and worked to get the conviction overturned. I got lucky, plain and simple. I was in the wrong place, with the wrong people, at the wrong time. But then I got lucky, and I got my life back. The day I was released, I went back to the island. I met Irene, we were married, and had Dante a year or so later." As he finished his speech, the words racing past his lips, he exhaled, blowing out air that he'd been holding on to for dear life.

"Wow," Camille muttered, the details of Vincent's confession spinning through her thoughts. "Wow. Whatever happened to your brother's friend?"

"I don't know. I never saw Joe again. They never found him. I did his time, and he just disappeared."

"That had to hurt."

"Camille, hatred is an ugly emotion to have to carry around, and prison can surely make you hate a man. I spent a number of years wanting to get even with Joe. I wanted to make him pay for Maurice dying, and for the time I spent behind bars. But after a while I realized that it wouldn't have made much difference. It wouldn't change what happened or make it different. Back then, here in the South, I would still have been guilty of something whether I'd done it or not. They would still have sent me to jail. I was blessed that they didn't kill me, and that there was someone who cared enough to make it right. But there is a part of me that still wants him to hurt. I won't lie to you. There are times I still think about making that man pay for all he did."

Camille reached out to wrap her arms around the man, pressing herself against his body. "You did a collection back in the early eighties. *Innocent Men.* If I remember correctly, it was a series of busts. You did facial images of men who were angry, and sad, and raging. It caused quite a stir as I recall."

Vincent hugged her close. "One of my first major shows. Those images came right from my experiences in prison."

In the darkness, Camille smiled up at him. "Thank you for sharing that with me," she said. "I know it wasn't easy."

Hugging her again, Vincent kissed the side of her face. As he brushed his skin against hers, she could feel his tears, went against her face. Camille reached a tentative hand up to wipe at the moisture, then leaned to kiss the salty dampness away.

Their kisses were light exchanges at first a brush of his lips along her brow, against an eyelid, atop the tip of her nose. When Camille wanted more, she tilted her mouth up to his, pressing her lips to his. The exchange was long and slow and Camille felt as if she were kissing him for the very first time, finding her way through unexplored territory. She eased her tongue past his lips, over the line of his teeth, tiptoeing her way toward the back of his throat.

Vincent welcomed her advances. He was intoxicated by her presence, wanting to fill himself with every ounce of her. Outside, the rain had stopped, and the humidity hung like a thick cloud around them. "I just want to hold you," he finally whispered, wrapping his long body around hers, gently stroking the length of her frame. "I don't ever want to let you go."

As the sun's rays peeked out in the distance, they were still talking, light chatter and laughter washing over their many hopes and dreams. When the new day spread its wings up and over the vast land, morning brought an expectation of more to come, more for them to explore and share. Instinctively, both for new, rules or no rules, ninety days or ninety minutes, what existed between them was more than either of them could ever have hoped for.

CHAPTER 13

Camille reached for the telephone, ticking off the last name and number on her list of callbacks as she dialed. Three rings later, Dr. Jon Howard picked up his private line, breathing heavily into the receiver. "Hello?"

"I hope you're doing something interesting to be breathing so hard," Camille said.

The man laughed. I was lifting some weights. Got to keep in shape, you know."

"Why? The wife complaining?"

"The wife never complains. I know how to keep my woman happy."

"So you say."

"Where have you been? I called you twice at home, and when I finally called the gallery, Darrow said you were taking a holiday."

"What? I'm not allowed to take some time off?"

"Who is he?"

"Why does a man have to be involved?"

"You saying a man wasn't involved?"

"I'm saying it's none of your business what man I spent the weekend with."

"Did he leave you happy?"

"Very happy. The man is a dream come true."

"You didn't come back marriage too, did you?"

"Funny. Brother got jokes."

"So did Gina break the news to your old man yet?"

"What news?"

"I know she's pregnant. She had to be pregnant to get married like that."

"You are such a fool. She is not pregnant. She's in love."

"In love with what?"

"In love with her husband. Like you love that woman you are married to."

Jon laughed into the receiver. "So what else is new with you, my friend, since you won't tell me about this man you spent the weekend with?"

"Not much. How about yourself?"

"Busy as ever. No time for myself lately."

"But that should be a good thing for you. Means you're making money."

"Trying hard, woman. Trying real hard."

"I hope so. I definitely want to help you spend some of it," Camille said.

"You're worse than my wife."

"I'm better than your wife. I get to spend your money and I don't have to sleep with you."

"You don't know what you're missing."

Camille snickered. "Now we both know you don't have a thing to be bragging about."

"Says who?"

"Says me."

"How would you know? Zina telling lies again?"

"Because a man who brags as much as you do is usually more hot air than anything else. Like that car of yours. What is it you drive?"

"My Corvette?"

"A little red one, right? With a stick? To compensate for the stick you don't have."

"That was ugly. That was so ugly."

"But I still love you, and I'll still spend your money."

"So, what are you spending my money on now?"

"Zina has a new show opening at a gallery in Bermuda in two months. She is doing a collection of new routes. One of them would look sensational in your bedroom. And she's exhibiting with Vincent DeCosta."

"Impressive. Sister's gone big time, I see."

"Very. And I think one of Vincent's sculptures would be a great compliment to sit on your nightstand."

"You call him Vincent?"

"It is his name."

"Why are you smiling?"

"Who says I'm smiling?"

"Girl, that beam of light coming from the center of your face is so bright it could light up the galaxy. Blinding me through the telephone here."

"Ha, ha, ha," she said sarcastically.

"Mr. DeCosta is an old man, isn't he?" Jon asked, emphasizing the "Mr."

"How old do you think he is?"

"Seventies, eighties. He's been around forever, hasn't he?"

"You really need to study more when you're reading up on your artists. The man isn't close to being seventy. You are so sad."

"That's why I've made you my personal curator. You're supposed to keep me up-to-date on these things."

"I just did."

"I didn't realize you knew him that well."

"I know him. That's all that's important."

"Must be, if you're calling him Vincent," he said, stretching out the man's name.

"I call you by your first name. So what's the big deal?"

"You never say my name the way I hear you saying Vincent's name. You say Vincent's name like Vincent got to see you naked."

"You've seen me naked."

"But that was an accident. I was looking for Zina."

Camille shook her head slowly, the memory of that moment and the ensuing embarrassment flashing before her. "You know you did it on purpose, so don't start lying."

"You truly know how to hurt a man's feelings."

"Please," Camille said rolling her eyes.

"Okay. Bermuda, huh?"

"Sounds like a romantic weekend to me. I doubt that Elise would resist. It'll give her a good reason to show off that great figure of hers on the beach."

"Is Vincent going to be there?"

"Both the artists, Ms. Martin and Mr. DeCosta will be present for the opening."

Jon chuckled into the receiver. "I might be able to work that. What's in it for me?"

"I won't tease you about that little car of yours anymore."

"Why don't you give my little car a test drive so you can see just how big it really is?"

"Please, and ruin your wife's good thing? If you ever got a taste of this, you go crazy. You wouldn't know what to do with yourself, and poor Elise would have to suffer the consequences."

Jon blew a kiss into the receiver. "I love you too, woman. Email me the dates of the opening. We'll be there."

"Knew I could count on you, Jon. Your invitation is in the mail. And bring cash. Lots of it."

"Don't I always?"

"It's a pleasure, Dr. Howard."

"It could be, Ms. Martin. It truly could be."

Camille laughed. "Goodbye, Jon. Tell Elise I said hello. Tell her to call me if she's got any questions about Bermuda."

"I will surely do that. Talk to you soon, my friend."

On the fourth ring, Vincent reached for the telephone, dropping the polishing rag onto the table beside him as he pushed the piece of sculpture into the middle of the desk.

"Hello?"

"Vincent, how are you?"

"Lydia, hello. What can I do for you?"

"Hadn't heard from you in a few days. Thought I'd see what you've been up to."

"I actually just got back. Went to the States for the weekend."

"Visiting the boys?"

"Visiting."

There was an awkward pause. Vincent tapped a pencil against the top of the desk, leaning to run a finger along the edge of his sculpture. *Needs more smoothing*, he thought to himself.

"I was thinking that we might get together for dinner this evening?" Lydia asked.

Vincent inhaled. "I appreciate the gesture, Lydia, but I really need to finish some work here in the studio."

"I could bring dinner to you."

"You know I rarely eat when I'm working."

Vincent could hear the woman breathing heavily on the other end of the telephone. "What's the matter, Lydia?"

"I just feel as though you're ignoring me lately."

"No, I'm not ignoring you. I'm ignoring your efforts to move our relationship toward something more personal. That's not going to happen and I have no intentions of giving you the impression that it's possible.

"Well."

"Don't play hurt. We've had this conversation before."

"Are you seeing someone?"

"It doesn't matter if I am or not."

"Vincent, you and I could be very good together. You know this."

"What I know is that many years ago you and I attempted to make a relationship work and it didn't. In fact, it was bad. Very bad. We both learned an invaluable lesson, and we moved on. So why should we endeavor to make the same mistake again?"

"Do you have to be so harsh, Vincent?"

"I'm honest, Lydia."

"Are you seeing that woman?"

"What woman?"

"Camille Martin. You two seemed very close."

Vincent shook his head, heaving a deep sigh. "Would it make a difference, Lydia? Whether I'm seeing Camille, or Bambi, or whomever, would it make a difference?"

"Who's Bambi?"

Vincent laughed. "My new woman. Doe eyes with skin like soft leather. She's truly a four-legged knockout."

"It's a good thing we're friends, Vincent. I might not take your teasing so kindly otherwise."

"And we can remain friends, Lydia, as long as you accept that we will never be more than that. And I don't say that to hurt you."

"Well, will you have dinner with me next week? I hear the Black Horse Restaurant in St. David's has a wonderful new chef."

"Next week's good. Lunch would be even better."

"Fine. I'll put you on my calendar for lunch next week. Tuesday work for you?"

"I'll meet you at noon."

"Call me that morning to confirm."

"I will."

"Oh, by the way. I have the copy and proofs for the invitation. They did an extraordinary job. You need to decide which image you like best so I can order them in time for the show."

"Let's discuss it Tuesday."

"Goodbye, Vincent."

"Talk to you soon, Lydia."

Zina glanced down at the caller ID on her cell phone, then flipped open the utensil and pulled it to her ear. "Hi, Daddy."

"Hello, baby girl. How are you?"

"I'm good. Working on one of my paintings for the show."

Louis nodded his head into the telephone. "Very good. Camille took care of all our tickets already. We're all very excited to be going. It will be a nice getaway."

Zina continued to paint the canvas before her, the phone propped between her ear and her shoulders.

"Have you spoken to Camille today?" Louis asked.

"No. Is she back from her trip?"

"She was supposed to get back last night. DO you know where she went?"

"Said she was meeting a friend in South Carolina for the weekend. I guess she was just hanging out with the girls."

"Must be that Jackie girl, or what's her other friend's name?"

"Janet?"

"That's her. Probably with one of them."

Zina nodded into the telephone. "I guess. I didn't ask."

"You need to ask. You and your sister need to let people know who you're with when you go away in case something happens to you."

"Uh-huh."

"Something could happen and we wouldn't know what to tell the police. Wouldn't know who you're with or where you went. Fine not telling me, but the two of you need to tell each other."

"Uh-huh."

"Antione treating you okay?"

"Antione and I are fine, Daddy. You don't need to worry." Zina dropped her paintbrush into a can of water and stepped back to review her work, pulling the cell phone from her shoulder into the palm of her hand.

"You know you can tell me if things aren't going well. We could get you out of this if there's anything wrong."

"Uh-huh."

"Zina Michele, *uh-huh* is not a proper response. You will answer yes or no when someone is speaking to you."

"Uh-huh…I mean yes, sir, Daddy," Zina said, inhaling deeply.

"Does Antione have any lawyer friends he might introduce your sister to?"

Zina laughed, tears rising to her eyes. "Daddy, Camille doesn't need to meet any of Antione's friends, lawyers or otherwise."

"Is she dating someone?"

"Camille is a big girl. She can find her own man without any help from us. I don't think she's got any problems in that area."

"Some input from her family might keep her from making a mistake she might regret later on in life."

"Uh-huh."

Annoyance pulled at Louis's brow. Zina seemed to enjoy testing his nerves, he thought to himself. "Did you hear what I said to you about answering people properly."

"Daddy, I have to go. I just spilled paint on my carpet," Zina lied. "I'll call you tomorrow, okay?"

"Why are you painting on the carpet?" You know you're supposed to put a drop cloth down if you're not painting in your studio."

"Love you, Daddy. I'll call tomorrow."

"I love you, too, baby girl."
"Bye, Daddy."
"Goodbye, Zina."

CHAPTER 14

Camille rushed from the shower into the bedroom dripping atrial. The telephone is ringing incessantly.

"Hello?"

"Hi. I catch you at a bad time?"

A wide smile rose to her face. "Vincent. No. Not at all. How are you?"

"Excited that I'm going to see you tonight."

Dropping onto the bedside, Camille pulled her knees to her chest and a hand through her freshly permed hair. "Me too."

"So you have everything under control? Is there anything Nana or I can do to help?"

"No. I think were already."

"I'm looking forward to meeting your father. He seems like an interesting man."

"He said the same about you."

"Well, I think we'll get along just fine."

"Until he finds out you have designs on his youngest daughter."

Vincent laughed into the receiver. "Maybe we shouldn't tell him."

"I'm scared it's going to show all over my face."

"I know it'll be all over mine."

"What are we going to do?"

She could feel him smiling into the telephone. "We aren't going to worry about it. Everything is going to be just fine."

"Vincent?" Camille inhaled deeply, blowing the warm air past her lips. "Come here before we have to be at the reception. Can you get away?"

"I don't see why not. Nana's addressing now and Dante is here so, he can escort her. I'm ready, so I can leave now if you want me to."

"I want to see you first. Without a crowd around us."

"I'm on my way. What's the address?"

After giving him directions, Camille bade him goodbye, then dropped the receiver back onto the hook. Taking a seat at the dressing table, she quickly applied her makeup.

She and Vincent had spoken daily since her trip to the farm. Vincent had initiated the first calls, and now, like clockwork, they didn't miss an opportunity to speak with one another, sometimes talking two and three times a day. Just thinking about it made Camille smile. Thinking about him made her drunk with wanting.

For the past four weeks, Vincent had been privy to every intimate detail about the impending reception, an event Zina and Antione couldn't have cared less about. The saga had seemed endless, until now, culminating in the black-tie gala they were all about to periods.

Pulling her hair into an intricate French twist, Camille pinned it loosely atop her head, pulling at a few strands that spiraled over her forehead, along the nape of her neck, curling ever so subtly over the curve of her diamond-studded earlobes.

The dress her father had selected, a David Meister silk chiffon evening gown, lay across the bed. Camille fingered the delicate fabric gingerly. Both she and Zina have balked at the extravagant Neiman Marcus price tags, but Louis had insisted, his duty, he'd said, since their mother was not there to help select the bridal gown and the maid-of-honor attire they'd been denied with Zina's elopement. Although both women had argued vehemently, they both loved the dresses that had been selected. Hers was a wonderful print, the strapless, smocked bodice and the double-layered skirt with its inverted pleat lined in vibrant red fitting her size-ten frame with relative perfection. The three-inch Manolo Blahnik black suede sandals were a nice complement, elevating her five-foot-eight-inch stature with ease.

Camille loved to dressing up. She loved the excitement of formal events. Since she and Zina were little girls, their father had made it a monthly ritual to dress them in pretty dresses and escort them out on the town. When they were eight and ten, they'd go in full-skirted dresses with white socks and patent leather shoes to dinner at upscale restaurants and an early movie or children's theater production. When they were teens, there had been at the ballet, the opera, and a host of events he had introduced them to. He had lavished them with exquisite clothes to parade about in, and Camille had loved every moment of it. As much as Camille had loved it, Zina had hated it with a passion, preferring jeans, a T-shirt, and a comfortable pair of sneakers.

Slipping on her dress and stepping into her shoes, Camille appraised herself in the full-length mirror. Even with its skirt that fit snugly around her small waist, the dress couldn't hide the curves of her plentiful hips, or the round of her behind, which seemed to tease the length of fabric that encircled her. Camille couldn't help hoping that Vincent would take due notice.

When the doorbell rang, nervous energy seemed to swell up and over her. Making her way to the front door, Camille could feel the rise of dewy perspiration forming under the line of her breasts. *Please, God don't let me sweat,* she thought, reaching for the doorknob. On the other side, Vincent stood resplendent in a charcoal tuxedo, red vest, and matching bowtie. He carried a dozen yellow roses in hand, a wide grin pasted on his face. The moment she saw him, Camille could feel the anxiety lift off her shoulders, an easy calm wrapping itself around her like a welcome comforter.

"You look beautiful," Vincent purred, as Camille pulled him inside. With the door closed behind him, he pulled her into him with his free hand, his mouth meeting hers. The kiss was easy, their tongues are reuniting like long-lost friends. Camille was awed by the power of it, the sensation driving the breath from her body. She seemed to float, her body having no desire to settle back down on the ground. Pulling away, she smiled up into his eyes, her body waving from side to side with pleasure.

"I missed you."

Vincent smiled back. "Not nearly as much as I missed you." He kissed the side of her mouth, then her cheek, resting his face against the curve of her neck. "You smell good too."

She laughed. "Thank you."

"These are for you," he said, passing her the roses.

"Oh, Vincent, these are beautiful!" she exclaimed, clearly pleased.

"You deserve them. I know how hard you've worked to prepare for tonight."

Camille gestured for him to follow her inside, leading the way into the kitchen to pull a vase from the cabinet. As she filled the crystal container with water, dropping the cut flowers down inside, Vincent stepped back into the living room, taking in his surroundings.

"Someone else has a nice art collection, I see."

"Getting there. Trying to model mine after yours," she responded.

He chuckled. "So are you ready for this evening?"

"Ready for it to be over."

They both laughed.

"Did you speak with Antione?"

Vincent nodded. "He and Zina will meet us at the entrance. They both seemed to be pretty excited."

"Well, I hope so," she said. "I'm nervous myself."

Vincent went back into the kitchen, approaching her from behind as she neatly arranged the flowers. He wrapped his arms around her body, leaning down to kiss the back of her shoulder. "Why?"

Camille leaned back against him. She shook her head. "I don't know. I just am. Worried that things won't go well. Worried that my father will be disappointed. Worried about you."

"Me?"

"Just nervous how things are going to go for us, if people will read what's going on in our faces."

Vincent spun her around. "Would it bother you if they did?"

Camille paused before responding. She looked up into his eyes, searching the emotion on his face. As she shook her head, her facial muscles lifted the curve of her mouth ever so slightly. "No. But I do worry about their reactions when our families find out. I surely don't want my father to be blindsided by this. I don't want there to be any surprises that neither of us is prepared for."

Vincent took a deep breath. "We won't let that happen. But don't you worry about it tonight. Everything will be okay. I promise."

As he hugged her tightly, Camille sank deep into his chest. *I hope you're right*, she thought, trying to will the unsettled feeling from her abdomen. *I really hope you're right.*

Vincent let her into the grand ballroom of the Raleigh Marriott, his arm curved easily around her waist. Neither of their families was in sight, and as she scanned the room, she was thankful that they arrived before the others. Taking in the decor, Camille was pleased. The hotel's catering department had followed her directions to a T. The room was beautiful. White linens adorned the tables, complemented by ivory place settings atop gold chargers. White roses and candles, woven in elegant centerpieces, sat in the middle of each table. Place cards, original Zina Martin designs, added bold touches of color that complemented the entire setting. A team of staff was lighting the last candles and Camille breathed a sigh of relief.

"Ms. Martin. Good evening."

Camille turned toward the voice calling out her name. Janine Long, the hotel's catering director, came rushing in her direction.

"Hello, Janine. The room looks spectacular. You've done a beautiful job."

"Thank you. We're delighted that you're pleased. Everything is on schedule in the kitchen. Will be laying out the hors d'oeuvre buffet shortly there are bars set up in each corner of the room, and my staff is ready to serve your every need."

Camille nodded her head. "Thank you. Did my father call to give you a final headcount?"

"He did. We're prepared for 350 persons. Is that correct?"

"Yes."

"Well, if you need anything, please don't hesitate to let me know. Any of our wait staff will be able to get me."

"Thank you again, Janine. You've really outdone yourself."

The woman smiled broadly, extending her hand in a firm handshake.

As she walked off, Vincent laughed. "Just a few close and personal friends, I see."

Camille shrugged. "What can I say? This is half the reason Zina and I have been butting heads this past month. She and Antione didn't want all this nonsense. A beer and peanut party would have suited the two of them, but Daddy had to have his way."

"You always do what your father wants, don't you?"

"Usually."

"What will happen when he doesn't want you to have anything to do with me?"

Camille looked at him. Before she could respond, Antione and Zina waved at them from the entranceway. Grateful for the distraction, Camille smiled widely, waving back as she and Vincent headed over to greet them. Zina looked ravishing in a satin slip dress with a full six-gore skirt. Intricately embroidered detail flowed across her bust line and down one side to the hemline, complementing the soft fabric. The color was stone, a pale taupe that shimmered against Zina's rich complexion. Her dark hair fell in long wisps down past her shoulders. Diamond and pearl clusters hung from each earlobe.

"Zina, you look so pretty," Camille said, reaching out to hug her sister. "Hi, Antione. You're looking pretty spiffy yourself," she said, admiring the flattering tuxedo, his dreads falling loose against his shoulders.

"Thanks, Camille. Hey, Pop. You're here early."

Vincent nodded. "Wanted to make sure Camille had everything under control."

Antione stared at his father intensely, the muscles along his jawbone tightening. "Where's Nana?" he quipped.

"She and Dante should be here shortly," Vincent said, his response edged in rising tension.

"Did you talk to Daddy?" Zina asked, noting a sudden change in her husband's mood.

Camille nodded. "He's on his way."

The two women exchanged a look as their gazes raced from Antione to his father and back again.

"Would you two excuse us? Camille and I are going to go to the ladies room to freshen up." Zina leaned up to kiss her husband's cheek. "You two play nice while were gone."

Grabbing her hand, Zina led the way out the door and down the hotel corridor to the large restroom. Once inside, hidden behind the closed door, Zina dropped down onto the chase lounge in the sitting area. Camille inhaled deeply, holding the warm breath before letting it escape. "What was that all about?"

"You."

Camille sat down next to her sister. "What about me?"

"Antione isn't happy about his father being interested in you."

"He told you this?"

Zina nodded. "We've had a few discussions about it. Nana told him how you two have been talking on the phone every day. Then last week Dante told him that Vincent stopped through town for the day, but didn't bother to tell them he was here. Seems the only person he saw was you. Got you a real-life romance going on, huh, little sister?"

Camille rolled her eyes. "Don't start."

"Hey, it doesn't bother me. I'm happy for you. But you knew it had to come out sooner or later, and you knew there were going to be some folks, namely our father and my husband, who weren't going to be happy about it."

"Why tonight? I don't want this to spoil your evening."

Zina laughed. "Look, don't worry about me, and don't worry about Antione. I'll keep him happy. Just do what you want to do. It's obvious you and Vincent care about each other. Why not share it with the rest of us?"

Camille dropped her head into her hands as Zina wrapped an arm around her shoulder and pulled her close. "Are your ninety days up yet?"

Breaking out in laughter, Camille cut her eyes in Zina's direction. "No, and I'm about ready to break that rule. Did you see how good he looked in that tuxedo?"

Zina laughed with her. "Now that's a family of men who know how to wear the heck out of a suit."

"We better get back. Daddy should be here soon and I don't want him to walk in on any tension between Antione and his father."

Rising, Zina pulled her sister to her feet, clutching the woman's shoulders. "Don't let Daddy stop you from loving Vincent. If this feels right, then go for it. Daddy may not like it, but he will get over it. He will still be here for you. Just don't throw it away to try and make him happy."

"Zina, please…"

"No. You promise me. If Vincent makes you happy and being with him is what you want, then you do it. Promise me, Camille."

The pressure of Zina's nails against her skin was unnerving.

"Promise me."

Opening her eyes, she studied her sister's face, noting the rise of tears in Zina's eyes. Nodding her head, she smiled. "I promise."

Zina grinned. "Good. Now come and throw me this fancy party. We look too good to be in here. No point in wasting all this beauty on a bathroom mirror."

Both women took one last look at their reflections, giving their make up a final touch-up, and then

Camille headed out the door with the Zina close on her heels.

Vincent and Antione were standing in heated conversation when Louis Martin walked through the door. The exchange between them was intense, and neither of them noticed Louis's entrance. He stood off in the distance, quietly observing, wondering where his daughters had disappeared too, and what had happened to cause the quiet commotion with his new son-in-law. As Antione swept past the man in front of him, ready to storm off in rage, he noted Louis's presence, inhaled deeply, then turned back abruptly to make one final statement to the man at his side. Vincent turned to stare where his son had gestured, and almost simultaneously Vincent DeCosta and Louis Martin felt the brunt of history long forgotten flash between them.

CHAPTER 15

Vincent could feel the large room swell with tension. The pressure seemed to rise out of the hardwood floors like morning mist on a dreary day. Its thick swell clouded his thoughts, spinning his movements in slow motion. His son's voice seem to float from some place far away as the young man spun background to utter one more statement at him.

"We'll drop it for now, Dad, but we need to finish this conversation later. This is far from being finished." The man paused, taking a deep breath. "I should introduce you to Zina's father."

Vincent shook the haze from his head, his gaze still locked on the man across the room. "No. I would use myself. You need to find your wife, and you need to calm down before your guests arrive."

He turned to look at his son, his expression hard.

"Look, Dad. I didn't mean--" Antione started.

Vincent lifted his hand to still the words about to spill from his son's mouth. "Just find your wife."

Nodding his head, Antione pushed his hands into his pockets and headed across the room, pausing to shake his father-in-law's hand. The two men exchanged a brief greeting before Antione headed out the door. Crossing over toward the corner bar, Vincent ordered himself a double scotch. Clutching the glass tightly, he took a hard swig of the bitter spirit, inhaled deeply, then turned to stare once again at Louis.

Louis suddenly felt warm, a hollow pit forming in his midsection. He looked quickly over his shoulder to watch Antione leaving in search of the women. As the door closed behind the younger man, Louis and Vincent sauntered toward one another, meeting each other halfway.

"Joe Louis. You're still alive."

"Hello, Vincent. It's been a long time," Dr. Louis Martin responded.

Vincent nodded. "Not long enough."

Louis bristled, fighting to keep the tone of his voice even as he struggled to make conversation. "You look good. Older, but you haven't changed much." Vincent shrugged, his fingers digging into the palm of one hand. "Since this isn't the time or the place for us to rehash old memories, how would you like to handle this?"

"As far as anyone needs to know, we're meeting for the first time. We can be as polite as we need to be."

Vincent stared at the man, his expression stoic. "And if I don't agree?"

"I mean, neither of us wants to do anything to spoil the evening for Zina and your son, do we?"

"Or Camille," Vincent said, the expression on his face frozen with tension.

Louis nodded, taking a deep breath. An uncomfortable silence filled the space between the two of them. Louis glanced over his shoulder toward the closed door, then focused his gaze on a waiter setting a massive tray of shrimp on a table. Vincent cleared his throat, his eyes pausing on the same table where Louis's gaze rested.

"It was my intent to be here until Tuesday. I think you and I should get together to talk before I leave," Vincent said, still focused on the table being set with food.

"I'll be in my office first thing Monday. We can meet there. I'll get you the address before you leave."

The two men met each other's eyes again. Louis extended his right hand, taking note of the empty scotch glass clutched between Vincent's fingers. Vincent hesitated, his eyes locked on Louis's face; then finally he reached out to shake the man's hand. Just then, the doors swung open, Camille leading the way as Antione and Zina followed, with Nana and Dante bringing up the rear.

Eyeing each other one last time, Louis and Vincent turned toward their families and smiled, neither giving any indication that the past between them could very well bring all they'd known shattering down around them.

CHAPTER 16

As Camille pulled her car out of the hotel's parking garage, she wasn't quite sure what to make of the evening. She knew all their guests had thoroughly enjoyed the party. The food was exceptional, and everything seemed to have gone smoothly. But she had no understanding of her father's serious mood, and Vincent had become distant and preoccupied, claiming to have a migraine as he'd said an early goodbye and made a hasty retreat up to his hotel room.

Where she had half expected her father to hold Vincent hostage at one of the tables for a game of twenty questions, it was as though he'd gone out of his way to avoid the man instead. Until Vincent's sudden departure, she had flitted back and forth between the two of them trying to lighten the moment and engage them in conversation, but her efforts had been futile. Neither had responded, and she'd finished the evening as frustrated as she was confused, most especially when the hotel operator said the occupant of the presidential suite wasn't accepting any telephone calls.

To make matters worse, Antione had then seen fit to lecture her about her interest in Vincent. The memory, a fresh irritation, caused her to bite down against her bottom lip, breaking the skin, as she eased her car onto the highway.

"Camille, we need to talk," Antione had said, pulling at her elbow in the hotel lobby. Across the way, Zina sat laughing with Nana, the two women chatting quietly about the guests who'd come and gone.

"Is everything okay?" Camille asked, concern dressing her brow. "There's nothing wrong with Vincent, is there?"

Antione took a deep breath, glancing quickly toward his wife before meeting Camille's anxious case. "Look, I'm not going to beat around the bush. I don't think it's appropriate for you and my father to be seeing each other."

"Excuse me?" Camille could feel the sudden rise of annoyance creeping into the pit of her stomach.

"It's disgusting, Camille. He's old enough to be your father, and the two of you know better. What can you be thinking?"

Her concerned expression changed quickly, ire flooding her face. "I'm thinking that who I choose to date, and what is or isn't happening between me and your father, is none of your business. That's what I'm thinking." Camille's blood pressure was on a steady climb as she and Antione stared at each other.

"Camille, this is awkward for me but someone needs to say something."

"Mind your own business, Antione. Not mine. And not Vincent's."

"It is my business, Camille. It affects my family. How do you think this looks?"

"Looks to who?"

"Everyone. My father has a reputation to uphold. His dating a woman young enough to be his child won't look good for him. And what about me and Zina?"

"What about you? How in the world does this affect you two?"

"Because when it doesn't work out, Zina and I are going to have to deal with the fallout. And what about your father? Have you even thought about how he's going to take this?"

Camille lowered her eyes, pulling her hands to rest against the round of her hips. She tilted her head ever so slightly, anger seeping from her eyes as her gaze raced across Antione's face. As she spoke, her voice was calm, her tone edged in ice.

"I'm only going to say this once, Antione. I don't care what you, Zina, my father, or anyone else thinks about me being with Vincent. What happens between him and me is none of anyone's business."

"Are you that desperate for a man?"

Camille bristled, the low anger rising to a deep rage. "You don't want bad blood between us, Antione. So, consider yourself warned. If you know what's good for you, you will stay out of my business."

She turned, lifting the hem of her skirt as she walked away.

Antione reached out to grab her arm. "Camille--"

Camille snatched the limb back, causing Zina and Nana to turn abruptly, curiosity guiding them in their direction. Zina rose from her seat, walking briskly to stand by Antione's side. "What's the matter with you two?"

Deborah Fletcher Mello

"You'd better tell your husband to check himself. He doesn't have license over me or Vincent, and the sooner he figures that out the better off he'll be," Camille hissed, storming off toward the exit doors.

"Camille, don't--" Zina started, glaring at Antione before rushing behind her sister. "Stop, Camille."

The two women faced each other as Camille pushed the illuminated button for the elevator.

"Please, don't be mad, Camille. I'll talk to Antione."

"Antione needs to mind his own business. I'm not it," she spat, rage painted down the lines of her face.

"He's only concerned about the two of you," Zina responded, her soothing tone attempting to defuse the situation.

"No, he isn't. He's concerned about how it's going to make him look. Nothing else."

"That's not true, Camille," her sister said, shaking her head. "He just doesn't want to see you or his father hurt."

"Zina, I love Vincent. I love him, and I don't care who approves or who doesn't." Camille whispered, moisture pressing at the edges of her eyes, the tears threatening to spill down her face. "I love him."

Zina pulled Camille into a deep hug. "I know you do. Everything is going to be fine. Go home, little sister. Get some rest. We will make this all better in the morning. I promise we will."

Camille nodded her head as Zina brushed a tear from her own eye. As Camille stepped into the open elevator, Zina smiled, blowing her a kiss through the door. Behind them, Antione stood with his head hanging down, his grandmother shaking a wrinkled finger in his face.

Pulling her car into the driveway, Camille sobbed, the flow of tears finally flooding past the length of her lashes. She had told Zina she loved Vincent. The words had spilled out of her mouth as easily as if she'd been telling her sister the time of day. She'd been avoiding putting a label on what she felt for Vincent. She hadn't wanted to name what she thought he felt for her. She had simply relished each and every occasion they'd been able to spend together, and the countless hours they burned up on the telephone. But the truth of what was happening between them lay exposed like the open pages of a book. Together they had eased past the "once upon a time" of the first chapter, and were now waist deep in the story, rushing blindly to get to the last page, and the "happily ever after." And just like the heroine in the fairytale, Camille Martin knew she was in love, and knew that Vincent was her Prince charming. Pulling her cell phone from her purse, she dialed the Marriott Hotel and waited patiently for Vincent DeCosta to answer the phone in the presidential suite.

CHAPTER 17

As he made his way through the doors of the Martin Medical Building, Vincent had no clue what he planned to say to Dr. Louis Martin. Since Saturday evening, he'd replayed countless scenarios over in his head, and not one of them had ended well. He still had no idea how to finally end the nightmares that had plagued him since the night his brother lay bleeding to death on the side of the road with a dead white man beside him. He couldn't fathom how to find vindication for the childhood he'd lost in the squalor of the state penitentiary. He only knew there could be no revenge if he had any hope of walking off into the sunset with Camille at his side.

He paused, stopping in the lower lobby to read the building's occupant directory, searching out the floor and office number where Joe Louis sat waiting for him. As he rode the elevator to the fifteenth floor, he tapped his foot nervously, wishing there was some way to avoid the confrontation that was about to take place. Wishing instead that he was back home on the island, pink sand dusting his black complexion, blue water brushing against his thighs as he waded hip high with Camille.

Camille. He'd lost count of the number of calls she'd placed to his room trying to check on him.

Finally, when he'd composed himself enough to call her back, the hurt in her voice had devastated him. Her tone had been muffled behind the tears she had tried to hide from him, but he could hear the pain in her voice. What plagued him most was that he was responsible for putting that hurt there. Even with his assurances that everything was fine, and that he was well, he could tell that she'd hardly been convinced. She had seen right through the shallow façade he'd tried to assume, and she'd been hurt. He had promised her honesty, and thus far the only thing he had been able to give her was his silence.

Now he had to face her father. Two weeks ago, he had planned to tell Louis Martin how deeply in love he was with the man's daughter, but today, as he made his way out of the elevator, he didn't know what he intended to say.

As Vincent entered the office reception area, easing his way past the frosted glass doors, the nervous energy that had plagued him seemed to dissipate with each step he took. A sudden calm dropped over him, embracing him easily, and he couldn't help fearing the storm that threatened to follow.

The receptionist, a robust woman with a pecan complexion, greeted him warmly. She turned from her typing, pushing the keyboard that sat on the desktop out of her way as she rose to her feet. "Mr. DeCosta?"

"Yes, ma'am."

"Dr. Martin is expecting you, sir. Can I get you a cup of coffee?"

"No, thank you."

"Right this way then, sir. Dr. Martin said to bring you right in when you arrived."

Vincent smiled politely, brushing his palms against the sides of his black slacks. He followed behind the woman as she led him through another set of doors and down a short hallway. At the end of the corridor she pushed the large wooden doors open and gestured for him to enter. Thanking her, Vincent smiled as she closed the door behind him. Inside, Louis came to his feet, the friend sitting beside him also rising to stand.

"Vincent."

"Joe Louis."

"You remember, Lawrence Chambers from the other evening, don't you?"

"I do." Vincent extended his hand. "Mr. Chambers."

"Lawrence is my attorney, and under the circumstances I felt he should join us," Louis continued. Vincent shrugged, shaking Lawrence's hand briefly before allowing his arm to fall back to his side. He turned to face Louis, who suddenly appeared visibly shaken by his presence.

"May I sit down?" Vincent asked.

"Please," Louis said, gesturing toward the tailored gray sofa that sat against the wall.

Vincent made his way to one of the upholstered office chairs that sat before a large conference table in the center of the room. Taking a seat, he made herself comfortable and waited as the other two men made their way over to join him.

Louis eyed Lawrence nervously, twisting his hands in front of him.

"Dr. Martin has apprised me of the unfortunate circumstances that bring you here today, Mr. DeCosta. I think we need to ask what your intentions are," Lawrence said, pulling a pen from his breast pocket, and setting it atop a yellow-lined notepad that sat before him.

Vincent glanced at Lawrence, and let his gaze fall on Louis. He hesitated before speaking, an unwelcome silence flooding throughout the room.

I was thirteen years old, and instead of high school I served five years of hard labor because of you," he finally said, ignoring Lawrence as he directed his comment to Louis.

Louis it dropped his gaze to the table, his bottom lip trembling. He swayed his head from side to side, then took a deep breath before responding. "I'm sorry. If I take back that night, I would. But I can't change what happened. It was an accident."

"You killed a man, and my brother lost his life because of what you did. How do I let that go? How do you expect me to just let that go?"

"We were both young. I was only seventeen myself. I was stupid, and I was scared. I reacted, and I ran. I'm not proud of that, and I've lived with it every day of my life since. But you were there. You know how fast it all happened. All I knew was I needed to get away. That cop would have killed all three of us, and I did what I thought I had to do to protect myself."

Vincent dropped his head into his hands, pushing his fingers against his forehead. "What about me? I was just a kid. And what about my brother? He was supposed to be your best friend."

"I have cried every day for Maurice. But if it hadn't been for him and all the crap he was into, neither one of us would've been there that night. That wasn't my gun. Maurice stuck the gun in my pocket when the police pulled us over. Once they pulled us out of that car, I didn't know what to do. I just knew that once they found that gun, I was a dead man. A dead man who'd been pretending to be cool just to be friends with Maurice," Louis said, an edge of contempt rising in his voice.

"So, what you saying? Are you blaming all of this on Maurice?"

"No, of course not." Louis heaved a heavy sigh catching the intonations of his voice before he continued to speak. "I made the choice to pull that gun. I pulled the trigger and I don't even remember doing it. Did I plan to kill that man? No. All I wanted was to buy us some time to get the hell out of there. I was young, and stupid, and…" Louis's voice dropped, the man choking back the rush of anguish that dripped from his spirit. "I'm sorry. I am so sorry."

Vincent watched as Louis fought to compose himself, fighting back the wealth of tears that threatened to dampen the front of his gray silk suit. He watched in slow motion as Lawrence reached a wide hand out to tap his friend's arm, neither of them saying a word.

Lawrence is booming voice broke the silence. "Mr. DeCosta, I think I should ask again what your intentions are. Do you plan to turn Dr. Martin in to the authorities?"

Vincent rose from his seat and pushed his chair in neatly. He studied Louis momentarily before responding, then turned to direct his comments at Lawrence.

"Mr. Chambers, I intend to return to Bermuda today to prepare for the opening of my new show in two weeks. This is a very important showcase for my daughter-in-law, and I want to ensure that the event is successful for us both. I don't want there to be anything that might spoil the moment for her, or her sister. They've both worked far too hard for me to allow that to happen. Besides that…" He paused, pushing his shoulders up toward the ceiling, then continued. "I don't know if I have any other intentions. If I do, though, I'll be sure to let you know."

Vincent turned, heading for the door, then did an about-face, spinning around toward Louis. "Right now I don't know how I feel about you or this situation. But I do know I don't want to see you in Bermuda. Under the circumstances, I'm sure you won't have a problem making up some excuse with your daughters about not being able to come. And for the sake of our children, I guess we'll just figure out the rest of it as we have to."

Across the way, Louis nodded his head pushing his hands into the pockets of his pants. As Vincent disappeared out the door, closing it gently behind him, Louis dropped back down to his seat, laid his head on the table, and cried.

Since Vincent had called to say he was on the way over, Camille could do nothing but pace of the floor in anticipation. After Saturday night's fiasco she needed to see him, needed to look into his eyes to understand what could have possibly happened to dull the feelings between them. She peered anxiously out the window, looking up and down the street for his car.

The ringing telephone was an unwanted distraction, and though she wanted nothing more than to ignore the annoying ring, she felt obligated to answer when she saw her godmother's name reflected on the caller ID.

"Hi, Aunt Kitty."

"Hello, Camille. How are you, darling?"

"I'm okay."

There was a short pause as each woman waited for the other to expand upon the conversation.

"What happened, Camille? I could see that things weren't going well Saturday," Kitty finally asked.

Camille fought to suppress a sob, the older woman's inquiry stirring up her emotions. "I don't know, Aunt Kitty," she whispered into the receiver. "Things started well, and then it all seemed to fall apart."

Kitty nodded into the telephone. "Do you and Mr. DeCosta speak with your father at all? He seemed upset."

"No. In fact, I spent the better part of the evening trying to get them together. They were polite enough, but neither seemed interested in having anything to do with the other."

"Has Mr. DeCosta said anything or did he do something to hurt you?"

"No, ma'am, he didn't. In fact, he's on his way over now so that we can talk."

Camille could sense the woman nodding into the receiver.

"Camille, I know you don't want to hear this but I have to say it. Maybe you should end things with Mr. DeCosta now, before it goes any further. I understand that you have feelings for him, but I am really concerned that you are going to be hurt by all of this."

She continues, "Obviously, the two men aren't interested in getting to know each other. I don't doubt that Louis harbors some resentment about Zina marrying Antione, and Mr. DeCosta not doing more to stop them. You know how your father can be."

"Aunt Kitty, I love the Vincent," Camille said. "I love him. I don't understand what's going on, but I'm confident that he and I can work through whatever it is. Maybe he and Daddy had words when they met. I don't know, but I'm not going to let that affect my relationship with Vincent."

"Sweetheart, this thing between you and Mr. DeCosta is too new for you to be saying you're in love. I don't doubt the man has his own agenda. He's got far more experience than you, Camille."

"Vincent loves me, Aunt Kitty."

"Has he said so?"

"Not in so many words, but I can feel it. I know his heart."

Kitty sighed deeply. "Camille, baby, what could you possibly see in that old man? Heavens, child!"

Camille paused, peering again out the window, before dropping herself onto the cushions of the loveseat. She knew her godmother was waiting for an answer and she knew that her response would either ease her concerns are cause her greater frustration.

"Aunt Kitty, Vincent makes me feel special. He is comfortable with the woman I am and he allows me to be comfortable with myself. He doesn't pass judgment and when we're together, he makes sure that there is peace between us and around us. I'm sure his age has a great deal to do with it, but Vincent isn't like other men I've dated. He isn't all over me is if I owe him my body because he brought me a meal. He makes me laugh, and just being in the same room with him makes me feel safe and protected. He has never put up any barrier between us as if he thinks I have some hidden agenda he needs to protect himself against. He opened up his heart, and he trusted me with it, and he allowed me to return that favor. I see nothing but love and goodness in Vincent and when I look into his eyes I feel like that's all he sees in me."

"Oh, Camille! I am so worried about you."

"Aunt Kitty, don't, please. Vincent just pulled up in the driveway. I need to go."

"I want to talk with you more, Camille. I think it's important."

"Yes, ma'am. But it won't change my mind."

"Maybe not, but I think you really need to see this from all sides. I will call you later. Better yet, you call me as soon as you're free."

"I will."

"I love you, darling. Uncle Lawrence and I are both here for you."

"I know that. Thank you."

"Call me now."

"By, Aunt Kitty."

As he pulled his car into Camille's driveway, Vincent felt numb. He knew he needed some distance between himself and his past. Staying in North Carolina, with Joe Louis in striking distance, would more than likely cause problems that neither of them wanted to deal with. He knew he needed to go home.

As he rang the doorbell, he stared out across the road noting the bloom of roses in her neighbor's yard. The weather had not been kind to the summer foliage and the florae appeared to be agonizing under the summer heat. Vincent felt as weak as the thin stems that struggled to hold up the bright heads of the withering blooms. Everything about him felt heavy, and the weight of his burdens sat high on his shoulders. He'd not felt this way since prison, when the man he was thought to be had been identified by a sequence of numbers across his chest. Numbers that had said he was nothing but waste to be eliminated. When Camille opened the door, he was still staring out at the flowers.

CHAPTER 18

Florence Gibbons had given birth to six children. God had taken two of them, her eldest daughter from breast cancer, and her son a victim of senseless violence. When their times had come, destiny returning them to their eternal home, she had found solace in God's word, knowing that where their spirits now rested was a brighter and better place awaiting them all.

Standing at the kitchen door, Nana watched as her youngest son struggled. She had no clue who or what had moved him to the place of unrest he now found himself settled in, but she could sense the demons he battled were monumental. Vincent had not found ten words to speak to her since they'd returned from the States. His mood had been sour, a touch shy of toxic, and she had felt how heavy the burdens were that weighed down upon his shoulders.

Well before she'd given birth to her babies, when each had lain nestled in the security of her womb, she had wanted them, had felt what they felt, their energies tied as tightly to hers as the umbilical cord that connected them. They had fed on her emotions and she upon theirs, and it was that eternal bond of motherhood that now moved her to her son's side in search of answers.

Vincent looked up in surprise as she sat down beside him, adjusting her seat to move herself out of the bright afternoon sun. He smiled weakly as she placed her hand on his, nodding her gray head as she spoke.

"Tell me what's the matter."

Vincent dropped his dark eyes down towards his lap, heaving a deep sigh. His gaze darted back and forth as he struggled to tell his mother what plagued him. He opened his mouth, then closed it, fearing the emotion that would come, its raw intensity wrapped in a fountain of tears that threatened to fall.

"Is it Camille?" she asked.

He looked up quickly, his gaze meeting hers.

"Has something happened between you two that you weren't prepared for?" Nana asked, her questions probing. She continued, I know how you feel about her. I hear the love in your voice each time you two are on the telephone with each other. But you've not spoken in a few days so I can only imagine that something has happened to tear you apart."

"It's about her father," he finally uttered, the sound of his voice vague and dull, its tonality ringing strangely in his own ears.

His mother nodded her head. "Did you two have words?"

"It wasn't pleasant."

"I'm sure, because he loves his daughter, he is just worried why an old man like you would be interested in her." Nana laughed softly, trying to ease the tension on her son's face.

Vincent shrugged his shoulders. "We never got that far."

Nana raised her eyebrows. "Oh?"

"No. He doesn't know about me and Camille."
Vincent paused. "Mom, Camille's father is Joe Louis,
the man who killed Maurice."

Nana inhaled sharply. "Are you sure?"

Vincent nodded his head, tossing her a look of
acknowledgment. "Positive. We recognized each
other the night of the reception."

"But you never said a word, Vincent."

"He and I agreed to pretend like we were meeting
for the first time. Then I met with him that Monday
morning. Him and his attorney, that Mr. Chambers
you met. They wanted to know what I intended to
do."

Nana sat back in her seat, crossing her hands in
front of her. "What did you say?"

"Nothing, really. I didn't have an answer."

"Does anyone else know?"

Vincent's head waved from side to side. "No," he
answered.

"And you do not know what you want to do
because you are in love with Camille." Nana smiled,
reaching out once again to stroke her son' s hand.

"I love her so much, Mom. Since Irene died, I
didn't think it could be possible for me to love
anyone as much. And I don't know what to do. Tell
me what to do, Mom. Please. Tell me what to do."
Vincent implored, tears rising in his eyes.

Nana's smile was comforting as she stroked his
arm, leaning over to wrap her arms around his solid
frame. She held him tightly as he fought the tears, not
wanting his mother to see him cry. Sensing the wave
of emotion passing, Nana patted him gently on the
back, then rose to her feet.

"I will say a prayer, Vincent. God will lead you where you need to go."

Vincent shook his head. "I think I need more than prayer, Mom."

Nana pondered his comments before speaking. "Vincent, I made peace with your brother's death many years ago. I loved Maurice very much. He was my child, but he was a difficult to young man, and no matter how your father and I tried, we couldn't make him do right. It just wasn't in him, and he was never willing to try. When you went to prison over Maurice's mess, it broke my heart because you for everything your brother refused to be. There was never a day that went by that I didn't say a prayer for you. There is great power in prayer, son. Great power," she repeated. "And I think you being here right now is proof of that.

"The Louis Martin I met is not the boy who made the mistakes that took your brother's life and put you in jail. He has paid for his mistakes. He's a decent man. He has raised two beautiful daughters who are loving, successful women. Somehow, some way, he found the goodness within himself to change his ways. I saw that when he and I sat down and spoke at the party. I see it in his children, and how they love him, and how he returns that love. I didn't see anything in him that remotely resembled that boy you hate so much. If I can forgive him, then so can you."

She took a deep breath, continuing to study the lines of her son's face as he struggled to understand what she was trying to say to him. "When you came home from prison, I was scared to death that you were going to allow your anger and bitterness to consume you, but you didn't. You fought past it and found your own goodness. Don't let that hatred overcome you, Vincent. You let it go once, you can do it again. Allow what you feel for this young woman to help you to do what's right. And I can't tell you what that is. But I know that if you pray long and hard enough, God will."

Vincent watched as his mother made her way back inside the house. His eyes were still searching for answers, long after the afternoon sun had disappeared out of the cloudless sky, as he was sending prayer up to the heavens as fast as his mind could form the litany.

Camille had never been the type of woman who lingered in a bad relationship, hanging on to promises with both hands. She'd never been one who thought she could will a bad man into tolerable and tolerable into "it's not so bad after all." Early on her mother had taught her and Zina how to run from the venom of any relationship that brought them more heartache than it did joy. From the simplest of friendships to the deepest relationships, Camille knew that overcoming a challenge was one thing. Overcoming continued heartbreak was something else entirely.

What she and Vincent had shared had been special. Together, they'd just discovered a side of themselves that few others had ever been privy to. For Vincent, his late wife had been his only witness, and no man had been privileged to experience Camille as Vincent had. Love did that to you. Allowed you to open up the depths of your inner self to expose the hollow of your being for that one special person to see and explore. Peeling away the shell and cutting through the deepest of flesh required a significant to trust in one's self and in that other person. That kind of trust didn't come without a significant price and touch of sacrifice. Camille was certain that she and Vincent had shared that kind of trust.

As she lay sprawled across her bed, she pulled a pillow over her head, wanting nothing more than to drop into the ensuing darkness until whatever was happening with her and Vincent was over and was nothing but a memory for them to learn from. This was a challenge to overcome, she thought to herself, believing Vincent when he had said he would never purposely bring her any heartbreak. Throwing the pillows across of the room, she reached for the telephone, intent on calling him. Thinking better of it, she dropped the receiver back down onto the hook, not even bothering to dial. *No,* she thought. She couldn't fix this until he was ready to tell her what the problem was. The ball was in his court and the best thing she could do was wait until he was ready to play.

CHAPTER 19

Dante, Antione, and Zina talked exuberantly, Zina leaning over her husband to tell tales with his brother. Although she'd tried to concentrate on the conversation, Camille could not will herself to focus on their chatter, finding the noise of their laughter annoying. Thankful for the window seat, she feigned sleep, occasionally opening her eyes to peer out into the distance to marvel at the rise of clouds that sat like a cushion beneath the airplane's wings.

The last two weeks had wreaked havoc with her nerves, and she was anxious to see Vincent, to feel him next to her, his arms wrapped tightly around her. When he'd left her that Monday following Zina and Antione's reception, he'd promised that things would be well when she arrived in Bermuda. He'd said that he would be well, and whatever apprehensions she thought she'd felt would be better. She had witnessed the tension that bore deep lines into his brow, creasing the bronze of his skin with distress. She'd traced a manicured finger along the edges of anxiety that had shown itself in the lines of his face. She had held him, and he her, and then he'd kissed her goodbye, promising that things would be better. They'd not spoken since, and Camille now wondered if it was possible for anything to be better at all.

Zina had told her not to worry. Antione and Kitty had said maybe it was for the best. Even Dante and Nana had ventured an opinion, both advising her to be patient, to let things fall where they might fall. But what she needed to hear, she needed to hear from Vincent, and he wasn't' saying much of anything at all. Nervous energy numbed the pit of her stomach, and she was afraid that she might spew the remainder of her breakfast against the back of the seat in front of her. Just as she struggled to crawl over Zina and Antione, racing for the bathroom, the pilot announced their descent into Bermuda.

Louis and Lawrence had just settled down for lunch when Louis glanced at his watch, noting the time. "It's one-thirty. They should be landing right about now."

Lawrence nodded his head. "What did the girls say about you not going?"

"Camille wasn't happy, but Zina didn't seem to be too disappointed."

"Do you think they believed you?"

"How often have I had to cancel on them for a patient? They accepted it like they always accept it. They understand that my work is important, and that there are times my patients have to take priority."

"I arranged for a large bouquet of flowers to be delivered from Kitty and myself."

Louis smiled warmly. "They'll both appreciate that."

Lawrence lifted his glass to his lips, sipping the cold soda as they waited for their meals. "Have you heard anything from DeCosta?"

Shaking his head no, Louis shrugged his shoulders. "I need to resolve this, Lawrence."

"What do you want to do?"

"I don't know. You're my attorney. What do you suggest?"

"There is no statue of limitations on murder, Louis, accident or not. And under the circumstances, with the man being a police officer, you don't have many options. You can still be tried, convicted, and given the death sentence in this state. At best, you'd get life behind bars."

Louis stared off into the distance, his fingers brushing against the moisture on his glass. The last remnants of sweet tea, watered down by too much ice, sat in the bottom of the container. "He had two children," Louis finally said, muttering softly under his breath.

"Excuse me?"

"The cop. He had two children. A boy and a girl. But you already know that."

Lawrence nodded. "I remember."

Louis continued. "David was two when his father died, and Rachel wasn't quite three months old. They were both just babies."

His friend stared at him intently, allowing him to repeat the story he'd heard the first time, when he and Louis had become friends. When their bond had become deeper than that of some brothers, he had taken him into his confidence. It was the same story repeated again and again, ever since he'd become Louis's attorney, and his friend had needed to face the demons that continued to haunt him.

"It was an accident," Louis said, still staring into space. "It happened so fast. I didn't mean for that gun to go off, and when it did I ran. I didn't bother to look back, just willed my legs to get me as far from that spot as they could. Somehow, I made my way to Hollis Booker's farm. Mr. Brooker hit me in his barn for three days, then got me a bus ticket out of the state, and away from this place. I rode in the trunk of his old Ford all the way from here to Maryland, and then he put me on a Greyhound bus, and told me to disappear.

"My grandma used to tell me stories about her great-granddaddy. He was an honorable, decent man named Martin, Martin Louis, and I decided right then that not only would that be my new name, but I was going to do whatever I had to do to live up to it. So, I became Louis Martin, and I swore I was going to make amends for that man's death, and for Maurice, and for his little brother. Didn't know how I was going to manage it, but I knew that I would die trying."

"You didn't do too badly," Lawrence interjected, meeting his friend's gaze. "You went on to become a fine doctor. How many other people can say they put themselves through medical school while working three jobs? Not only did you make a very nice life for your own family, but you took care of those other children. Both of them received wonderful college educations thanks to your generosity, and their mother has never wanted for anything."

Louis chuckled, a nervous laugh that echoed strangely around the room. "Remember when Sarah found out about that woman and the money I was sending her? Almost cost me my marriage."

Lawrence smiled with him, shaking his head. "That was a rough time, but you got through it. You finally made her understand."

The duo went silent as a young girl with a peach-toned complexion, and a mop of carrot-colored hair, placed two salad and sandwich combos in front of them. They both nodded, holding back their conversation until she'd disappeared back in the kitchen.

"Louis, you did better than most would have done under the circumstances. You shouldn't have any regrets. Convincing Albright to help me work on DeCosta's case was a major accomplishment. I was barely out of law school, and here he was, one of the most influential white attorneys in the area. You nagged that man to death to get him to take on that case, and the fact that he worked for free was something else."

"Yes, but he worked you near to death, not only on that case, but half a dozen others. That man never gave you one red dime for any of the work you did for him, and you never complained once."

"It needed to be done. I understood that and I believed in what you were trying to do. The fact that we were able to get the conviction overturned and he was set free was a true blessing. Besides that, I learned a lot. Albright showed me what to do and more importantly what not to. Made me the lawyer I am today. What more could we have asked for?"

Louis shook his head. "I was worried that DeCosta was going to recognize you."

"We never met. Old man Albright didn't want anyone to know that he had a black man doing his work for them. Most folks just thought I was the janitor." Lawrence took a bite of the sandwich and chewed, wiping at his mouth with a paper napkin before he continued to speak. "I was surprised that I didn't know who he was. He changed his name, and time has been very good to him."

Louis nodded his head. "He dropped his last name. Started using his mother's name when his art career took off. Gave the boys his wife's name. Guess he was trying to get as far away from the past as I was."

Both men grew silent, playing with the food upon their plates. Louis sighed as he finally spoke. "I promised Sarah I'd never let the girls find out about this. She always said that it was important that our daughters never find fault with me."

"She wanted them to have a strong example to compare other men to. You know that. She wanted to make sure the girls found good, decent men to care about them, and you were supposed to set the example. Sarah loved you, and those girls were everything to her. That's the only reason she asked you to make that promise."

"So, how do I keep it, Lawrence? Because I don't think I can. At some point, they're going to have to know the truth. They're going to have to find out that most of my life has been a lie, and that I'm not half the man they think I am. And when that happens, it is going to break my heart."

Nana greeted them at the door, pulling each of them into a warm embrace. As she leaned in to wrap her arms around Camille, her warm smile soothing the young woman's anxious nerves, she whispered into Camille's ear, "He's in the studio."

After dropping her luggage onto the bed in the guest room, Camille headed out the door and across the road. Outside, the summer heat had risen to full height, the intense sun bearing down on her bare shoulders. The warmth felt good and she welcomed its embrace against her skin, stilling the nervous chill that had consumed her since the taxi drive from the airport.

Knocking before she entered, Camille stepped inside, the cool fresh of the air-conditioned room seeping past the opened the door to the outside. Vincent sat at his worktable, a sketchpad in his hand.

Staring, Camille suddenly found herself speechless, not knowing what to say. Words escaped her until Vincent rose from his seat, coming to stand in front of her, his own nervousness trickling from his eyes. Then she asked the question that had troubled her since his departure, needing an answer before she could even think about moving on.

"Vincent DeCosta, what kind of a man are you? Why are you trying to break my heart?"

CHAPTER 20

Vincent and Camille walked hand-in-hand along the shoreline, kicking a trail of fine sand with their bare feet. Warm seawater brushed against their ankles, the spray of water racing in with the tide to kiss the edge of the beach.

"I don't know that I have all the answers you want, Camille."

"Vincent, I just want to understand. You promised that you'd let me know what it is you're feeling, and then I feel like you're pushing me away. You tell me everything is all right, and clearly it's not. I could see something was wrong, and you refused to tell me what it was."

"I didn't mean to hurt you."

"Well, you did. You hurt me a lot. If this is how things are going to be between us, then I don't know that I want to be with you."

Vincent stopped walking, turning to face Camille. He placed his hands against her shoulders, staring deep into her eyes. "Camille, I don't want to lose you. I have spent the last two weeks coming to terms with just how much you mean to me, and what I'm willing to do to hold onto you. This isn't about us testing the waters to see where our relationship might go. Right now, it's about forever. You have every right to worry about it not being easy for us. To be concerned about Antione, and your father, and how they might feel about us. I had to understand that their feelings were going to have a significant impact on how we deal with our relationship. I had to know that I was willing to fight whatever might lie ahead for us if I was going to do right by you."

Camille shook her head slowly. "If there's going to be any us, Vincent, then I don't want it to be a secret anymore. I want everyone to know how much I love you. Because I do. I love you, Vincent DeCosta. I love you and I want us to be together."

Vincent pulled her against him, dropping his face into her hair, his hands dancing along her back, brushing down the length of her arms. He clasped his hands against her cheeks, pulling her lips to his, kissing her hungrily. "I love you too, Camille. I love you so much," he finally whispered into her ear, a rush of wind blowing around them.

The Foggo family sat in the family room chatting quietly when Vincent and Camille finally returned to Art-House. The couple had lost all track of the time, not caring about the hours that had passed since Camille's arrival. Outside, the sun had quieted down nicely, a cool ocean breeze replacing the incessant heat.

Zina looked up from the magazine she was scanning and smiled, meeting Nana's gaze as the two women grinned widely. Antione shook his head with concern, rising from his seat to shake his father's hand, as Dante stood at his elbow.

"Hey, Pop. We thought you two got lost."

Vincent pulled his son into a warm hug, then turned to embrace Dante. "Camille and I need to say something to all of you," Vincent started, dropping down to sit in a plush wing chair. Camille sat beside him, perching her buttocks against the chair's arm. Vincent reached up to take her hand, gripping it tightly.

"Wait," Nana said suddenly. Rising from her seat, she crossed the room to the door where Savage stood patiently waiting for someone to let him outside. "Okay," she said, after closing the door behind the animal and sitting back down. "Go on."

Vincent chuckled lightly, tossing his hands up and mock exasperation.

"I said go on," his mother chastised. "Don't get an attitude with me," she said with a laugh. "Say what you have to say."

Clearing his throat, Vincent started to speak. "I love Camille and surprisingly it seems that she loves me. We've decided that we want to be together. Even though we know not all of you may agree with it, we're hoping you will at least respect our decision, even if you don't feel you can give us your support." He looked directly at Antione.

The room was quiet as Vincent and Camille looked from one face to the other, trying to gauge their reactions. Zina reached to take her husband's hand, squeezing it tightly. Nana was the first to speak.

"People will say that she is too young for you or that you are too old for her. How will you respond?"

"We will say that our love for each other is ageless." He looked up at Camille, meeting her gaze. "We will say that what we feel is a love for all time."

Camille smiled, leaning down to kiss the brow just above his eye.

Nana nodded her head, pleased. "All I have ever wanted is for my children to be happy. All of you. If you two make each other happy, that I can't help being happy for you. Camille, baby," Nana rose from her seat, crossing over to kiss Camille's cheek. "You be good to my son. He's a wonderful man, and he deserves the very best."

Camille smiled. "I will, Nana."

Antione came to stand before them both, extending his hand toward Camille. "I'm sorry if I was out of line with you. I did see how serious you two were. But if my father says he loves you, and it's obvious that you love him, then you both have my full support. Congratulations."

Zina clapped her hands excitedly, giggling as she rushed up to hug them all. "This is so cool. I am so happy for you. We have to call Daddy."

Camille shook her head. "No, not yet, Zina. Vincent and I want to tell Daddy ourselves, in person."

"Okay, but you better do it soon. You know how bad I am at holding stuff like this in."

Everyone in the room laughed. Dante cleared his throat. "So, how does this thing work? Are you two getting married, or what?"

Camille and Vincent grinned. "We went to the registrar's office this afternoon. They'll be posting our marriage intentions this week." Vincent said. "In fourteen days we'll have a marriage license, and soon after that, a wedding.

Zina shrieked with joy. "This is so exciting!"

Dante nodded in agreement. "So, now Camille is not only Antione's sister-in-law, but she'll be his stepmother, and Zina's sister and mother-in-law and—"

"And nothing," Antione interrupted. "She's family and that's all we need to know. Stop trying to confuse the matter."

"Who's trying to confuse the matter? I just want to know if I can call her Mom or Mommy or Mother or what."

"Both of you need to stop," Nana laughed. "Is anyone else hungry? My dinner is getting cold."

"I think we all are, Nana," Antione said, following her into the kitchen, the rest of the family on his heels.

As Vincent came to his feet, he wrapped his arms around Camille's waist, pulling her against him. "I love you," he said. "I would do anything for you."

Camille tilted her head to kiss his lips, reaching her arms up and around his neck. She hugged him as tightly as he held her. "I love you, too."

He tapped her on the behind, pushing her toward the kitchen. "You go on ahead. I have a quick telephone call to make, and then I'll be right there."

"Are you sure?"

"I'll be right there. I just have something important I need to do."

CHAPTER 21

Louis Martin sat on his living room sofa, darkness starting to fill the large room. The home's usual quiet seemed more pronounced to him, and he did not find the silence nearly as comforting as he used to. He sighed deeply his gaze falling to the large family portrait that sat over the mantle above the fireplace. The image of him, his wife, and their daughters smiled down at him. He remembered the moment well, when the photographer had commanded them to say, "Cheese," and Sarah and her daughters had screamed out, "Daddy" instead. There was pure joy shining in each of their faces, and even then he had seen Sarah's spirit reflected in Camille's and Zina's eyes.

He'd always found it hard to imagine other women loving their children as much as Sarah had loved her daughters. That woman had doted on each of them, setting the standards she demanded of them, and being the prime example that they were meant to follow. She had placed heavy demands upon him as well, continually imploring him to be the ideal that she wanted her daughters to idolize. She had left a wealth of footsteps for each of them to follow, and he had always known he could never fill her empty shoes, no matter how hard he may have struggled to try. There had been something uniquely special about his precious wife. Something so utterly special that he had never once thought about any other woman taking her place. Sarah had been the love of his life, and even before her death he had known that no one else would ever again fill his heart as she had.

He sighed again, thinking of how much she missed her, wondering how she would have advised him to handle the mess he now found himself wading knee-deep in.

Rising from his seat, Louis sauntered into the kitchen, pulling open the refrigerator door to peer inside. Finding nothing that stimulated his appetite, he pushed the door closed, then stood with his forehead pressed against the stainless steel compartment.

He had worked diligently to keep each and every promise he had ever made to Sarah. When the cancer had been diagnosed, her want-list had increased tenfold, every detailed instruction revolving around their two daughters. He had made her many promises, and now, for the first time, he knew there was one pledge he was going to have to break. Sarah had never wanted them to know about his past. She had implored him never to reveal his secret, fearing that if they knew their father had been responsible for killing a man, the knowledge would somehow shatter the gilded shield of protection she fought to keep around them. And he had sworn to her, had crossed his heart in promise, that neither Camille nor Zina would ever learn the awful truth if there was any possible way for him to keep it from them.

Reaching behind the bar, Louis pulled a bottle of aged scotch from the shelf and cracked the seal.

Filling a glass, he gulped down three shots of the burning liquid before flinging the glass and the bottle across the room. As shards of glass and the flow of amber fluid settled against the slate floor, the telephone rang, beckoning him to answer it.

Lawrence and Kitty sat deep conversation, huddled close around the kitchen table as they pored over the papers and files before them. Kitty was jotting down notes as Lawrence dictated instructions to her.

"How bad do you think it will get?" Kitty asked her husband, dropping her pendant to the table as she turned to stare at him.

"I don't know. It could get messy."

"This will devastate Camille. She adores him."

"What about Zina?" Lawrence asked, pulling his glasses from his face and setting them on the table.

"Zina's got a tougher skin than Camille. She's not quite as sensitive. She's like her mother was. There is a tougher foundation with that one. The outside may seem soft, but don't let my girl for you. Zina can hold her own with the best of them."

"She's never been as mesmerized by her father the way Camille has been either," Lawrence added.

Kitty nodded in agreement. "Is he going to tell them?" she asked quietly.

"Only if he absolutely has to. It will all depend on what Mr. DeCosta does."

Kitty rose from her seat, reaching to fill the teakettle with water. After setting it on the stove to wait for it to simmer, she sat back down beside her husband. She looked at them curiously before speaking. "Did you say anything to him?"

Lawrence glanced at her briefly, then allowed his gaze to fall back onto the paperwork for him. "Woman, please. I still think you're wrong."

"Don't dismiss me. I know what I know."

"I cannot believe that there is anything going on between DeCosta and Camille. In fact, I'm sure that there is nothing happening between them."

Katie chose her words carefully, not wanting to betray Camille's confidence. "Lawrence, I saw how she looked at that man the other night. Mark my words, something is happening there. That child is head over heels in love, and by the way he was looking back at her, I don't doubt he feels the same way."

"Kitty, stop. I don't know what you saw, but if there is one thing we don't need right now, it's that. Besides, that man is too old for her. It would be like me trying to go out with her."

Kitty rolled her eyes. "Well, I still think you should say something, or have at least. If you don't want to say something to Louis, but maybe you should speak with Camille. Tell her that you were curious since they seemed so close at that night."

Lawrence stopped to stare at his wife. "Do you know something you're not telling me?" he asked.

"If I do, then you will just have to understand that I can't say anything. But trust me when I tell you there is something between Camille and that man and we need to do something about Louis."

"Darling, what I think is that we're going to leave it alone. Louis might be facing prison, or worse, the electric chair. If that happens, then you can rest assured that if there is something going on with Camille and DeCosta, it will be over before the trial even gets started. Now, would you help me go through that list of evidence, please? I really need to be prepared for whatever we might find ourselves up against."

Kitty studied him momentarily as he pulled his glasses back onto his nose and buried his face back into his paperwork. Rising once again, she poured boiling water into two teacups. As she reflected back to the reception, and the exchanges she'd witnessed between Camille and Vincent DeCosta, she instinctively knew that she would write to want to prepare Louis. And although she trusted her husband's instincts, she also knew, trial or no trial, what was happening between the couple was far from being over. The shrill ring of the telephone startled both of them, and as Lawrence reached for the portable receiver that lay on the table top, Kitty felt the need to say a prayer for them all.

CHAPTER 22

Vincent and Camille lay side-by-side under the large shade tree that shielded one corner of the rear yard. In the distance, Zina, Antione, and Dante were playing Frisbee with the dog. Nana was exercising in the pool, performing a series of water aerobics to maintain her limberness and keep her muscles toned.

Behind the dark lenses of his sunshades, Vincent's eyes danced along the length of Camille's elongated body, his appreciation of her beauty hiding behind the faintest of smiles that crossed his face. He inhaled deeply, trying to will away the dull throbbing that was beating in his loins.

Camille noted his sudden tension as he moved to pull his body away from hers, throwing his legs off the side of the lounge chair. She smiled coyly, amused by his embarrassment.

"Are you okay?" She asked, running her fingers down the length of his arm.

Vincent lifted his shades slightly, peeking beneath the bottom edge of the wire frames. "Sorry about that," he said.

"What do you have to be sorry for?"

"You know," he said, crossing his legs in an attempt to hide the raging erection that had risen in his shorts.

"No, I don't know," Camille said, sitting up to wrap her arms around his torso. Reaching around the front of them, Camille raked her fingers lightly against his upper leg.

"Woman, you need to stop. You know what you're doing to me and it's not fair."

Camille laughed, leaning up to bite lightly against his ear. "You want me, don't you?" Camille said teasingly, whispering enticingly into his ear.

"You know I do," Vincent replied, capturing her hands beneath his. "And you know that you are driving me crazy. You need to stop teasing me."

Camille moved to sit in his lap, pressing her mouth to his. "So, why do you want me?" she asked, finally pulling her face from his. "Why do I excite you?"

Vincent shook his head from side to side. "Are you serious? he asked.

She nodded. "Tell me."

Pushing her off him, Vincent spun his body around to face her, holding her at arm's length.

"You amaze me. You're incredibly beautiful. You have dynamic energy. I love to hear you laugh. I love the way you bite your bottom lip when you're in deep thought and how you twirl your index finger through your hair when you're nervous. You make me feel special. I feel like you want me as much as I want you. Even when we're just sitting side-by-side, lost in our own thoughts, I feel comfortable next to you. I feel warm. Everything about you excites me."

Vincent's hands had dropped down to his sides. He stared off toward his family, avoiding her eyes. His pulse vibrated throughout his lap, the swelling of tissue desperate for relief.

Camille leaned to kiss him again, reveling in the fullness of his lips, which felt so soft against hers.

"I do want you," she finally said. "I want you as much as you want me, if not more. I am so excited at the prospect of our being together it's all I can do not to bust. I want to make love to you, Vincent. I want to show you just how much I love you, how in love I am with you."

As Vincent pulled her toward him, they both fell into the embrace. Across the yard, Zina called out both their names.

"Hey," she shouted. "You two stop that mess over there. We've got a reception to get ready for."

Neither Vincent nor Zina had seen each other's work for the exhibition. With everything on his mind, Vincent had avoided the gallery, allowing Lydia to display and hang the artwork as she saw fit. With him and Camille announcing their engagement the night before, the entire family had spent most of the day relaxing by the pool, discussing wedding plans. Only Camille had been privy to both collections, confident that each would complement the other beautifully.

As they prepared for the opening reception, the excitement bounced off the walls. Laughter rang from one room to the other, the infectious energy spilling out into the yard. Leading her down the hallway to her room, Vincent held on tight to Camille's hand. At the door, he leaned in to kiss her, pressing himself against her and her against the wall.

"We aren't coming back here this evening. Pack an overnight bag. Just a few things to carry you over for a couple of days," Vincent said, smiling coyly.

Camille eyed him curiously. "Where are we going?"

"It's a surprise. You don't need much. Very casual and comfortable."

"T-shirt?"

Vincent laughed. "Need to borrow one?"

Camille joined them, giggling into his ear. "Will I need one?"

"No."

Opening the door, Camille tucked into her room, as Vincent attempted another kiss. "Go get dressed, Mr. DeCosta," she said. "We have a reception to get to."

Vincent beamed. "Yes, ma'am."

An hour later the family was gathered in the front foyer. The three men were decked out in matching black Armani suits, the ebony silk atop snow-white dress shirts opened at the neck. A boutonniere graced Vincent's lapel, the single white rose a nice accent. Camille wore a simple ankle-length tank dress, the camel-colored silk draping her body like a second skin. Zina stood beside her, dressed in a black crewneck shirt with silk chiffon sleeves and wide buttoned cuffs, her nose pressed into the newly opened long-stemmed rosebuds that Vincent had presented to her. Black leather pants hugged the woman's firm hips. Gathering them together for a group photo, Nana commented on how smart they all looked.

Vincent handed Dante the keys to his grandmother's vehicle. "Dante, you will need to drive Nana's car. Camille and I aren't coming back here tonight. This way the four of you will have a ride home."

"Where are you two off to?" Antione questioned.

His father looked at him sideways as Zina punched him lightly on the arm. The man blushed, feeling the wealth of color tinting his dark cheeks. "Oh," Antione said, visibly flustered as he turned toward the door.

Nana started to hum a low hymn as she followed behind him. Dante brought up the rear, laughing aloud.

Zina giggled. "Them ninety days must be up."

Camille shook her head, rolling her eyes at her sister. "Shut up, Zina."

As they pulled into parking spaces outside Somerset Gallery, parking Vincent's car beside Dante's, they could see that a small crowd had already gathered inside. Vincent and Camille entered hand-in-hand, Zina and Antione close behind them. Lydia was right there to greet them at the door, her anxiety gracing her pale face.

"Vincent, Camille. It's about time. You two look good?" the woman gushed hugging them both. "And you must be Zina," she said, extending her hand in greeting.

"Hello, Lydia. It's a pleasure to meet you," Zina said.

Camille beamed. From the entranceway, the display was spectacular. Bright color leapt off the walls. Zina's paintings lent an exciting ambience to the space, and in conjunction with Vincent's sculpture, the showcase was mesmerizing.

"Oh, Vincent!" Zina sang, racing to see the sculpture up close. "They're beautiful!"

Camille stepped back as people rushed over to acknowledge Vincent and to meet the young new artist that were showing with him. Making her way toward the back of the gallery, Camille was pleased, confident the reviews would be incredible. A familiar voice suddenly called out to her.

"Congratulations, daughter. Job well done."

"Daddy!" she exclaimed, throwing herself into her father's arms.

This hugged her closely.

"When did you get here?" she asked excitedly.

"I arrived on the afternoon flight."

"But we thought you had to work."

"Well, Vincent called me last night and said it was imperative that I be here. He arranged my transportation, and here I am."

Camille looked across the room to Vincent, who was staring back. She smiled as he nodded his head, then lifted his hand to give a slight wave to her father.

"I was worried that something had happened," Louis said, nervousness rising in his voice.

"A lot has happened, Daddy. I have so much I want to tell you, but first, did Zina see you?"

"No. Let me sneak over and say hello, and then we can talk."

Camille nodded her head as Louis made his way over to his older daughter. He and Vincent passed each other midway, shaking hands and exchanging a polite, and very brief, greeting. Vincent came over to her side, leaning to kiss her cheek as he took her hand into his.

Surprised?"

"Very. Thank you."

"I knew that we couldn't make any more plans until we've had an opportunity to talk with your father. I know how important it is to you to have him involved and hopefully to have his approval."

Camille squeezed his hand tightly. Lydia tapping her on the shoulder interrupted their conversation. "Camille, darling, there's someone I want you to meet. George Wye is head of the British Arts Council, and is absolutely charmed by your sister's artwork. He wants to speak to you about Zina doing an exhibition in London with a group of artists. It's a show Vincent has done many times, and should be quite beneficial for her career. Vincent, dear, you need to excuse us."

"Thank you, Lydia," Camille said.

Vincent nodded his head as he waved them both off. As he stood staring out into the crowd, Louis caught his eye, nodding in his direction. Walking toward him, Vincent gestured for Louis to follow him outside. Standing together in front of the gallery, the two men faced off. As the gallery door opened and closed, more bodies entering to experience the show, noise spilled out onto the sidewalk.

"Thank you for inviting me," Louis said.

"I did it for Camille and Zina. It was important to them that you be here."

"Well, I appreciate it. They're both very excited."

"Zina has done an outstanding job. Her work is remarkable and Camille is the best advocate an artist could wish for."

Louis glanced over his shoulder, his attention captured by a young man and woman who seemed to be arguing as they exited their vehicle. Vincent's eyes followed his as they stared the couple.

The gallery door opened and Camille stuck her head out to look for them. "There you two are. I was wondering where you both disappeared too."

Both men smiled warmly in her direction. "Didn't mean to cause you any worry," Vincent said. "Your father and I thought we'd catch some air and get away from the noise for a few minutes."

Camille came to stand beside them.

"How's Zina doing?" Louis asked.

"She's in her element. Your daughter is a center of attention, and she is happy."

"That's my baby girl. I guess I should go back inside. I haven't had an opportunity to speak with Antione yet and I wanted to spend some time with your mother, Vincent. So, if you two will excuse me."

"We'll be right there, Daddy."

Camille watched as her father made his way back inside. When the door closed behind him, Vincent hugged her close, his lips lingering against the side of her face. "So," he asked, finally letting her go, "when do you want to tell your father?"

"When I couldn't find you two, that's what I thought you were doing."

Vincent smiled ever so slightly. "I wouldn't do that without you, unless you wanted me to."

"No. I think it's important that he hear it from me first; then we can talk with him together."

Vincent nodded his agreement. "Whenever you're ready."

"So what do you have planned for us tonight?"

"Ohhh," Vincent cooed, tossing back his head slightly. "Curiosity is killing you, isn't it?"

She grinned, grabbing him around the waist, her hands clutching the waistband of his pants. "I hope it's been worth my weight, Mr. DeCosta," she said seductively, her voice low and enticing.

Vincent inhaled deeply, his gaze weaving a path from her eyes, down the span of her body, and back again. Taking in the full lips that begged to be kissed, the round of her breasts pressed anxiously toward him, falling along the line of her hips that swayed easily in the light breeze, he hummed with appreciation. "Hmmm. I think it will be, Ms. Martin."

Camille reached up to press her mouth against his, lightly biting at his bottom lip. As Vincent pulled her closer, his hands trailing across her buttocks, they both felt the tremors of anticipation racing through their loins. Vincent pulled himself away, trying to suppress the first twitch of a rising erection. Stepping down off the sidewalk, he spun himself around in a circle, laughing loudly as he felt the quivers of excitement throughout his body.

Camille laughed with him, swinging her arms from side to side as she watched him. Stepping back toward her, Vincent brushed his palm against her face. "Woman, you are driving me crazy. I love you so much."

The smile on Camille's face was illuminating, her grin spreading from ear to ear.

"Are you ready to get out of here?" Vincent asked.

"Should you be leaving this early?"

"I've been ready to leave since you walked out of the bedroom in that dress."

Camille shook her head from side to side. "You are so bad."

Vincent kissed her quickly. "I'll tell Lydia we're leaving."

"Okay. But I think we should talk to my father first."

"Do you think that's a good idea? We may need a bit more time. He may not take it well."

Camille considered Vincent's comment briefly, then nodded her head. "You're right. What if we do it sometime tomorrow?"

"I think that would be better." Vincent glanced over his shoulder toward the gallery door. "I'll tell you what, will stay a bit longer and then we'll sneak off when the coast is clear."

Nodding in agreement, Camille smiled at him warmly. "We should go back inside and make nice with your guests," she said, leading the way toward the front door. "Go be a good artist now."

Vincent laughed loudly behind her. "Yes, Ms. Martin."

Together the duo reentered the gallery. Looking around briefly, Vincent found Lydia in deep conversation with a prospective buyer. Looking at Camille, he made his way to the other woman's side, engaging her and his patron in conversation. Camille searched for her father and found him sitting with Nana, the two laughing together with Zina and Antione. Strolling over to join them, Camille grabbed her sister's elbow, squeezing it gently.

"Hi there. Everyone doing okay?

"I've sold for paintings," Zina said excitedly.

"Very nice," Camille said, hugging her warmly. "Congratulations."

Antione smiled. "Zina and Dad are doing very well. Five of dad's sculptures have also sold."

"I told you it would be a great show, and as a bonus I just booked two exhibits for you in London," Camille said.

Zina squealed, jumping up and down against Antione's arm. "You are the best, Camille."

The woman smiled, winking in appreciation. So, Daddy, are you enjoying yourself?" Camille asked, turning to face her father.

"I am, daughter. I'm having a very nice time. I am so proud of both of you girls. Zina, as always the artwork is wonderful."

Both Zina and Camille smiled, the two women leaning in on either side of him to plant a kiss on their fathers cheek.

"So, where are you staying, Daddy?" Zina asked.

"I checked into the St. George's Club. Vincent made the arrangements for me."

"You know you're more than welcome to stay at the house," Nana said, tapping him lightly on the knee. "There is no reason for you to stay in any hotel. We have more than enough."

"I appreciate that, and Vincent did offer, but I'm only here until Thursday. Then I'm going to head back home. I wouldn't want to inconvenience anyone."

It wouldn't be any inconvenience, Louis."

"Thank you, Nana, but I think I should stay out from underfoot. My daughters get annoyed when they think I'm in their way."

Zina swatted her hand that her father. "We do not, Daddy."

"Zina, please." He laughed. "Your jaw gets tight real quick when something doesn't go your way.

Especially if I'm involved. And you can get evil with me in a heartbeat."

Zina sucked her teeth, rolling her eyes in her father's direction.

"See what I mean, Nana? There she goes now."

The group chuckled, Antione pulling Zina into a tight hug, kissing her pouting lips.

Out of the corner of her eye, Camille could see Vincent headed in their direction. As he joined them, Vincent moved to stand by his mother's side, consciously avoiding being too close to Camille.

"Have you made dinner plans, Louis?" he asked, reaching to squeeze his mother's hand.

"I really hadn't given it any thought," he replied. "I'm actually more tired than I am hungry. Not really feeling all that well this evening."

"You've had a long day." Nana said, studying him intently. "You should probably get some rest so that you don't make yourself sick."

"I think you're right, Nana," Louis said. "Thank you for asking, Vincent, but I don't think I'd be good company this evening."

"What time is your flight tomorrow?" Camille asked.

"I'm on the eight-thirty flight to Atlanta. There's a short layover before we head back to North Carolina."

Camille glanced from Vincent to her sister before she continued. Taking a deep breath, she asked, "Do you think we can meet for breakfast? I would really like to talk with you before you go."

Louis eyed her curiously, noting the grand that crossed Zina's face. "Of course. Everything is okay, isn't it?"

"Of course," Camille answered. "I just wanted to spend some time with you before you left."

Louis nodded his head.

"Well, I'm buying dinner if anyone's interested," Vincent said, looking from one face to the other.

"I'm going to pass, Pop," Dante said. "I'm joining some friends."

"What about you two?" Vincent asked, looking at Antione and Zina.

"I've actually planned a private dinner for the two of us," Antione answered, leaning to kiss his wife. "Thought I'd give my wife a special celebration."

"Nana?" Vincent queried, looking down at his mother.

"I'm not feeling that great myself. Dante and his friends are going to drop me off home."

Vincent shrugged his shoulders. "What about you, Ms. Martin? Can I interest you in dinner?"

Camille rolled her eyes. "Well, looks like we're stuck with each other this evening, Mr. DeCosta."

"That should be painful," Dante said jokingly.

"Louis, can we give you a ride back to your hotel?" Vincent asked.

"Thank you, but I'll be fine. Your friend Lydia said she'd arrange a taxicab for me when I was ready to leave."

Vincent nodded his head, glancing quickly toward Camille. "Well, why don't I go to tell her that were all about ready to leave? I think I've had my fill of schmoozing this evening."

"You and me both," Zina echoed. "My feet hurt."

"Well, let's go get you out of those shoes," Antione chimed, grabbing her by the hand.

"Goodnight, people," he sang, pulling Zina along behind him.

"Bye," Zina called out, waving in their direction.

Louis shook his head. "Have mercy," he said. "I don't know what we're going to do with those two."

Nana laughed. "You said a mouthful," she said.

Louis waved a finger at Lydia. "Let me see how long that taxi will be," he said, making his way toward her.

Camille and Vincent caught each other's eye, holding the stare. Nana looked from one to the other and shook her own head. "You two be careful. You hear me?" she said.

Vincent nodded, breaking the gays between them. "We will. Dante, get your grandmother home safely, son."

"I will, Dad."

Outside, the couple watched as Dante and Nana climbed into another young man's automobile, Nana displacing the rider who rode shotgun to the backseat. Camille and Vincent laughed as she busied herself fussing at the trio of young men. Antione and Zina had disappeared in Nana's car. Coming up behind them, Louis cleared his throat, catching their attention.

"Thank you for having me," he said, extending a hand to Vincent.

"Thank you for coming. It was important to your daughters for you to be here."

"What time is breakfast?" Camille asked.

"I have to be at the airport by seven-thirty."

"Why don't we pick you up at six forty-five? We can grab something quick and get you to the airport on time."

Louis nodded his head. "There's my taxi," he said, gesturing toward a short bald man who waved in his direction. He leaned to hug and kiss his daughter goodbye. "I'll see you in the morning," he said, waving at them as he made his departure.

"Good night, Daddy," Camille called out after him. "I love you."

"I love you too, daughter."

CHAPTER 23

After making polite conversation with the few remaining clients, Camille and Vincent bade Lydia goodbye. She stared after them, wanting to ask Vincent to stay a bit longer, but a client's offer on one of the artworks proved to be a distraction. By the time she was able to look up again, the duo had disappeared out the door.

As they drove back toward the center of the island, Camille looked over at him and smiled. She reached out to run her hand against his arm. "I am so excited about tonight."

Smiling back, Vincent leaned over to give her a kiss careful to keep his eyes on the roadway. "Tonight's our night," he said. "And I want it to be special."

Minutes later, as they entered Hamilton Parish, Vincent turned, guiding his Peugeot 206SW toward the marina. Entering the gates of the Royal Bermuda Yacht Club, he turned and drove to the Point Pleasant Dock. From her opened window, Camille inhaled the rich scent of the ocean air, the salty aroma tickling her nostrils.

Parking the car, Vincent stepped out onto the road and headed for the rear of the vehicle. Reaching into the trunk for both of their bags, he slammed the top closed, then grabbed her hand and pulled her down the wooden planks behind him.

Camille treaded cautiously, careful not to hook her heels into the open planks for fear she might fall flat onto her face. At the end of the third dock Vincent stopped and tossed their luggage over into the backside of a very large sea craft. Camille's mouth dropped, taking in the sight of the seventy-foot yacht, the name, *Work of Art,* scripted in black on the ship's stern. Vincent laughed at her surprise as he held out his hand to help her aboard.

"Might be easier if you kick off them heels."

"Is this yours?" she asked, reaching down to slip the three-inch sandals off her feet, passing them to Vincent by the thin leather straps.

He nodded. "Just one of my favorite toys."

"This is a big boat, Vincent!" she exclaimed, visibly awed.

"Baby, this is no boat. Don't insult my gem. She's a full-fledged luxury yacht."

As Vincent helped her onto the dock, Camille laughed. "Boat, yacht, ship, whatever. It's huge!"

Grabbing her hand, Vincent took her on the tour. "Come on. Let me show you around."

Guiding her along, he pointed out the many amenities available to them. From the posh salon with its cherry interior, to the galley with its marble countertops and state-of-the-art appliances, each room was wrapped in pure opulence.

The U-shaped settee, which ran the full-length of the salon, called out to her, the supple white leather seat wrapping itself around her body as she threw herself across its length. Vincent laughed as he walked back for their luggage, depositing it at the door of the master stateroom below.

Returning to the salon, Vincent lowered his body above Camille's, kissing her warmly. "Do you like it?" he asked, rolling over to lie beside her.

"Very nice, Mr. DeCosta. I'm quite impressed."

He smiled. "We can take her out if you want. But I thought we'd just hang out here in the dock. I went shopping, so there's plenty of food on board, or we can go down to Front Street and try any of the restaurants. Your choice."

"At the moment, I'm really not hungry. I can always make us something to eat when we get ready.

He nodded. "Works for me. Come on," he said, pulling her to her feet. "You can't miss this."

Leading her topside to sit on the fly bridge, Vincent pulled her into his lap, wrapping his arms around her waist. He pressed his mouth against her shoulder, leaning his head against her neck. He pointed toward the skyline and the setting sun in the distance. The view was incredible as they sat watching the flaming red orb kiss the clear blue water at the edge of the earth. The last of the sun's rays reflected off into the water and Camille swore she could hear the faint hiss of the sun's heat as it dropped into the cool water. Camille turned her head, reaching round to kiss him, brushing her closed mouth lightly over his.

They sat quietly together as darkness filled the clear sky. Hands entwined, their fingers played an erotic game of hide and seek. They reveled in the night noises, the whisper of water hitting against the shore. With the lights from the harbor and the neighboring vessels lighting the sky, Vincent pushed her onto her feet, then walked her back down below.

Back in the interior of the salon, Vincent pulled her into a warm embrace, his lips boldly searching hers. His tongue danced inside her mouth, performing an impromptu tango as it pranced against the line of her teeth. Camille wrapped her arms around his chest to his broad back, losing herself in the kiss. The exchange was soft at first, growing in intensity as desire surged between them.

Pulling away, Vincent looked deeply into her eyes, drawing the essence of her into his soul. He wanted this night to be perfect. Without another thought, he knew it couldn't be anything but.

"I need to get out of this monkey suit," he said, his hands still lingering against her body.

"I'd like to slip into something more comfortable myself," Camille whispered, sliding her cheek over his lips to his chin. Vincent inhaled the scent of her, filling his nostrils with the sweetness of her aroma.

Leading the way, Vincent headed down to the staterooms. Reaching into the first room on the right, he flicked on a light switch. "You can change in here. There's a shower in the bathroom. I'm going to fix us a snack, and then I'll meet you in the back room."

Nodding her head, Camille smiled sweetly, closing the door behind her as Vincent stood on the other side.

After a relaxing shower, Camille was awed when she entered the large master stateroom, calling out his name. Vincent had transformed the interior setting into a romantic getaway. Candles flickered soft light from one corner to the other, pillars of scented wax covering every conceivable surface. The bed had been turned down, revealing the ivory-laced bedding. On the nightstand, a platter of fresh fruits and cheese had been spread in abundance. A silver tray held two champagne flutes brimming with fluid, and an uncorked bottle resting alongside.

With her hair falling loose over her shoulders, Camille pushed a stray strand out of her eyes and behind her ear. Making her way to the bedside, she inhaled the view, intoxicated by the beauty of it. Reaching for the fruit, she pulled a peach into her hand, guiding the luscious fruit into her mouth. As she bit into the ripe flesh, lapping at the sweet nectar that ran down the length of her hand, Vincent opened the bedroom door, stepping back inside the room. Wrapped only in a lush white towel, he glistened from the warm mist that swirled behind him, his skin still damp from the hot water he'd just bathed in.

Camille met his gaze as he reached behind him to close the room's door. Want was carved in the lines of his face as he stared at her with much appreciation. Camille stood before him, dressed in nothing but one of his white dress shirts, the tailored garment opened down the front. The brown of her body peeked out from the folds of white fabric, beckoning him forward. Wanting only to stand and stare at her, Vincent could feel his control melting, his body taking over his mind. Cocking her head ever so slightly, Camille smiled, a seductive bend of her lips that welcomed him warmly.

Dropping the peach back onto the platter, Camille lifted herself onto the bed, crawling toward its center. Resting on her knees, she pulled her right hand to her mouth and licked her fingers, beckoning Vincent to her with her left hand. Easing his way toward her,

Vincent could feel the pull of muscle tightening between his legs, his pulse throbbing in his manhood.

Camille kissed him with the whole of her body, the front of her thighs meeting his, the flat of her stomach pressing against his, her breasts leaning into his chest, her lips to his. He could taste the sweet sugar of peach nectar in her mouth, and as he reached to pull the line of cotton fabric from between them, tossing the towel to the floor, the sensation of her naked flesh against his made him quiver with excitement.

Easing the shirt off her shoulders and pulling her arms from its sleeves, Camille kneeled naked before him. Vincent marveled at her beauty, admiring the curves of her body with his hands. Camille caressed his shoulders, running her fingers down his arms and over his chest. Her palms paused to press against his nipples, the tissue standing firm beneath her touch. She brushed the back of her fingers against his abdomen, tracing a circle against the line of his bellybutton. She reveled in the sheer majesty of her dark hands against the rich brown of his skin.

Vincent cupped her left breast with his palm, leaning to suckle from her right. His tongue felt incredible against of the rise of dark brown nipple that floated in his mouth. When his hand trickled past her stomach, easing its way between her legs, his mouth remaining wrapped around her breast, Camille heard herself moan, the low murmur of her voice breaking the quiet of their breathing. Vincent smiled, leaning up to relish the excitement on her face. His fingertips danced against her, exciting every nerve ending throughout her body. Camille acknowledged his performance by opening herself wider, allowing him easy access into her secret place.

Their mouths touched, each hungry for the other. Locked in the embrace, Vincent eased her back against the bed, relaxing his weight against her. Reaching between them, Camille pulled the length of his manhood into her hand, stroking him as boldly as he continued to stroke her. They both moaned with pleasure, the sensation of each other's touch more than either could ever have imagined.

Unable to hold off any longer, Vincent reached for a condom and pulled himself above her. He entered her easily, their moment of connection intense. Camille clutched at the covers beneath her as a Vincent pushed and pulled her body against his. His breathing was deep and heavy, mirrored by her own gasps for air. Riding the waves of the ocean beneath them, Vincent shouted her name, the impact of his love spilling deep beneath the waters of her sea at the exact moment hers crested against the rise of his tide.

They lay spent, their bodies still one, as Vincent rested above her. He whispered light kisses on her face, her neck, down along her shoulders, then leaned up on his forearms to peer down at her.

"You are so beautiful," he whispered.

Smiling up at him, Camille reached out her arms to pull him back close, holding tightly onto him. She felt as if her whole body was humming with pleasure, pure joy resonating throughout her veins.

"How's your heart?" she asked, running her tongue lightly against his ear.

Vincent chuckled. "Still ticking."

"Just checking. You promised to do this again on day ninety-two, remember?"

Vincent kissed her, his lips dancing against hers. "As soon as you catch your breath I plan to do it again tonight and I may not stop until next week," he said.

Camille laughed. "Are you sure your heart can take it?"

Lifting her leg against his side toward his back, his hand running down the length of her thigh to her buttocks, Vincent tickled her flesh, sending a wave of electricity throughout her body. "Baby, I'm not that old yet," he said, rotating his hips slowly against her pelvis. "The question is, can you keep up?"

Camille tossed her head back, inhaling him deeply as he moved against her. "Ohhh, Vincent," she moaned, before he pressed his mouth over hers, breathing in the essence of her.

"I love you, Vincent DeCosta," she whispered, wrapping her arms tightly around him.

"For all time," Vincent whispered back.

CHAPTER 24

The sun had just lifted itself into the sky when the sound of a boat engine pulled Camille from her slumber. The sharp noise startled her and for a brief moment she lay disoriented, unsure of her surroundings. As she lifted her body upward, extending her legs, her thigh muscles burned ever so slightly, a pleasant reminder of the previous evening.

Around the room, the candles had been extinguished, the faint hint of morning light peeking through the side windows, starting to brighten the room. The bed beside her was empty, the warmth of Vincent's body gone, and against the pillow lay two dozen yellow roses and a short note promising his swift return. Camille pulled the flowers to her nostrils, breathing in their aromatic scent, then pulled herself up and out of the bed and headed to the shower.

Minutes later, Vincent was calling out to her. "We need to hurry, or we're going to miss your father."

"Good morning," Camille said, pressing her damp body against him.

"Good morning."

"Where did you disappear to?"

"Stopped up to order a picnic breakfast from the club's dining room. It should be ready by the time you're dressed. Figure will probably have to grab a quick bite at the airport with your father depending on how the conversation goes."

Camille nodded. "You think of everything, don't you?"

Vincent smiled. "I try."

Minutes later, with a freshly filled basket of fruit and pastries resting on the rear seat of the car, Vincent and Camille made their way toward Louis. At the entrance to the St. George's Club, Camille pressed her hand against Vincent's arm.

"Vincent, I need to do this myself. Do you mind?"

He turned to stare at her, concern flashing across his face. "Are you sure?"

She nodded her head. "Let me talk to him. I can get a taxi back to the yacht. You can meet me there."

Tension burned against Vincent's face. "I don't think you should do this alone, Camille."

She shook her head. "I have to." Leaning to kiss him, she squeezed his upper arm. "I'll be back at the boat in an hour or so."

"I wait for you."

Camille watched as Vincent pulled off before entering the hotel lobby to call up to her father's room. A few minutes later the man made his way out toward her, a leather overnight bag his only luggage. Camille smiled up at him.

"How are you feeling this morning?" she asked.

"Very well, daughter. I slept nicely. Where's Zina?"

Camille shook her head. "She's with Antione. I wanted to speak with you alone." Looking around to the hotel grounds, Camille spotted an antique bench a few feet away from the hotel entrance, and led her father to sit down.

"Is everything okay, Camille?"

"Everything is wonderful, Daddy. I just wanted to speak with you before you left."

Louis raised his eyebrows. "This sounds serious."

"It is, Daddy. I've met someone and I wanted to tell you about him."

Louis looked at her with surprise. "Who is this young man? Is he here?"

Camille reached for her father's hand, clasping it between her palms. "Daddy, I can't remember when I've ever been this happy. I've become involved with an incredible man, whom I absolutely adore."

Camille could feel her father studying her reflection. The sun was just beginning to fill the sky, and a sliver of sunlight danced across her face.

"How long has this been going on?"

"We've been getting to know one another since my first trip here. And we've become very close." Camille paused, inhaling deeply.

Louis dropped his gaze, his eyes darting back and forth as his mind raced to take in what Camille was trying to tell him.

Looking back at her, he squeezed her hand. "Camille, you know more than anything in this world I want you and Zina happy. I might not like some of your decisions, but if they make you happy, then I can accept most of them. So, stop being afraid to tell me who it is. Is it Dante, Antione's brother?"

Camille shook her head. "No, Daddy. It's his father, Vincent."

Surprise drained the color from Louis's face as he gasps loudly. Vincent's name was not what he'd been prepared to hear and his expression reflected his shock.

Camille continued, "Daddy, I love the Vincent. He's become very important to me and I know as you get to know him better you'll understand why. I love him so much and I know he loves me. He has made me so happy."

Louis cleared his throat, trying to contain the tone of his voice. "Camille, I don't think…" He stopped, hunting for the right words but finding none that wouldn't betray his secret. Rising to his feet, he pulled his daughter up from her seat and hugged her tightly.

"I know it's a shock, Daddy, and I can imagine what you're thinking, but I promise you, Vincent and I have given this a lot of thought. We didn't just jump into a relationship blindly."

"I'm sure you didn't," he said, his words spilling out into the air behind her head. "But I really think we need to talk about this, Camille." He continued to hold onto her tightly, afraid of his reaction if he were to let her go.

"I know, Daddy. Vincent and I both want to talk to you, but I wanted to tell you myself first."

He nodded his head, the side of his face brushing against her hair. He inhaled deeply.

"Are you okay, Daddy? You're scaring me."

Louis laughed lightly, a veiled attempt to ease the rise of tension.

"I'm fine, daughter. Just shocked." He dropped his arms down to his sides, allowing Camille to draw back to stare up at him. He smiled a weak smile. Camille could feel her father tensing as he dropped her hand, clasping his palms together in front of him.

"I love him, Daddy."

He nodded his head. "I believe you, daughter. I'm sure you think you do."

"And he loves me."

"That's what I have my doubts about, baby." Louis reached out and kissed his daughter. "Don't you worry. Everything is going to be okay. You and I will discuss this when you get back to the States."

"Yes, sir, Daddy."

At the Bermuda International Airport, Vincent stood in the lower lobby, waiting patiently for Dr. Louis Martin. The first flight stateside was scheduled to depart at eight-thirty. Vincent looked down at the watch on his wrist, making a mental note that the time read seven forty-five. He passed from one end of the room to the other, anxious to have conversation that needed to be had.

At precisely eight o'clock, he watched as Louis and Camille pulled up in a hired taxi. As Louis exited the vehicle, Camille leaned out through the window to give her father a hug and kiss goodbye. Vincent continued to peer out through the glass as he watched Louis pay the taxi driver and send Camille on her way. As he entered the airport doors with his luggage, Louis spotted Vincent, stopped short as he collected his thoughts, and then headed in the man's direction.

The two men locked eyes. Vincent's face showed no expression, his eyes refusing to betray the emotion he felt toward Louis. Camille's father glared, rage seeping from his stare.

"Louis."

"Vincent. Camille tells me you two have been seeing each other."

"Yes, we have. Your daughter is a very special woman."

"I know that," Louis quipped, his response sharp.

Vincent nodded his head, gesturing toward a row of empty seats at the far end of the room. Louis followed behind him, dropping his bag to the floor beside him as they both took a seat.

"What did you say to Camille when she told you?" Vincent asked, glancing around to see who might be listening to them.

"I didn't say much of anything. I told her we needed to discuss it when she came home. I told her I didn't think she'd thought this whole mess through." Louis replied.

"Camille and I have given this a great deal of thought. I've asked her to marry me, and she's said yes."

Louis bristled, his anger rising. "You will never marry my daughter,' he spat at Vincent. "You don't love..." He stopped suddenly as he remembered that he was in a public place. He attempted to still his rage. "Is this your idea of some kind of sick revenge?" he asked.

Vincent shook his head from side to side. "I love Camille," he whispered under his breath, the two men inches from each other's face. "I love her."

"My daughter doesn't deserve to be caught up in our twisted joke. Fine, if you want to get even with me for what happened, but you need to leave Camille out of this."

"This isn't about you or what happened between us. I love Camille and this is about the two of us sharing our lives together."

"That's not going to happen. I will not allow that to happen."

"You don't have a choice."

"She's my daughter and I will have more say than you give me credit for."

"Your daughter is an adult and capable of making her own decisions, and she has decided that she loves me and wants to be with me."

The tension filled the room, pervading the air around the two men. They eyed each other defiantly, neither wanting to concede to the other. Louis bristled, his hands drawing up into tight fists at his side.

"Damn you," Louis spat, slamming his hand against his thigh, bruising the flesh along his leg. "You don't love Camille. You're only using her to get even with me."

Vincent rose to his feet, inhaling sharply. "I have spent most of my life hating you for what you did. And there was a time when it would have given me great pleasure to see you hurt. But over the last few months, wanting Camille happy, and loving her, has become more important to me. Your daughter loves you. She would like nothing more than to have you bless this relationship. And because that's important to her, it has to be important to me."

He took a deep breath before continuing. "I personally don't care whether you support us or not, but I want Camille happy. Now, I'm willing to work with you. I'm willing to let bygones be bygones for Camille's sake. But I will not give her up just to pacify you. I love her. Whether you believe me or not, I love her with all my heart."

"And what about our history? Do you plan to tell her?"

"If you think there's something Camille needs to know, then you need to be the one to tell her. She knows my past. I've shared all I feel I need to share."

Louis studied him intently, taking in all the man had just said. He shut his eyes, trying to ease the rise of tension that stretched the length of his shoulders and down his back. Opening his eyes, he stared at Vincent, then responded. "You are damn near as old as I am. My daughter deserves a relationship with a man who is closer to her own age and wants the same things she does."

"What makes you think I don't want what Camille wants?"

"You can't tell me you have the same interests my daughter has. What about children? Yours are grown. Her sister is married to your son! Camille deserves a family of her own."

"Camille can have as many babies as she wants."

"You'll be having your own grandchildren," Louis said sarcastically.

"No, we'll be having your grandchildren," Vincent replied.

The silence festered between them, both still eyeing each other with disdain. Vincent finally shook his head, heaving a heavy sigh. His voice was low, the easy quiet of a self-assured man.

"I don't want to fight with you. Your daughter love you and you love her. I don't want to come between that. But you need to understand that she means the world to me. She makes me happy and I want to make her happy. So, you do whatever you think you need to do. But don't get in our way. We've applied for a marriage license and expect it to be passed within the next two weeks. We intend to be married here on the island. She wants you to be a part of that. You decide."

As Vincent walked away, Louis sat back against the seat, deflated. Under his breath, he muttered to himself. "Hell will freeze first, DeCosta. Hell will freeze first."

CHAPTER 25

When Vincent leaned down to kiss her, Camille lay dozing on the yacht's deck. The discussion with her father had unnerved her, and it had showed , a shiver of emotion shaking her in her seat as she'd made her way back to the yacht. A second shower and a few yoga stretches had eased the tightness in her muscles and she felt more relaxed. The roses, arranged in a crystal vase, sat on a table beside her, the warm sea breeze sweeping their aroma through the air. A light snack of fresh fruit and apple juice had filled her stomach and she couldn't help imagining what it would be like to be this happy every day for the rest of her life.

"Hey there, sunshine!"

"Mmmm. Hello. Where have you been?"

"I was at the airport. I wanted to see your father before his flight left."

Camille rose up on her elbows, pushing the sunshades on her face up above her head. "Was he okay?"

Vincent shrugged, dropping down on the deck chair to sit beside her. "He was dealing with some issues."

"You shouldn't have gone without me."

"Yes, I should have. He and I needed to talk man to man. It was better this way. You and he will have an opportunity to talk more when you get back."

"He was angry, wasn't he? He didn't say much when I told him, but I knew he wasn't going to take it well." She shook her head. "I could tell he wasn't happy."

"No, he wasn't happy, but he took it better than I thought he would. I was half-expecting that he and I would have to go a few rounds before it was over."

Camille laughed. "You still might. We're not finished, remember?"

Vincent reached out to press his hand against her leg, squeezing the flesh gently. "I don't know that he's going to give us his support the way you would like," he said, his tone serious.

Camille hung her head, sighing deeply. When she looked up, there were tears in her eyes, one teardrop escaping pat her thick lashes to fall against her cheek. Vincent reached out to embrace her, pulling her tight against his chest.

"Don't get upset. He'll come around. He's just worried about you. He's concerned that by marrying me you'll be shortchanging yourself."

"Why would he think that?"

Vincent shrugged again. "He raised the issue of children. I have two and they are both adults. Most men my age are thinking about retirement, not diapers.

Camille leaned forward, pulling her knees to her chest, wrapping her arms around the front of her legs. "What did you tell him?"

"What I've told you. I want you happy and that means giving you anything and everything that you want. If you want babies, we'll have a hundred babies."

She smiled, reaching out to press her palm against the side of his head. "I have never felt so completely loved in all my life. You always say the right things, at the right time, and you make me feel so special."

I love you. It's what I'm supposed to do."

"I love you too, and I would love to have your child, Vincent, but it has to be right for both of us. Not just to make me happy, but it has to make you happy also."

Vincent's gaze was soothing, stroking warmth through her. He pressed his lips to the back of her hand, kissing her fingers. "I would be honored if you would be the mother of my child. I want us to have babies and be able to watch them grow as you grow old and I grow older," he said with a smile. "I want that with you."

Dropping her feet to the deck floor, Camille leaned to press her lips to Vincent's. She kissed him easily, the surface of her mouth comfortable against his. Rising, she extended her hand and pulled him to his feet, leading him back below deck.

"Where we going?" Vincent asked trailing behind her.

Camille smiled. "To celebrate day ninety-two."

Vincent and Camille lounged naked in the salon, enjoying the air-conditioned breeze that negated the rise of heat that burned outside. The morning had passed quickly, the duo giving no thought to how to spend the day other than side-by-side, loving each other.

Reaching for his cell phone on the counter, Vincent dialed to retrieve any voice messages that may have been left for them. Grabbing for a pen and a piece of paper, he jotted down messages and numbers, then pressed the off button, disconnecting the line.

"Anything important?" Camille asked, scratching at a mosquito bite on her leg.

"Lydia has left three messages, and Antione called. He says you and Zina have friends here from the States who want to meet for dinner. The Howards?"

Camille nodded her head and smiled. "Jon and Elise. Did he say whether or not they purchased anything?"

Vincent chuckled. "No, he didn't. Do you want to have dinner with them?"

"I actually would. Jon is a very good friend. He and Zina dated briefly, but we've all remained close. I want you to meet them. I think you'll like Jon, and Elise is very sweet."

Vincent raised his eyebrows. "He's one of Zina's ex-boyfriends?"

"I don't think they dated long enough for him to have been classified as a boyfriend. Zina had far too much energy for Jon to handle. They were through long before they got started."

Vincent nodded his head. "But they remained friends?"

"Well, he and I are probably closer than he and Zina. Jon and I actually have more in common than those two ever did, but since he dated my sister I obviously couldn't date him."

"Is that some unwritten sister rule or something?"

"Or something. It's just not the thing to do. Dating a friend or sister's ex-anything kind of breaks the female code of ethics."

"Okay if you say so," Vincent said with a wry laugh. "So just how close are you and this Jon person?"

Camille turned her body around to stare at him, her expression curious. "Are you jealous, Mr. DeCosta?"

Vincent shrugged his shoulders, purposely avoiding her eyes.

"I think you're jealous."

"Should I be?"

Smiling, Zina leaned up to give him a deep kiss. "No. Jon and I are just very good friends. He's great for conversation. We like to argue. Sometimes, we might flirt, and we spend a lot of time teasing each other. But he loves his wife and I consider her a friend. I love you and you are my best friend. You will never have any reason to doubt that. Never."

"Promise?" Vincent asked, wrapping his arms tightly around her.

"You have my word," she said, crossing her fingers over her chest.

"Well, dinner sounds like a good idea to me. I'll call the house and let them know we'll meet them. I guess I should call Lydia back too."

"She's probably not happy that we left when we did."

"I doubt that's the only thing she's unhappy about."

Camille raised her eyebrows, looking at him curiously. "Did I miss something?"

"No. Just that Lydia wishes she was here right now instead of you."

"So, I did detect a bit of jealousy there. I thought I was imagining it."

"You weren't. Lydia and I dated about six years ago. It just didn't work out."

"Why?"

Vincent stopped to choose his words carefully, stretching the length of his body against Camille's. "I've dated my fair share of women over the years. And the relationships have never been but so serious. The one thing I always knew was that any woman who captured my heart totally would encompass all the qualities my mother had."

Camille pushed herself onto her elbows, resting her chin in the palm of her hands. Vincent continued, "I knew she'd be intelligent, vibrant, talented, and have a remarkably huge heart. And I knew that she would be an incredibly beautiful *black* woman."

Camille twisted her body against his, resting her hand against his abdomen as she cradled her head in the crevice of his arm. "You keep talking like that, Mr. DeCosta, and you might have a hard time getting rid of me."

Vincent laughed. "Then we don't have anything to worry about, because I don't intend to let you go any time soon."

Vincent dialed his home, pulling the phone to his ear as it began to ring "I'll tell Antione to meet us here, and then we can drive over to meet your friends."

Camille nodded her head against his chest. "Tell Zina I said to bring me a dress or I won't have anything to wear except a T-shirt."

CHAPTER 26

Jon and Elise Howard were cuddled together in the lobby of the Waterloo Inn when Camille, Vincent, Zina, and Antione entered. Vincent had reserved a table for six on the Poinciana Terrace. Dining right on the water's edge, the group sat out under the stars, enjoying a candlelit meal and each other's company.

Camille had laughed when Vincent donned traditional Bermuda dinner attire: navy blue blazer, white shirt, necktie, Bermuda shorts, and knee-length stockings. She and Zina both giggled until they cried as they compared Antione's knobby knees to those of his father. The man had not been as amused.

"I don't know if I could get used to the look either," Elise chuckled "John's legs are just too, too skinny to be wearing knee socks."

Jon rolled his eyes. "I could sport the fashion no problem. Too skinny, my behind!" he exclaimed, giving his wife a light squeeze.

"That's a bit skinny too," Camille chimed, laughing at her friend.

Vincent shook his head. "So are you two enjoying your stay here in Bermuda?"

"We're having a wonderful time," Elise said hugging John's arm. "The island is so romantic," she gushed.

"What did you think of the show?" Camille asked.

"Zina, who was probably one of your best exhibitions," Jon responded. "Your talent continues to amaze me. And, Vincent, I was very impressed. Although I was familiar with your work, to see it up close and personal was truly an honor."

"Thank you," Vincent said, "and thank you for your purchase. It's the collectors who keep us artists working, and we truly value your support."

Zina reached out to squeeze John's hand. "Yes, thank you, Jon. You and Elise have been so good to me," she said, leaning to give Elise a friendly hug.

"What did you buy?" Camille asked, leaning on her hand, her elbow on the table as she studied the couple.

"We purchased Zina's painting *The Moaning After* and two of Vincent's sculptures, *Ecstasy* and *Ecstasy in Motion,,*" Elise said.

"Very nice. Those will look wonderful in your home, Elise. I'm so happy for you," Camille said.

Antione leaned to take a bite of Zina's dessert, the crème brûlée melting against his tongue.

"So, are you two enjoying married life?" Jon asked, as he and Elise shared a warm look at the couple.

Antione nodded. "It's the best thing that could've happened for us."

"Well, Zina you are absolutely glowing," Elise remarked. "If you two are half as happy as Jon and I are, then I know you'll be blessed."

Zina smiled. Did Camille tell you her news?"

"No," Jon said, smirking. "What news might that be, Camille?"

Camille cut her eyes at him, as Vincent reached for her hand, clasping his atop hers against the table.

"Camille and I are going to be married. Camille has agreed to be my wife," Vincent said beaming.

"How exciting!" Elise chimed. "Congratulations!"

"Yes, congratulations," Jon added, extending his hand to shake Vincent's. Reaching over the table, he kissed Camille lightly on the cheek. "Finally found you a man. I know Elise will sleep better at night. She had a list of men a mile-long she wanted to introduce you to."

Everyone at the table laughed.

"That is so untrue, Camille. Jon, you play far too much," the woman said, scolding her husband. "There was only one doctor I thought she'd be perfect with."

Vincent smiled, swaying his head from side to side. "Well, the good doctor is just out of luck," he said, laughing, "because this lady's all mine."

CHAPTER 27

Pacing the floor of his office, Louis recapped his trip Lawrence, emphasizing Vincent's final remarks about him not getting in their way. The man fumed, anger and spite stalling his spirit. Lawrence tried to calm him, to ease his mind as best he could.

"Louis, you need to relax. Getting angry isn't going to help the situation, and what you don't want to do is alienate Camille. Not now."

Louis tossed his hands up in disgust. "As soon as I can talk some sense into Camille, there won't be any situation. DeCosta has her head spinning right now, but I will set her straight. Camille will do what's right."

"When is she coming home?"

"They returned home last night. I spoke to Zina briefly and she said DeCosta came back with them."

Lawrence paused, eyeing his friend cautiously. "Look, this might not be my place, but you and I have been friends far too long for me not to say something."

"To say what?"

"Camille has always done whatever you wanted her to do. But there have been far too many times when, trying to please you, she was unhappy. Now, I didn't think it was fair then, and I don't think it's fair now.

You need to let Camille figure this out on her own, without your interference. She needs to make this decision on her own.

"Lawrence, I know my daughter better than anyone, and I know what will make her happy. That man doesn't love her. He's only doing this to hurt me. I can't let that pass. DeCosta won't get away with this. Camille is my child. Mine."

Lawrence rose from his seat, heading for the door. "Louis, you're wrong this time. Camille is an adult. When Zina married Antione, you were hurt. You said then that you wanted at least one opportunity to walk one of your daughter's down the aisle. Don't miss that opportunity. You fight Camille on this and we're going to have one more wedding that you won't be invited to. And I don't think either of us wants to see that happen."

As his friend exited the room, closing the door behind him, Louis dropped down into a seat, then reached for the telephone, dialing as he pulled the receiver to his ear.

As Camille dropped the telephone back onto the hook, she stretched the length of her body up and out, rolling to curve herself around Vincent. Dropping a light kiss against his broad shoulder, she sighed, a deep mournful expulsion of breath that fell heavy into the air.

"Are you okay?" Vincent asked, feeling the rise of anxiety that rested within her.

"That was my father. He's on his way over to talk."

Vincent nodded his head, rolling to hug her close against him. "I'll be right here if you need me. We'll get through this together."

Camille pressed her lips to his. "I know. But for now, I think he and I should have this talk by ourselves. You don't mind, do you?"

"No. I understand. I have some things I need to do anyway," Vincent tossed his legs over the side of the bed, rising to his feet.

Camille smiled as he scratched at the flesh against his left butt cheek. "You've got a nice rear view, Mr. DeCosta."

Peering over his shoulder, Vincent glanced down to his backside. "I do, don't I?" he said winking at her.

Extending his hand, Vincent pulled her up and out of the bed. "Let's grab a quick shower. How much time do we have?" he asked, kissing her as his fingers crept beneath the elastic of her bikini bottoms.

"We have exactly an hour and a half."

"Sounds like more than enough time to me."

"For that shower?"

"And for what I plan to do to you in that shower."

Camille giggled, following behind him as he turned on the warm water and stepped beneath the gentle spray of moisture. The rising heat trickled over them as Camille stood with her body pressed against Vincent's back, her hand washing soap suds over his torso. She cleansed the length of his frame, brushing her tongue against his nipples and abdomen, pausing to nibble against the taut muscles of his buttocks, stopping to linger along the length of his sex. Her attention to his direct member caused him to visibly shake with anticipation.

Regaining his composure, Vincent turned about to reciprocate the attention. His hands caressed her shoulders first, lathering soap around her neck and down the length of her arms. He paused to linger against her breasts, the palms of his hands dancing in small circles around the fleshy tissue. Vincent leaned in for a kiss, sliding his tongue into her mouth, hungry for more of her. His mouth drew a slow path down the length of her body as he fell to his knees, the spray of water bouncing against his shoulders, his tongue dipping in and out of her belly button.

Camille moaned, the sensation of his touch raining over her control. Vincent dropped lower as Camille pressed her palm against the top of his head, guiding him further down her body. As he clutched her backside, his fingers pressing into her cheeks, she felt his tongue tapping against her femininity, as though he were knocking, seeking permission to enter. Her fingers tangled in his hair as she pulled and pressed his face into her, his mouth dancing against her open orifice. Almost without warning, an orgasm ripped through her as he lapped hungrily at her juices, pushing his mouth greedily against her secret treasure. The vibration was intense and unexpected, shaking her foundation as she fell back against the shower wall, her legs locked around Vincent's head, and the strength of his arms beneath her rear end her only support.

When the doorbell rang, Vincent had just poured himself a cup of black coffee—two sugars and no cream. As Camille continued to primp in front of the dressing table mirror, he called out to her as he made his way to the door. "I've got it, Camille."

Louis stood on the other side, surprised when Vincent opened the door and welcomed him.

"Louis, good morning."

"What are you doing here?"

Vincent chuckled, shaking his head. "Can I get you some coffee?" he asked, gesturing with the cup of morning broth he held in his hand.

"Where's Camille?"

"She's still dressing. She'll be right out."

Vincent headed back to the kitchen, Louis on his heels.

"So what now? You've moved in?"

"I'm just here for the week. Camille and I have a lot to get ready for."

"You don't have a damn thing to get ready for. There isn't going to be any wedding."

Vincent dropped his cup against the counter, turning to face Louis. "Obviously, you think you know best, and you have something to say, so go right ahead. Get it off your chest. Say what you need to."

"I'm no fool. I know the only reason you're chasing my daughter is to get even with me. As soon as Camille sees what kind of man you are, she will come to her senses."

"And just what do you plan to tell her?"

"The truth. All of it. Every sordid detail."

"And you think that's the best thing for your daughter?"

"It's better than having her become tied to a man who cares more about getting revenge than about her well-being."

"You still don't get it, do you? This doesn't have anything to do with you. Not a thing. I love Camille. I want to be with her. This is about what she and I share and how we want our future with one another."

"Don't lie, you son of a—"

"Careful," Vincent admonished him, holding up his hand toward the other man. "You don't want to say something you're going to regret."

Louis glared, taking a quick look over his shoulder at his daughter's closed bedroom door. "Why don't you admit the truth? You don't love Camille. You hate me. You hate me so much you'd do anything to get even with me. Isn't that what this is all about? Isn't making me pay more important to you than anything else is? Isn't that the truth?"

"You arrogant fool! What do you know about truth? Vincent asked, the volume of his voice rising in ire. "When have you ever thought about the truth?"

The angry swell of their voices drew Camille out of her bedroom and down the hall toward the kitchen. Her father and Vincent were both enraged and she could hear the heated exchange as she got closer to where they stood.

Vincent 's anger flooded the air. "Making you pay for what you did would give me great pleasure. I don't have any love lost for you. I have thought about making you pay every day of my life, but that doesn't mean—"

"Make him pay for what?" Camille asked, interrupting. "What are you two arguing about?"

Louis's eyes met his daughter's, his own ire flooding his face and seeping out of his eyes. Vincent spun toward the sink, fighting to gain control over the rage that had managed to consume him.

"Vincent, I want an answer. One of you tell me what's going on," she insisted.

Louise clasped his hands against her shoulders, facing her inquisitive stare. "I'm so sorry, Camille. I didn't want you to be hurt but you need to know the truth."

Vincent turned back around toward them, tears spilling down his face. "Camille, baby, I love you, and—"

"No, he doesn't, Louis interrupted, shouting even louder at Vincent. "He only wants you to think he does. He's only using you to get back at me."

"Back at you for what?" Camille asked, looking from her father to Vincent, searching for an answer.

"Something bad happened a number of years ago, before I married your mother. I was the cause, and Vincent spent some time in jail because of it. He—"

"You're the man?" Camille watched her father intently, shock registered across her face. She searched the lines of his expression, then turned to Vincent and back to Louis again. "You're Joe Louis?"

Her father hung his head, unable to meet her gaze. "I dropped the Joe when I left the state. I didn't—"

Camille stepped back out of her father's grasp. She turned to Vincent. "How long have you known?"

"Since Antione and Zina's reception. We recognized each other at the party."

"That's what you couldn't tell me?"

"I didn't want—"

"What?" Camille interrupted. "You didn't want me to think that maybe you were with me to get back at the man you hated so much? Didn't you just say you wanted to make him pay for what he did? Isn't that what I heard?"

"You didn't give me a chance to finish. I don't hate your father. I hate what he did, and I hate that--"

"I don't believe this. How could this be happening? How could you do this to me?"

Vincent reached out for her, wanting to draw her close, but Camille brushed him aside, pushing his hands from around her. "Don't touch me," she whispered between clenched teeth. "Please, don't touch me."

Making her way into the living room, Camille leaned back against the oversized sofa, wrapping her arms about her torso. Visibly stunned, she fought to make sense of all they'd been saying. Her father followed behind her.

"Daughter, we'll get through this. Everything is going to be okay."

"No," Camille whispered, her voice barely audible. "No. Nothing is okay. It's not going to be fine. Nothing is going to be fine," she finally shouted, the onslaught of tears falling against her chest.

"Camille—" Vincent started.

"No. Get out. Both of you. I want the two of you out of my house. Now."

"Baby, we've got to talk about this. I love you," Vincent implored, his tone beseeching.

Camille stared at Vincent, emotions washing over her, the brunt of their deceit rolling the dice before her. She shook her head vehemently, holding the palm of her hand out toward him. "No. Please. Just go."

"Daughter, I need you to understand—"

"I don't understand, Daddy. I don't know if I'll ever understand. But right now you just need to leave."

Reaching for her keys and purse, Camille headed for the door. "I don't want to find either one of you here when I get back. If you're still here, I will call the police to remove you."

Broken, Vincent and Louise stood side by side as Camille slammed the front door, then spun her tires out of the driveway and as far away from the two of them as she could get. The two men stood like stone, heads bowed, chins resting against chests, trying to make sense of all that had happened.

With mere minutes feeling like hours, Vincent struggled to make his way to the door. With his hand on the doorknob, he turned to face Louis, tears spilling down his face. "It didn't have to be this way," he whispered. Turning to race down the drive, hoping to catch up to Camille, he shouted back over his shoulder. "It didn't have to be this way."

CHAPTER 28

Camille had allowed the morning hours to pass her by, not knowing how long she'd been driving before she found herself at the gallery door. Darrow greeted her warmly as she made her way inside, her head still spinning from the morning' s drama.

"Hey, boss!" he greeted, his expression changing as he studied Camille's face. "What happened? What's the matter?"

Camille shook her head. "Have you heard from Zina today?"

"She called looking for you. She wants you to call her the minute you get in. What's wrong?"

Camille continued to ignore his questions, heading to the rear of the building and the security of her office. "Anyone else call?"

"Your father, that Lydia woman from Bermuda, and Vincent DeCosta. His package arrived also. I guess he was calling to check on it."

"What package?"

"Big box. It's on the table in the studio."

Leading the way, Darrow went into the studio, Camille following closely behind him. The large box sat imposingly in the center of the table, the brown carton decorated with stickers identifying it as fragile, to be handled with care. Camille ran her hand along one corner, then shook her head.

"Return it. Call UPS and have them come pick it up."

"What's in it?"

"I don't know and I don't care. I just want it out of here."

"Must be man problems," Darrow said, snapping his fingers knowingly. "How many times have you been told you don't return gifts? Consider them investment for time served."

Camille rolled her eyes.

"At least open it and see what it is first."

"I told you I really don't care."

"Well, let me open it. I'll repack it nicely and then you can send it back."

"It is killing you to know what's in this box, isn't it?"

"You know it is, so why are you torturing me?"

Camille flipped her hands up to her shoulders and out to her sides. "Just shoot me. I know I'm going to regret this."

Darrow grinned as he pulled a box cutter from one of the storage drawers and proceeded to cut into the cardboard container. "So, why is this man sending you stuff?"

Taking a seat on one of the wooden stools, Camille dropped her head into her hands, brushing her fingers against her face, then pulling them through the thick of her hair. "We got engaged while I was in Bermuda."

Darrow stopped what he was doing to stare at her, his jaw dropping to the floor. "Engaged? How did this happen?"

"We've been seeing each other for the last few months. I thought we were in love."

"What do you mean, thought? What happened?"

Sighing deeply, Camille shook her head, trying to shake the rise of misery from her spirit. She didn't want to cry and she particularly didn't want to cry right then with Darrell watching. Biting her lip, she took a deep breath. "Let's just say it was a short engagement."

Darrow looked at her, peering intently over the top of his eyeglasses. "Girlfriend, you are too much for me." He continued to pull at the box until he could release the top and fold back the sides. Layers of bubble wrap spilled out onto the counter as he pulled at the contents inside.

"Oh, my word!" Darrow gushed, reaching deep into the box to pull at the object inside. "Girlfriend, help me here."

Camille extended her hand, reaching to pull at the bottom of the box as Darrow lifted the contents from within.

As Darrow laid the sculpture onto the table, she stared in awe. The woman in bronze had her face, the lines of her body all Camille's, the man at her side Vincent. Camille reached out to touch the metal of the woman's hand along the top of his head, running a manicured finger down the length of his torso, brushing at his lips pressed against her leg. The artwork was beautiful, her love for Vincent captured for posterity. Darrow handed her an envelope, the legal-sized mailer labeled with her name in Vincent's scribbled handwriting.

As she read the words imprinted in ink, Camille pulled her hand to her mouth, trying to stifle the sobs that consumed her. The emotions were overwhelming as she fought the rise of hurt within her. Darrow let her cry, easing his way out of the room, and minutes later her sister wrapped her in a tight hug and told her everything was going to be just fine.

Darrow had locked the gallery doors behind him, leaving Camille and Zina inside. The two women had sat in the studio for most of the afternoon, neither speaking, each waiting for the other to initiate the conversation. Camille had cried until she felt all cried out, her eyes bruised red, her nose stuffed as if she had a cold. Zina had cried with her, both shedding tears for themselves and each other. Quiet enveloped them, and from the small window they could see that the sun had disappeared behind a spread of dark clouds and rain had begun to fall.

"I'm sorry you had to find out about Daddy like that, Camille. I should have told you years ago but I always figured it was better that you didn't know."

"You knew? How?"

"Before Mommy died I overheard her and Daddy arguing about it. It didn't take a whole lot of detective work to know that he'd done something really terrible. He filled me and Antione in on the details right after you ran out this morning."

"Why didn't you tell me, Zina? Why?"

"Because you have always idolized our father. He walked on water as far as you were concerned, and I remember after Mommy died how much you needed to make him the center of your universe. I didn't have any right to take that from you."

"Is that why you and he have always butted heads?"

"I just knew he wasn't perfect and I wasn't going to pretend he was."

"Did you know about Vincent and his connection?"

"No. That came as a surprise. Like I said, I didn't know all the specifics, just that Daddy had heard someone and caused a man to die. I also knew that for Mommy and him to want to keep it a secret meant that it had to be extremely bad."

Camille hung her head, fighting to maintain her composure. "I can't believe Vincent used me like that."

"Stop being ridiculous, Camille. Vincent loves you."

"I heard him, Zina. I heard him telling Daddy that all he wanted to do was make Daddy pay for what he did."

"And he had every right to feel that way. But he also said that he loved you and that was reason enough for him to let go of his anger. But you're just like Daddy. You only heard what you thought you needed to hear. You heard exactly what Daddy wanted you to hear."

"That's not fair, Zina."

"Maybe not, but it's true. Think about it, Camille. Vincent told you about his incarceration at the beginning of your relationship. He didn't have to. But he did. He told you the truth. Then he meets Daddy and the past suddenly catches up with the two of them. But Vincent was sharing how he felt about you long before he and Daddy met. He was feeling when you first went to Bermuda, before he knew who your father was, and you know it. That had nothing to do with Daddy."

Camille shook her head as her sister continued to talk.

"If Vincent had really wanted to hurt Daddy, he could have just turned him over to the police. Daddy could be behind bars with his reputation ruined and his relationship with us completely destroyed. But Vincent didn't do that. He was willing to forgive the past because he wanted to be with you. All he wanted was for Daddy to support you and be happy for you so that you could be happy with him."

"Daddy should be in jail. He should pay for what he did. He was responsible for the deaths of two men."

"No. He wasn't."

"What do you mean?"

"Uncle Lawrence helped work on Vincent's case years ago. When Vincent recognized Daddy, uncle Lawrence apparently pulled the evidence file thinking that he would probably have to defend Daddy in court. He wanted to be prepared."

Zina rose from where she sat, strolling to the window to peer outside. "Daddy's lucky that forensic science has come a long way since the 1960s. They tested the bullets pulled from the body of the police officer, and those from Vincent's brother, and both came from the same gun. There was only one bullet fired from the gun Daddy had and Uncle Lawrence said they pulled it out of the car's tire. The others were fired from the other officer's gun. It turns out that this other cop used the predicament to kill his partner. Seems he thought the man was sleeping with his wife, and when Daddy pulled the gun he thought he could use the situation to his advantage and it worked. Until now. Uncle Lawrence says they'll be closing the case. Daddy may still face some charges for running and being a fugitive, but we won't know for a while. Uncle Lawrence is going to try to work out a deal with the district attorney."

Camille shook her head in disbelief. "How did you find all of this out?"

"After you took off, Daddy came to my house. He was so upset and I just couldn't handle it so I called Aunt Kitty. She and Uncle Lawrence came over and he filled me in."

"Why did this have to happen, Zina? Why?"

"I think some good needed to come out of this, for both of us. You needed to see that Daddy wasn't perfect and to learn that you could have an opinion that didn't agree with his. I needed to learn that even though he wasn't perfect he was still a decent man. And he is. Daddy tried to use what happened to do some real good for the people it affected."

Camille thought about what her sister said, nodding her head slowly. "What about Vincent? What am I going to do?"

"Do you love him, Camille? Do you really love him?"

Camille nodded her head yes, tears threatening to spill from her eyes.

"Do you honestly think he wanted to marry you just to get even with Daddy?"

Camille shrugged, shaking her head from side to side. "I don't want to, Zina. I really don't want to."

Zina looked down at the watch upon her wrist. "Vincent caught the twelve-o'clock flight back to Bermuda. He had a connection through Atlanta so I imagine he's landing right about now. You need to take a few days to clear your head and decide if you really want to be with him. If you do, then when they issue that marriage certificate you need to be on that island by his side."

"What about Daddy?"

Zina laughed, coming to shake Camille by the shoulders. "What about him? If you want to marry Vincent and be with him, I promise you Daddy will be right there to support you. He might not like it. He might not agree with it, but he'll still be right there."

Camille hugged her sister tightly. "I love you, Zina. You're the best big sister a girl could have."

"Don't you forget it." Zina chuckled. "I have to go. My husband has been sitting out front waiting for me since I got here."

Camille's eyes widened. "Zina, no!" She nodded, laughing. "I left him working on some papers in my office, but I'm sure he's stretched out on the sofa sound asleep by now."

CHAPTER 29

He'd been wrong and he knew it. He knew it the moment he'd witnessed the devastation on his daughter's face. He had felt the brunt of her anguish and had been bruised and battered by its impact. Adding insult to injury, when Vincent had raced out of the house, trying to catch up with her, he had seen something in the man's eyes that had brought tears to his own. It had never been about him, and now his little girl was having to deal with the ramifications of his selfishness.

Zina had not spared him when pointing out the error of his way. Her words had been harsh, bitterly brutal, and ever so reminiscent of her mother's straightforwardness. He'd felt like the child being scolded by the parent instead of it being the other way around. And then she'd hugged him and told him how much she and her sister loved him and that no matter what, their family would survive. All of them.

Lawrence had bestowed the good news on him, and his best friend's diligence and support had surpassed his wildest dreams. The dishonor and guilt he'd lived with had been washed clean and for the first time since he was seventeen years old, he'd felt that he could hold up his head with pride. Although he knew that his one moment of carelessness, where his actions had been most reckless, had precipitated the rise of events that he'd been running from, he was thankful that it had not been he who'd taken that man's life. It had not been he who'd pulled the trigger that killed his dear friend Maurice. Despite all he still needed to do, he was thankful for his blessings.

But he'd been wrong and now he had to figure out how to make things right with Camille. He needed to do whatever he could to make things right for her. Picking up the telephone to dial the airlines, he knew exactly what had to be done.

Vincent hadn't left the studio since his arrival back on the island. It had been six days and Nana had started to worry, not knowing what she could say that might ease the pain she knew he was feeling. Antione had called to tell her about the turn of events, and when she'd tried to speak with Vincent, had attempted to learn what it was he was feeling, he'd retreated into the studio, professing that there was nothing that needed to be discussed.

Doing what he knew he did best, Vincent spilled his heart into his work. Canvases were spread from one end of the room to the other, the smell of drying paint punctuating the air. He and Camille had spoken briefly since his return. The hurt and anger that he'd seen the last time they were together had begun to dissipate and he understood that she need time to resolve the uncertainty that plagued her. He'd regretted the words that had spilled out of his mouth that morning. He wished he could take back that single moment when Louis had pushed him to the brink of fury. But he couldn't and now he could only sit back and pray that Camille could find understanding, knowing that she consumed his heart and filled the very essence of his soul.

The knock on the studio door was unexpected and when he looked up to find Louise Martin standing sheepishly in the doorway, he was definitely surprised.

"May I come in?" Louis asked as he stepped inside.

Vincent nodded, wiping his hands against an old rag on the table. "What are you doing here?"

Closing the door behind him, Louis made his way toward the center of the room. As his gaze swept from one wet canvas to the other, he could feel his composure starting to fail him. At a loss for words, he could only shake his head as he took a seat opposite Vincent, his eyes still sweeping around the perimeter of the room. The two men sat in silence, music from the stereo the only noise.

Louis finally found his voice, his gaze coming to rest on Vincent's face. "I didn't know you painted."

The man shrugged his shoulders, tilting his head slightly. "Most people don't know that I started out as a portrait artist. Sculpture came later."

"These are incredible. You've captured her beautifully."

Vincent smiled slightly, an easy bend to his mouth, the muscles in his face barely moving. "Do you have a favorite?"

Louis looked around at the six paintings , each one a different image of his youngest daughter. His eyes rested on one composition that had her smiling, joy brimming at the edges of her eyes. "That one. It reminds me of when she was a little girl. You've captured her innocence and her vulnerability."

They both stared, the imagery reminding them of a moment with Camille that was unique to each of them.

"And your least favorite?"

Louis smiled, then laughed. "It's probably the one in red there," he said, pointing to a three-quarter view of his daughter's face that reflected an intensely sensual come-hither look. "That's a look that says her father is no longer the apple of her eye. Another man has captured her attention there."

Vincent laughed with him, nodding his head.

"I owe you an apology, Vincent," Louis finally said. "I know how much you love my daughter and I guess I was afraid that you were going to take her from me. I was scared you were going to replace me in her heart."

"You're her father. No man could ever replace you. Camille's heart is big enough for the both of us."

"I know. I understand that now."

"Why are you here?"

"My daughter deserves to marry a man who's going to treat her well and loves her like she is the one and only thing in his world. She loves you and she believes that you are that man. Her sister seems to agree. I'd forgotten that I needed to trust my daughters. I'd actually forgotten how well I'd raised them. I guess I just didn't want to let go. I've never been able to do anything with Zina, but Camille was different. Camille allowed me to take care of her. I was so busy trying to take care of her I forgot that I'd taught her how to take of herself."

He continued, "It's hard to admit, but it hurt me when I didn't get the chance to walk Zina down the aisle. I don't want to make that mistake with Camille.

I fully intend to give my daughter away on her wedding day and I fully intend to give her to you, because it would seem that's where she wants to be."

Vincent shook his head. "I don't know if Camille still wants to marry me. I hurt her. That might not be too easy for her to forgive."

"Well, it's something we're both going to have to work on. But I'm willing to work on it with you, if you'll let me. I made this mess and I'm hoping you'll give me the chance to make up for it."

Vincent studied him intently, then, rising from his seat, made his way to the other side of the table. Extending his arm, he offered Louis his hand. Shaking it, Louis grinned broadly.

"As long as you understand one thing, DeCosta. I won't have you calling me Dad."

Vincent laughed. "Not a problem. But I hope one day we'll be able to call each other friend."

CHAPTER 30

"I thought I made you give me that key back." Camille yawned as Zina pulled the covers from around her, then flung open the room's curtains to let in the morning light.

Her sister laughed. "Get up. We're going to be late."

Camille pulled on the blankets at her feet. "Leave me alone, Zina. I don't want to go anywhere."

Reaching for her hand, Zina pulled her to her feet. "I didn't ask. This time I'm telling you and you're going to listen. Grab a shower and get dressed. We're making time."

"Where are we going?"

"Not your concern. Just be ready to leave in thirty minutes. Where's your overnight bag?"

"Why?""

Zina dropped her hands to her hips, exasperation gracing her face. "You ask too many questions."

Camille rolled her eyes, then pointed to the top shelf in the closet.

"Thank you. Finally some cooperation. Thirty minutes, now move it," Zina ordered, pulling open a drawer for Camille's clothes.

Shaking her head, Camille dragged herself into the bathroom. Turning on the shower faucet, she tested the water with her hand, then moved to turn the hot water up a notch. As she brushed a spread of toothpaste across her teeth, vapors of mist clouded over the room, warming the chamber nicely. The rise of heat felt good and Camille welcomed the spray of water that fell down against her shoulders, settling between her toes.

Since the episode with Vincent and her father, she'd spent most of the time alone, occasionally welcoming Zina's company, sometimes with Antione, most times without. She'd answered only one of Vincent's calls and they'd talked briefly. Although she had yearned to reach out, to welcome him back to her, she'd fought the inclination, knowing that there were still some unresolved issues that she needed to face.

For as long as she could remember, she'd idolized her father. Dr. Louis Martin had been the next best thing to air as far as she'd been concerned. Now she had to face the reality that her father was only a man, and one who'd made mistakes. She had found it difficult to face him, afraid that anger would betray her, and so she'd not bothered to contact him and he had be, not wanting to push. There was a shadow that now lingered along the gold armor she'd wrapped him in and Camille was learning how to see him for who he truly was and not who she'd thought him to be.

She had doubted Vincent, and the truth of that fact confused her. She questioned how she could doubt the man she professed so dearly and still claim to love him. Zina had told her to stop overanalyzing the situation, because love didn't always make sense. Camille was working hard to do that, but was finding old habits difficult to break.

She smiled, the warmth of the water bringing back
memories of her and Vincent in the shower that last
morning they were together. Touching herself,
Camille remembered how his hands had stroked the
nervous energy from her muscles as he'd glided a
soap-filled sponge over her flesh. His kisses had been
sweet murmurs against her skin and they had lingered
like silk beneath the spray of water that washed over
them. She missed him and his hands and the round of
his sweet lips that tasted like nectar against her
mouth. Maybe, if she let it be, things could be as well
boot cut as Zina had said they would.

Zina's banging on the bathroom door interrupted
her flow of thoughts. "Hurry up in there. I told you
we're making time."

Minutes later, when Camille entered the living
room dressed in a tangerine-colored Ellie Tahari
beaded, crinkled chiffon top, sleek, boot-cut taupe
trousers, and low-heeled Ferragamo mules, Zina was
scanning the July issue of *Essence* magazine, with
Whitney Houston on the cover. She was flipping the
pages haphazardly as she read the captions of the
pictures, forgoing the articles altogether. Camille
peered over Zina's shoulders. "Turn to page 136," she
said.

As Zina flipped into she reached the photograph
that Camille wanted her to see, Camille reached for
her handbag, pulling the leather strap up against her
shoulder.

"Wow. What a beautiful couple," she said of the
man and woman posed intimately together.
Supposedly, the duo was promoting the khaki shorts
and print blouse the woman was wearing, but the

chemistry reflected off the glossy pages seemed to be selling much more than that.

"It's striking, isn't it? I love the composition."

The other woman nodded her head. "It's very hot. Gosh, they are a beautiful couple!"

"I need Vincent, Zina. I need my man."

Her sister smiled. "I'm glad you said that," she said, dropping the magazine down against the sofa.

"I don't know what it is you have planned down, but I want to see if I can get a flight to the island. I have to go see him."

Rising from her seat, Zina glanced down to her watch. "Our plane leaves in one hour. We need to hurry because you know how testy those airport people get about you checking in late."

Camille grinned, shaking her head. "I don't believe you. We're going to Bermuda?"

Zina nodded. "Yeah. My baby sister is getting married Sunday. Figured we needed to get there early to make sure everything is under control."

"Sunday?"

"That's the plan, unless you intend to give us a difficult time."

Camille paused, her eyes darting back and forth as she comprehended what her sister was saying. Resolve settled easily within her, dropping an easy calm against her shoulders. She nodded her head. "What were you going to do if I refused to go?"

"Hit you over the head and toss you into my luggage if I had to. But we can discuss it on the way to the airport. We are going to miss this plane if we don't hurry it up." Zina reached for the overnight bag as she headed for the door.

"What did you pack for me?"

"Very little. Vincent said all you needed was a couple of T-shirts."

Camille laughed. "I hope you told him I didn't own any."

"I did, and I brought you a couple of mine. Consider them a wedding present."

As they headed down Interstate 70 toward the Raleigh-Durham Airport, the two women laughed and chatted comfortably. Camille could feel her excitement mounting as she thought about being in Vincent's arms shortly after lunch. The prospect left her feeling warm and fuzzy all over.

"Camille, remember when I went on my first date?" Zina asked, guiding her car onto the ramp toward Highway 85.

Camille laughed, throwing her head back at the memory. "Remember how devastated I was when I found out I couldn't go with you!"

"You were just so sure that I wouldn't know what to do or how to behave. You and Daddy both just knew it was going to be a disaster."

"It was!"

Zina laughed with her sister. "That's beside the point. How was I to know the boy was an alcoholic in training? And he threw up on my shoes!"

"Those were my shoes!"

"They were, weren't they?" Zina chortled, tears raining down her cheeks.

Camille passed her sister a tissue from the blue-flowered Kleenex box in the center console. By the time Zina pulled the car into the long-term parking lot, they'd both calmed down, the roaring laughter nothing but an occasional spattering of giggles.

"We've come a long way, Camille," Zina said, patting her sister against the knee.

Nodding her head in agreement, Camille leaned to hug the older woman's shoulders, and then both women raced inside to the check-in counter.

CHAPTER 31

Every time she approached Art-House, Camille was awed. The home seemed to welcome her, almost sensing that if this was where Vincent was, then it was assuredly where she belonged. As the taxi pulled into the driveway, Camille was perched on the edge of the seat, bopping up and down like an excited three-year-old ready to get outside to run.

As the driver pulled their bags from the trunk, Antione and Dante came down the front steps, Antione digging into his pockets for cash to pay the driver. Zina kissed him, wrapping her arms tightly around him as he passed the money in his hands to his brother so one of them could settle the tab.

Dante greeted them both warmly. "Welcome home, ladies!"

"Where's your father?" Camille asked, reaching up to plant a kiss on Dante's cheek and then Antione's.

"He's not here."

Camille's face fell. "Where is he?"

"Calm down." Antione laughed. "He's okay. He doesn't fly back until tomorrow. He had to take care of some business in the States."

"You mean I flew here and he's back there?" She tossed up her hands in exasperation. "Zina!"

Her sister shook her head, rolling her eyes up toward the sky. "Would you relax? He will be here tomorrow. Get over yourself. Go say hello to Nana and stop whining!"

"I have to talk to Vincent!"

"Tomorrow!" the three of them yelled at her in unison.

Pouting, Camille headed into the house, dropping her bags in the hallway she searched out Nana.

"Nana!"

"Hello, darling. You made it back safe," the older woman exclaimed, brushing flour from her hands as she reached out to hug Camille.

"They said Vincent's not here and he won't be back until tomorrow?"

Her future mother-in-law laughed. "That's right, precious. But he left something for you in your bedroom."

"Is he okay? I know how upset he was. Do you think he'll be able to forgive me?"

Nana chuckled. "Darling, he's worried about you forgiving him. You two will be just fine. Stop worrying. When he gets back, you will see just how much he has missed you. Now, where is that sister of yours? I need to make sure she's done everything she was supposed to do."

Camille pointed to the door just as Zina and the men entered.

Hearing her name, Zina gushed with excitement. "I did good, Nana. You'll be so proud of me."

"With what?" Camille asked. "What did you do?"

Nana and Zina cut their eyes at each other and then at Antione and Dante.

Nana shook her head, smiling. "Camille, you should go unpack. See what it is Vincent has left for you. Antione, take care of all the luggage. Zina and Dante can help me finish the meal and then we can go have lunch out by the pool," she quipped in one long breaths, dropping commands one by one.

"Yes, ma'am," Antione and Dante chimed, as Zina rinsed her hands under a cool spray of water.

"What do you want me to do?" Zina asked.

"Why don't you prep the salad?" Nana said, all of them clearly ignoring Camille.

Following behind Antione, Camille headed into the guest bedroom. Natural light flooded the interior, the warmth bouncing against the walls. A bouquet of roses lay spread across the center of the bed, tied with an elegant silk bow. A hand-printed note card sat in an envelope addressed to her, Vincent's neat penmanship in bold black ink.

The words warmed her, bringing tears to her eyes as she read the short message he'd left.

Camille, my love, you being here has made me the happiest man in the world. I hope that you know just how much I love you. When I return I shall ask you again if you will be my wife. I am praying with all my heart and soul that you will say yes.

Always, Vincent

The knock on the door startled her as a Nana and Zina pushed their way through the entrance. "Camille," Zina started. "There's a lot that is going to be happening over the next two days. We can't have you in the way."

"What's that supposed to mean?"

"It means that Antione is taking you to the yacht and he's going to leave you there. We'll come get you some time tomorrow."

"Tomorrow?"

Nana nodded her head. "It will be okay, dear. The refrigerator is stocked. There is a cell phone on board in case you have an emergency. You'll be right downtown in Hamilton so you can shop around if you like. Things will be fine. I will send Vincent the minute he gets here in the morning."

"I don't understand. If you two are planning my wedding, don't you think I should be involved?"

"No," Zina said, smirking. "You have always planned the big parties. Since we were little, all the birthdays and holiday events or your ideas. This time I'm in charge."

"Zina, I don't want pretzels and wine coolers at my wedding."

"Sounds like you don't trust me, little sister."

Camille cut her eyes at Zina, then looked beseechingly at Nana for assistance.

"I have to support Zina, dear. I promise you won't be disappointed."

"Well, since it looks like I'm outnumbered, I guess I don't have a choice."

Zina grinned. "No, you don't."

Nana shook her head at both of them. "You girls come eat lunch, and then, Camille, Antione will take you down to the dock."

Camille sighed deeply. "Yes, ma'am."

CHAPTER 32

When the sun rose Saturday morning, Camille was perched on the top deck, a warm blanket wrapped around her shoulders. Although she'd been anxious about Vincent's arrival and the pending events, she had slept well. The salt air had invigorated her spirit and she was thankful for the time alone.

Overhead, a commercial airliner flew low, heading into the airport. As Camille watched it pass above her, then disappear in the distance, she couldn't help hoping that Vincent was on board. Minutes later, the cell phone chimed, her sister on the other end.

"You okay?"

"I am," Camille responded. "How's it going there?"

"Picture-perfect."

"When can I come back? Why can't I come back?"

"Would you please just enjoy yourself and let me take care of the details?"

"I don't know about this, Zina."

"Camille, since you were twelve years old you have always talked about your wedding day. If there is anyone who has any idea what you would want and what you wouldn't want, it's me. Relax. You and Vincent just need to enjoy the time together. I'll see you later."

"This is absolutely crazy, Zina."

"What else is new! Wouldn't be any fun if it wasn't," Zina exclaimed. "Call me if you need anything." She disconnected the line before Camille could respond.

Heading back below deck, Camille pulled a container of yogurt from the refrigerator, shoveled it and a bowl of fresh melon into her stomach, and then headed for the shower. The water was cool, but felt good, refreshing her spirit as she bathed herself.

Stepping out of the shower, she wrapped herself in Vincent's bathrobe, drawing the terry fabric closely around her. Studying her reflection in the mirror, she rubbed a palm full of his Cetaphil moisturizing cream onto her face, bathing her flesh with the rich emollient. Opening the bottle of cologne that sat on the counter, she sniffed its fragrance, drawing the familiar scent of him deep into her nostrils.

As Camille came into the room from the bathroom, Vincent sat perched on the edge of the king-sized bed, the unmade sheets and blankets still tangles from the night before. He jumped anxiously to his feet, his excitement gracing the curves of his face. Startled, Camille took a quick step back, and then realizing who was standing before her, leapt into the bend of his outstretched arms. Their mouths sought out familiar territory, nestling in the fullness of each other's lips. Vincent hugged her close, his hands sneaking beneath the folds of the terry covering to press against her naked skin. As he held her tightly, his grasp just shy of bruising, Camille could feel herself melting against him.

"I have missed you so much," Vincent whispered in her ear, dropping his face into her hair.

"I am so sorry, Vincent. I was such a fool."

"No, baby. No. You had every right to be angry. I hurt you. I'm the one who's sorry. I was so afraid I'd lost you for good."

Camille leaned back, parting her torso from his, her hands still holding tightly to his. "I love you so much. I don't ever want us to be apart again. Promise me that nothing will ever come between us."

He smiled, cupping her chin in the palm of his large hand. "I promise. All I want is to take care of you, to love you and have you love me back. For all time, remember?"

Tears in her eyes, Camille pressed a kiss against his lips, nodding her head as her mouth met his.

"Make love to me, Vincent," she whispered, pressing one palm against his chest as the other fell to the waistband of his slacks. "Make love to me right now."

Vincent laughed, the sound a low, deep, sensual vibrato that resonated through both of them. "It would be my pleasure, woman. It would surely be my pleasure."

It was half past seven when the cell phone vibrated against the table. Vincent reached for the receiver, pulling it to his ear.

"Hello?"

He nodded his head as though the person on the other end could see, glancing at Camille as he listened intently.

"Okay... Right... I'll tell her... Okay... If we must... All right... See you soon."

"Who was that?" Camille asked, slipping back into the bathrobe at the foot of the bed.

"That was Antione. He is on his way over to pick me up. He says he's bringing Zina and dropping her off here to stay with you."

"You're leaving me?"

"According to them, I can't see you again until tomorrow."

"Do you have a clue what's going on?"

He smiled, the gleam of a co-conspirator gracing his face. "I know a few things."

"Tell me, Vincent," Camille implored, clutching at his chest.

"No, ma'am. You have to wait."

Rolling her eyes, Camille fell back against the bed, turning onto her stomach. "Have you at least had some say in this?"

"I've been able to get one or two ideas in, but Nana and Zina have been in control for the most part."

"Well, do you know if--?"

"I know that I can't tell you anything more," he said, cutting her off short. "Let's get dressed. They should be here in a few minutes."

"You are just as impossible as they are!"

"And you are enjoying every minute of it, aren't you?" Vincent asked, kissing the crest of her back, just above the rise of her buttocks.

Camille grinned. "Shhh. Don't tell Zina," she said, pulling her index finger to her lips as she whispered.

Vincent laughed.

"I am enjoying this. For the first time my sister is doing all the work and I get to sit back and relax."

"But it is your wedding. It really doesn't bother you?" Vincent asked, concern etched across his brow.

Camille shrugged. "Surprisingly, no. I wouldn't care how we get married. Just committing myself to you and having you give that back to me is what's most important to me. We could pledge our love on the back of a turnip truck and I'd be the happiest woman in the world."

Vincent nodded. "Well, I can promise you there are no turnips involved." He leaned down to kiss her forehead. "Come on. We can grab a quick shower before they get here."

Camille followed him into the bathroom as he led her by the hand. "That does sound promising, Mr. DeCosta. Promising indeed."

Loud laughter and a wave of chatter greeted them before the crowd did. Off in the distance, Camille could hear her name being called. Staring toward the gated entrance to the docks, she could feel the grin on her face spreading as Zina waved excitedly to them, a parade of Camille's closest friends following behind her. Darrow and Antione brought up the rear.

Vincent burst into laughter at the excitement painted on her face. Wrapping his arms around her, he hugged her tightly. "Surprise! I was told a woman has to have a bachelorette party."

"You did this?"

Vincent shook his head. "I can't take the credit for this, darling. This is all your sister's doing."

As Camille and Vincent climbed down to the deck, the group reached the side of the vessel. "Permission to board, Captain?" Zina shouted, bringing her hand up to salute.

"Permission granted," Vincent said with a soft chuckle.

"Ahoy, matey!" Darrow exclaimed, as Camille reached out to give each of them a hug.

Janet Daye shook her head in Camille's direction. "Hey, girlfriend! I hope you're surprised!"

"I am," Camille responded. "Very surprised."

"So, introduce us to your man," Jackie Bradley chimed in, winking toward Vincent.

Vincent waved, tossing his hand up in the air like an eager student.

"Everybody, this is Vincent. Vincent, this is everybody," Zina said for her. "Now, Vincent, you and Antione have to go." She looked down at her watch. "The bachelor party starts in thirty minutes. Can't have the guest of honor late."

"He gets a bachelor party, too?" Camille quizzed.

"I even got him a stripper," Zina chimed teasingly.

"I know you didn't," her sister gasped.

"Oh, yes, I did. She's jumping out of a cake and will shake her booty for exactly forty-five minutes, and then my Antione is going to put in a taxi and send her on her way. Isn't that right, honey?" she said, leaning up to kiss Antione's cheek.

The man rolled his eyes. "There is no stripper, Camille. Don't pay any attention to your sister."

Zina laughed.

Bridget Wallace chuckled beside her. "You better watch yourself, Zina, before Camille has us all showing up at your funeral and bright red dresses and high-heel hooker shoes."

The women roared

Antione gestured toward his father. "We better get out of here before things start to get really ugly."

Vincent nodded in agreement. "Well, ladies, it was a pleasure to meet you all."

Bridgette winked, batting her eyelashes at the two men. "The pleasure was all ours, Mr. Fiancé."

Jackie laughed. "Someone cool this woman off! Camille, where's the water hose? Girlfriends on fire!"

"Hey, Vincent," Janet called after them as he and Antione stepped off the boat. "Do you have any brothers, another son or two or three? Preferably unmarried and independently wealthy?"

"Or just plain wealthy will do," Jackie interjected.

Camille blew him a kiss, waving them off. "Ignore them, baby." Then turning to her friends, she said, "I swear. We can dress you up, but let you out and y'all still don't know how to act."

Janet hugged her. "We are so happy for you. I just about bust when Zina call to give us a news."

Darrow piped in, "you came close, but your girl Bridgette blew an absolute gasket over the telephone."

"What did you expect?" Bridgette responded. "The last time I spoke to Camille she was whining about not having a man. Then suddenly, not only does she have one, the brother is fine."

"Here, here," Jackie chimed in. "Didn't I hear Zina say there was another brother? Is he married?"

Zina shook her head.

Darrow giggled. "Boyfriend may be a touch too sweet for your tastes, Miss Thang."

Jackie rolled her eyes. "Darrow, you make me sick!"

Camille laughed, warmed by the presence of those she loved most. "Come on, everyone. Let's go downstairs."

"The girl has got herself a personal cruise ship," Bridget exclaimed, shaking her head from side to side as Camille led them below deck.

"Zina, what's in the bags?" Camille asked, reaching to take a package out of her sister's arms.

Zina smirked. "Food, girl, and a drink that will have you women slapping your mamas. We got us some Bermuda rum swizzle!"

"What's rum swizzle?" Bridget asked.

"Well, let's just say if Camille survives it, we're going to have us one heck of a wedding tomorrow!"

Camille shook her head. "I don't want to have a hangover on my wedding day, Zina."

"You won't. And by the way," Zina added, "we're not only your 'giving up the player's card' committee, but we are your official wedding party. Say hello to your bridesmaids." The women all fell into a tight circle beside her."

Camille nodded her head. "I couldn't have picked a better bunch if I'd done it myself."

Her friends grinned with her, each dropping a hand toward the center of their circle, fingers clasping together.

Camille grinned. "To good friends," she said.

"To family," Zina added.

"To Camille," Bridget, Janet, and Jackie sang in unison.

And from behind the bar, pouring the first round of rum swizzle, as he pursed his lips to blow a low whistle, Darrow said, "Lord, have mercy. Y'all gone make me cry."

Time passed quickly as the women and Darrow shared stories of their latest exploits and caught up on the relationship between Camille and Vincent. Laughter rang around the room, voices chiming in unison over one anecdote after the other.

Jackie stretched her arms above her head. She yawned widely. "I'm tired."

Bridget nodded in agreement. "I'm about to fall out myself."

"Thank you," Camille said, smiling at her friends. "Thank you all for coming and being with me. I can't tell you how much it means to me."

"We wouldn't want to be any other place," Janet responded.

"You're a lucky woman," Camille," Bridget said. "Vincent seems like a good man."

Camille's eyes widened, satisfaction flooding the contours of her face. "He is a good man."

"And he's the lucky one," Zina interjected. "My sister's quite the catch."

"Hear, hear," Darrow said, lifting his glass in salute before tossing back the last of its contents. "You women don't get much better than my girl here."

Camille rolled her eyes, still grinning.

"So, what's the secret?" Janet asked, setting her own empty cup on the table. "How did you and Zina both manage to find such good men?"

"Because there sure aren't many of them out here," Bridget said as she shifted her body around in her seat, pulling her legs beneath her buttocks.

Janet and Jackie both nodded with her, turning to stare at the Martin sisters.

Zina shrugged. "I guess it was just our turn."

Bridget tossed her head from side to side, her ebony braids swinging against her shoulders. "Had to be more than that. I mean, Zina, we know you have gone through some brothers and Camille here has always been picky when it comes to men. The few she did date weren't bad. In fact, they weren't bad at all."

Janet continued. "It was like neither one of you was willing to settle for 'not bad.' You two were looking for close to perfect and you seem to have found it."

Camille and Zina exchanged glances, both breaking out into a wide grin. "Louis and Sarah Martin!" they exclaimed in unison.

Jackie looked confused. "What did your mama and daddy have to do with it?"

Zina answered. "Probably from the moment we were conceived, both of our parents were adamant about teaching us how to marry well."

"That's putting it mildly," Camille interjected.

Zina nodded. "Mama had a list of attributes she said a husband needed to have and she read it to us daily."

"She used Daddy as her example," Camille added. "And he wasn't much better, with all of his lectures."

"They were like clockwork, the two of them, timely and consistent," Zina said.

"Your father needs to write a book then," Jackie said, "because if there's one thing that's for sure, we women do not teach our daughters how to marry well."

"But can you truly teach that?" Bridget said.

"Oh, yes, you can," Zina said. "If we teach our daughters from the jump how they should be treated by a man, then most will look for those qualities in a man."

"We need to teach these hardheaded boys, too," Janet said. "If they learned early how to care for and treat a woman, there would be stronger relationships and fewer children growing up in single-parent homes."

Darrow joined in the conversation. "Clearly, though, one's social and economic influences have an impact on what one does."

"True," said Camille, "but just because you have money doesn't mean you have to marry money, or if you're poor you have to marry poor. What my mother always stressed was that a man should be willing to work hard and find satisfaction in supporting his family, no matter what he did to do that."

"And Daddy says a woman can't expect a man to support her, if she's unwilling to support him. He says a man doesn't want to work hard all day long to come home to a woman who ignores or mistreats him. And vice versa, a woman doesn't want to go out of her way to pamper and care for her man to have him be unwilling to return the favor."

"But money always seems to find money," Bridget said. "Look at you two. Y'all didn't grow up in the projects like I did. You were raised around people who had. Now you're marrying a man who has as much, and the same with Zina's husband."

Zina sat forward in her seat. "True, but I have never limited myself when it came to men. And you know that. I didn't care what a man did for a living, as long as it was legal, and he did it well. Antione could have worked in a fast food chain for all I cared. I just needed to know that he was willing to work to build a life for himself and a family. He also needed to respect what I did and what I wanted for myself."

"Exactly," Camille said. "A man can have a lot of good qualities, but if he doesn't respect your needs and your dreams, then what good is he?"

Janet laughed. "My mother used to say a piece of man was better than no man at all."

Bridget laughed with her. "I guess it just depends on which piece you got," she said, slapping a high five with Darrow.

"Like I said," Jackie said with a chuckle, "we don't teach our children how to marry well."

When Camille rose the next morning, the sun was already perched high in the sky, the bright blue ceiling void of any clouds. Outside, the temperature was warm and rising and Camille instantly knew that she had slept through most of the morning.

In the salon, the other women were bustling about getting ready. A row of curling irons were plugged into the vacant electrical outlets and her friends were busy getting themselves primped and curled.

"Good morning, sleepyhead,' Zina chimed as Camille made her way into the room.

"Why didn't you wake me?"

"We wanted to make sure you got plenty of rest. You were wild last night."

"I was not."

"Yes, you were," Janet said. "You even made me blush a few times and that's not easy to do."

Camille smiled, shaking her head from side to side. "Blame it on the rum swizzle."

A strange woman was painting nail polish on the tips of Jackie's toenails. Camille pointed in her direction, lifting her eyes questioningly to Zina.

"Oh, Camille, this is Teresa. Teresa, this is the bride."

The woman smiled up at her. "Hello. It's very nice to meet you."

"You, too," Camille responded. She sighed. "Is there any coffee?"

"You don't need any coffee," Zina answered. "It's bad for your skin. Here," she said, passing her sister a glass of orange juice. "Drink up and then go get in the shower. Teresa will be ready to do your nails as soon as she's done with Jackie and Janet."

"If you're hungry, Camille, I'll fix you something to eat," Janet volunteered.

Camille shook her head. "No, thank you. I'm fine." She dropped down onto the leather settee. "So, Zina, what am I wearing today?"

The roomful of women glanced from one to the other as Bridget came to pull her fingers through Camille hair.

"Up or down?" she asked, looking at Zina.

"Up," she said.

"Hello. Remember me. The bride?" Camille said jokingly, waving her hands in front of her for attention. "Do you have something for me to wear today?"

"Of course,' Zina said, cutting her eyes at her sister. "Your dress should be here in a few minutes."

Camille shook her head. "Why is my dress—?"

Zina interrupted her. "You ask too many questions. Go get your bath, please, or you're going to be late."

Jackie laughed, leaning down to inspect her pedicure. She smiled at Teresa, nodding her head approvingly. "I am having way too much fun here. Camille Martin isn't in control and it's absolutely killing her," she said.

"She can't handle it, can she?" Janet chimed in, all of them nodding in Camille's direction.

"I will get even." Camille grinned, rising from her seat. "One of these days—"

"Well, until then, just do as you're told," Bridget interjected. "And hurry up. I need to get to the house to do Mrs. Gibbons' hair. I promised her I'd be there before one o'clock and I need to make sure your hair is finished before then."

When Camille finally emerged from the bedroom, bathed and newly revived, the noise in the outer room had subsided substantially. It was a twilight zone experience, Camille thought, curious as to why her friends were no longer bantering loudly between themselves.

As she stepped into the room, dressed only in Vincent's bathrobe, they all stood in a row, staring at her. Tears rose to Camille's eyes. The bridal party looked exquisite in the formal wear Zina had selected. Adorned in the palest shade of peach, each woman wore an asymmetrical lace tunic with a modest V-neckline over matte-jersey pants. The lace fabric's faint touch of color was a true complement to the variations of their brown and black complexions. Zina's tunic was a richer shade of mango that sat beautifully against her dark skin. The wide legs of the slacks were understated yet stylish, with a slit that ran from the hem to the knee.

"You each look so pretty,' Camille exclaimed.

"Don't you cry," Bridget said, wiping a tear from her own eye. "If you mess up my makeup I will hurt you."

Camille laughed.

Bridget gestured to a seat by the counter. "Here, sit down, so I can finish your hair and makeup. We've got to get a move on it."

Camille did as she was told, making herself comfortable as her friend proceeded to pull a comb through her hair, and Teresa began to do her nails.

Janet peered out the window. "It that our car, Zina?" she asked, pointing toward the parking lot.

"Yes, Zina said as she looked over the woman's shoulders. "He's early."

Darrow headed up the steps to the top deck. "I'll take care of it,' he said eyeing Zina. "You ladies head in that direction when you're ready."

The women nodded, gathering their remaining possessions scattered about. "Everybody ready?" Janet asked.

"I think so," Jackie answered.

"What do you think, Zina?" Bridget asked, adjusting a vine of white silk rosebuds around the large chignon she'd crafted with Camille's hair.

Zina beamed, reaching out to squeeze Camille's hand. "It's perfect."

Darrow stuck his head back through the door. "A certain person is starting to get antsy up here," he exclaimed.

Zina laughed as Camille looked at her questioningly. "We're almost ready," she said, watching as Teresa touched up Camille's French manicure.

Minutes later, Teresa nodded her head, packing up the last of her supplies. "I'm all set," she said. "Do you like?" she asked Camille.

"They're perfect. Thank you."

As Zina gestured toward Janet, who handed Teresa a plain white envelope and pointed her to the door, Camille rose from her seat, attempting to peer outside to see what was going on.

Jackie and Bridget broke out into laughter, Janet and Zina joining in.

"You are so nosy," Zina cried, wiping at the corners of her eyes. "Would you sit back down, please?"

"Zina, what is going on?" Camille said in a whining tone. "Just tell me something, please."

"I told you to sit down. You'll see in a minute." Zina turned to the other women. "If you will, please tell him we're ready."

Bridget nodded. "We will see you two at the house." She leaned to kiss Camille's cheek. "We love you, girlfriend."

Jackie and Janet each squeezed her hands, winking in her direction. "Congratulations," Janet exclaimed.

"We're so happy for you," Jackie added.

Camille watched as her friends headed out the door. Within minutes, there is a loud knock against the wooden frame.

As he pushed into the entrance, Louis Martin's voice filled the room. "Hello. Can I come in?"

Camille's eyes darted from her sister to the entrance and back again. Zina nodded her head, a wide smile gracing her face.

Making his way into the salon, Louis handed Zina the large garment bag slung over his shoulder. He stood awkwardly, his gaze meeting Camille's as she stared in his direction.

"Hello, daughter."

Camille smiled, rising from where she sat. "Hi, Daddy."

"I hope it's okay for me to be here?"

Tears spilled down Camille's cheek. "I wouldn't want you to be any other place, Daddy."

He shook his head. "I'm so sorry, Camille. I didn't mean—" he started.

Camille pressed her fingers to her father's lips. "I love you, Daddy. You're my father and no matter what happens between us, I will always love you. That's the only thing that's important right now."

Louis wrapped his arms around Camille's shoulders and hugged her tightly. Reaching out with his hand, he pulled the Zina into the embrace, both of his daughters holding on to him and each other.

Zina wiped the moisture from her face. "Look what you two have done to my makeup," she said with a laugh. "Enough of this now, we have a wedding to get to."

Zina cupped her palms against Camille's cheeks. "Daddy and I have a surprise for you. Now, you know I don't stand on tradition—"

Louis laughed. "That's putting it mildly, baby girl," he said interrupting.

She waved a hand at her father before continuing. "I knew that you would want that whole 'something old, borrowed, and blue' nonsense for your wedding. So, I wanted it to be really special." She took a deep breath.

"First, the something new," Zina said, reaching for a small turquoise box with a large white ribbon that sat on the table. "This is from Antione and Dante," she said, passing the container to her sister.

"You do us proud. Welcome to the family. Love, your future stepsons," Camille read out loud from the small card affixed to the package. Her eyes widened as she noted the delicate Tiffany's inscription across of the container. Pulling at the white ribbon, she opened the box, revealing a diamond-encrusted, deco-styled bracelet. Camille gasped loudly as she pulled the delicate, arabesque-patterned gem toward her.

"My man's got taste, girl! He picked it out all by himself."

Louis nodded his head. "I do like that boy."

The women burst into laughter as a Zina helped her sister fasten the bracelet around her wrist.

"Okay, now for the something borrowed." Zina reached for another jewelry box against the counter. "My baby bought these for me, and I want them back before you and Vincent take off for your honeymoon, you understand?"

Camille nodded her head as she opened the lid, revealing a pair of two-carat, diamond-stud earrings. "He does have good taste, Zina. I hope he got it from his father."

Zina grinned. Louis narrowed his eyes, a mock glare crossing his face. "You two should be ashamed of yourselves," he said, shaking a finger at them, the pretense of annoyance gracing his face. "You both act like you've never had fine jewelry before."

"Bad girl. Bad girl." Zina said, giggling, as she slapped at Camille's hand. "Now for the something blue," she continued, pulling a lace garter with blue trim from a bag. I can't get you married without one of these." She winked at her sister.

Louis glanced down at the watch on his wrist. "We need to move it, girls."

Zina side, rolling her eyes. "Okay, well, Daddy has the something old." She smiled at her father.

Reaching for the garment bag that Zina had laid carefully against the settee, Louis pulled at the zipper and carefully eased its contents out of the enclosure.

"I promised your mother that if I lived to see you two married, I'd make sure one of you wore her wedding gown. Camille, the day I married your mother she wore this gown. She was the most beautiful woman in the world. Sarah's mother, your grandma Janie, wore it first, and before your mother died she put it away for you two. I'd be honored if you'd wear this when I escort you down the aisle this afternoon."

Louis held the delicate lace and silk chiffon gown before her. Camille could feel the wealth of tears flooding her cheeks and she tried to stifle her sobs.

Zina fanned her fingers in front of Camille's face. "Don't cry, Camille. Please, don't cry," she said, "you can't get married looking like a red, puffy crybaby. It'll ruin the pictures. Stop it right now! You going to make me cry," she finished, fanning at her own eyes.

Louis kissed Camille's cheek. "Your mother loved you very much and I know she's right here, watching over both of you."

"Let's get you dressed," Zina finally said, guiding Camille and the dress toward the bedroom. "Daddy, we'll be right back."

Behind the closed door, Camille fingered the delicate fabric. "It's so beautiful, Zina."

"It's so you."

Stepping into the dress, Camille adjusted it against her body as Zina buttoned the length of pearl buttons that ran down the back. The dress was a simple A-line gown with an elegant boat-cut neckline and open-laced sleeves. The ivory silk chiffon fabric lay beneath the fine lace that fell down to the floor, the lines of a simple train trailing behind her. The two women stared at Camille's reflection in the full-length mirror. They had seen photos of their mother in this dress, but neither of them had ever imagined wearing it herself.

"It's absolutely perfect," Zina purred. "I was worried about the fit, but Daddy said you were the exact same size Mommy was when they were married."

"Do you think one of us will be able to pass it on to a daughter of our own?" Camille asked.

Zina chuckled. "Watch. I don't doubt that it will be my daughter who will probably be the one to wear it. Your child is going to be hell on wheels, like her auntie. I can see your child now, getting married in my hot-pink miniskirt with a black-lace bra top while my daughter wears this gown. It will drive us both crazy."

Camille laughed loudly, throwing her head back with glee. "Is that really what you wore?"

Her sister nodded. "Of course! I keep telling you about my aversion to tradition!"

Camille shook her head. "You're probably right, Zina. I can picture it now."

The two women stood clasped arm in arm, each lost in her own thoughts. "Thank you, Zina," Camille said, tears welling up in her eyes again. "Every time I thought I was taking care of you, it seems that you were taking care of me. I don't know what I would have done without you when Mommy died."

Zina smiled, a faint bend of her lips, as she hugged her sister's shoulders. "We had each other, Camille, and we had the good doctor out there. We will always take care of each other. No matter what."

Camille squeezed her sister's hand. "Would you get me married, please, before I start crying again?"

"Yes, ma'am," Zina responded. "Let's go do your father proud."

CHAPTER 33

Louis Martin beamed with pride as he escorted his youngest daughter down the aisle. Camille looked exquisite in her mother's wedding gown, and as her father placed her hand into Vincent's, nodding warmly in the man's direction, he truly believed that things would be well for all of them.

Vincent's love for Camille was written all over his face, emotion spilling out of his eyes like water flowing from an open faucet. The man's devotion for her rained down upon them like a welcome shower on a hot summer's night. As a Louis turned, taking a seat beside Nana, his eyes locked with Lawrence's, and his best friend nodded his head with approval. Beside him, Kitty grinned at both of them, tears pressed against the woman's eyes.

There weren't enough words to express the emotions that swept up and over Camille, consuming her like brush fire. From the moment she stepped out of the car, and Zina led her through the house to the rear yard, she'd been in awe of the home's transformation. From the pitched tent with its high canopy that took over the gardens, to the floral arrangements of cascading yellow roses that graced the guest tables, it was more than she ever could have imagined. Zina had successfully managed to take every wedding fantasy Camille had ever shared, and had turned them into a dream come true. As she and Vincent exchanged vows, pledging to love and protect each other for eternity, she couldn't imagine herself being any happier.

EPILOGUE

Nana, Louis and Kitty sat around Louis's kitchen table laughing and conversing over everything and over nothing. Time had been good to each of them, the lines of age only vague reminders throughout each of their dark faces that any time had indeed passed. When the two women had joked about still looking good for their ages, Louis had reminded them of that adage about black not cracking. The three had laughed joyously until tears ran down their faces.

It had been a full year since Lawrence had died. An abrupt stroke had driven the spirit from his body, the sudden loss a shock to them all. It had been almost two full years since they'd all been witnesses to Camille and Vincent's wedding, the day bringing closure to the past the families had shared and opening the doors to the future that lay before them. Louis missed his best friend as much as Kitty missed the love of her life, and the two had relied heavily on their bonds of friendship to help them survive the turmoil that always follows the death of one loved as much as Lawrence had been loved. The telephone rang just as Louis stepped out onto the patio to brush barbecue sauce atop the spareribs cooking on the gas grill. Nana picked up the receiver.

"Hello? Martin residence."

"Nana. Hi. It's me. Antione."

"Hello, baby. Everything okay?"

"You all need to get down here to the hospital."

"Lord have mercy! Is it Zina?"

Antione laughed. "No. It's Camille."

After Nana passed the message on to Kitty, the two women laughed excitedly, rushing out to the patio to give Louis the word. Leaving the spareribs where they lay, Louis turned off the flames that simmered beneath the partially cooked meat, then rushed both women and himself to the local medical center.

At WakeMed Hospital, Dante and Antione were pacing the carpet on the fifth floor, the brightly decorated waiting room welcoming the new arrivals. Louis rushed in excitedly, the two women following closely behind him.

"Where's my daughter?" he asked, shaking hands with Antione and then Dante.

"In delivery," Dante responded, excitement gracing all their faces. "Dad and Zina are both with her."

"They promised to come get us as soon as there's some news," Antione added.

The two women had taken a seat in the corner, both pulling magazines from the tabletop beside them.

"You three might as well sit down," Nana said. "This may take some time."

Antione glanced down at his watch. "I hope it doesn't take too long. I don't think I can stand it."

"Me neither," Louis said slapping him against the back as they all broke out into laughter.

Two hours later, Vincent made his way into the waiting room, a wide grin across his face. "Congratulations," he said, extending his hand to Louis. "You've got two beautiful granddaughters. Camille had girls. Twin girls."

Nana and Kitty both shrieked excitedly, wrapping each other in a warm hug.

"Knew those babies were girls," Nana said with a chuckle, Kitty nodding her head in agreement.

"How is Camille, Pop?" Antione asked.

"She's wonderful. Tired, but doing really well."

Louis smiled, tears welling up in his eyes. "Thank you, Jesus," he said embracing Vincent, Antione and Dante in turn. "Thank you, Lord."

"As soon as she gets settled in her room, you can all go up to see her and the babies," Vincent said. "I need to get back, so I will see you all in a few minutes."

"Vincent," Kitty called after him, catching him before he disappeared out of sight. "What did you name the babies?"

Vincent shrugged, his grin widening. "Can't tell you. Promised Camille I'd wait until we were all together," he said before spinning back out the door and racing down the hallway.

Zina held her sister's hand as they wheeled her into a private room on the maternity ward.

"You done good, girl," she said with a smile, squeezing Camille's hand warmly. "You done real good."

"And I did it first," Camille said, reaching out to brush her palm against Zina's bulging belly.

"That's only because you went into labor early. You were still due two weeks after me."

"Says you."

"You do have me beat with that two-baby thing, though," Zina said, grinning at her sister. "Twins. I can't believe you had twins, and two girls at that."

Camille smiled widely. "Every girl needs a sister," she said. "My two just saved me from having to do this pregnancy thing again."

Zina nodded, stepping to the side as the nurse made Camille comfortable on the bed. When the blankets were adjusted around Camille, Zina joined her on the mattress, the two women lying side by side, hand in hand.

Minutes later the nurse rolled in baby girl DeCosta one and baby girl DeCosta two, the two chocolate bundles of new life sleeping peacefully, one pink and one yellow skullcap adorning their small heads. The two women leaned over the bassinets to peer down at them.

"He kicked," Zina said, grabbing at her own pregnant stomach. "This boy is making mincemeat out of my insides."

"He can't wait to meet his two cousins," Camille said, beaming at her daughters.

The two women looked up as Vincent came rushing into the room. Wrapping his arms around Camille, he hugged her tightly, pressing his lips against hers as he planted a kiss on her mouth. Zina shook her head, waving a hand at the two of them.

"That's what got you two into this predicament," she said, giggling. "Them ninety days went by and you didn't know how to act."

Vincent slapped lightly at the back of her head. "You should talk."

Within minutes, the rest of the family had pushed their way into the room, Nana and Kitty both grabbed a baby, hugging the infants tight to their chests as the men oohed and aahed in delight.

Louis stood nervous against the wall, his arms folded tightly against his chest.

"Are you okay, Daddy?" Camille asked.

He nodded. "I'm fine, daughter. Just fine. I'm so proud of you."

"Do you want to hold your grandchild, Louis?" Vincent asked, reaching to take the baby from her grandmother's arms.

Louis shook his head. "They're just a touch too tiny for me right now."

Kitty laughed. "He was the same way when Camille and Zina were born. "Not one of us could believe that a grown man like Louis Martin was afraid of a tiny infant."

Louis rolled his eyes. "Who says I'm afraid? I just don't want to break them is all. That's why I didn't become an obstetrician."

Vincent laughed, pushing the child into Louis's arms. "She won't break, my friend. She's in good hands."

Nana beamed, pulling a camera from her large pocketbook to take a picture. "Well," she said, "we get to welcome your grandchildren this week, Louis, and hopefully, your grandchild next week, Vincent. Life doesn't get any better than this."

The group laughed, everyone in agreement.

"So," Dante asked, "what have you two named our baby sisters?"

Sitting back down on the bed, Vincent pulled Camille back into an embrace, the two of them beaming with pride as everyone stood staring at them.

"Well," Camille said, "it wasn't an easy decision, but we really think we picked the perfect names."

Vincent nodded his assent.

Gesturing toward the baby Kitty's arms, Camille said, "Everybody, we'd like you to meet our oldest daughter, Irene Gibbons DeCosta," and then as she pointed to the child her father was hugging, she finished, "and her baby sister, Sarah Louis DeCosta."

Both Dante and Antione exchanged a quick look, tears brimming at the edges of their eyes. Louis's tears had slipped past his lashes and were falling down his cheeks, landing on the printed baby blanket wrapped around the granddaughter named after her grandmother.

As Vincent kissed her, the two reveling in the love that surrounded them and their newborn babies, Camille knew how truly blessed she was. She had been promised a love for all time, and in her heart she knew that this love was eternal.

Dear Friends,

I love to write. Weaving a story from beginning to end is truly a thrill for me. I hope that you enjoyed *A Love for All Time*, because I loved writing this story. This tale is a true reflection of everything in my life that has special meaning to me. It parallels the dynamics of my family unit: the ideals and strengths of my parents, the camaraderie of my best friend and my sister, the love of my husband, a man fifteen years my senior, and my home and extended family in Bermuda. It has been my love for all these things, and the support of all these people that continually inspires and nurtures my creative spirit and allows me to write.

I pray that this story makes you laugh, smile, and reflect on the love of family, and the enchantment of passion. Thank you so much for your support, and please, visit me at my Website and continue to send me your comments.

With much love,

Deborah Fletcher Mello
June 2004

Hello, and welcome!

I am so excited to be able to re-issue my second book in both paperback and E-book formats! I am in awe of how so much has changed since it was first published twelve years ago. *A Love for All Time* remains one of my very favorite stories to have ever written. There is absolutely nothing I would change if I were to do it all over again.

In my original letter I extolled my love for and appreciation for the family that has continued to support me through this journey. The husband is no longer my husband, but my ties to my Bermuda kin remains strong, unbroken by our divorce. I still think of that beautiful island as home!

If you read *A Love for All Time* when it came out in 2004, I hope that you enjoy revisiting Vincent and Camille's story. If this is your first time, I pray that their love will inspire your own.

Thank you for your support and your love. Please know that I appreciate all of you who have been with me from the beginning and each of you who has continued to stand with me along the way!

Much, much love!

Deborah Fletcher Mello
September 2016

ABOUT THE AUTHOR

Writing since she was old enough to put pen to paper, Deborah Fletcher Mello firmly believes that for her, writing is as necessary as breathing. Her first novel, TAKE ME TO HEART, earned her a 2004 Romance Slam Jam nomination for Best New Author. In 2008, Deborah won the Romantic Times Reviewers Choice award for Best Series Romance for her ninth novel, TAME A WILD STALLION. Her publication, CRAVING TEMPTATION was named one of Publisher's Weekly Best Books for 2014 and was also nominated for a 2015 Emma Award for Book of the Year. As well, her novel PLAYING FOR KEEPS was a Library Journal Best of 2015 and won the Romantic Times Reviewer's Choice award for Best Multicultural Romance. Most recently, Deborah was named the 2016 Romance Slam Jam Author of the Year. Born and raised in Fairfield County, Connecticut, Deborah maintains base camp in North Carolina but considers home to be wherever the moment moves her.

41646092R00177

Made in the USA
Middletown, DE
08 April 2019